DEDICATION

To my children, Maria, Daniela, JoJo, Johnny

ACKNOWLEDGMENTS

My wife, Adelaide for her constant and pleasant support. For her suggestions, insights, and direction when I found myself lost in my writing.

My professors of Italian Literature at Fordham University Rose Hill-Dr. Palombo, Dr. Pallone, Dr. Perretta, Dr. Iannace who introduced me to the wonders of Renaissance Literature and to authors such as Dante, Boccaccio, Petrarca and the women they loved-Beatrice, Fiammetta, and Laura. Lessons never forgotten, still fresh in my heart.

CONTENTS

CHAPTER 1 *CASSANDRA*

He had found pleasure and satisfaction in his years at New York University. Professor Gianluca Morelli's deep understanding of European literature, his fair grading reputation, and his British accent had students filling his classes each semester. His ability to expose the essence from an author's work, to dig deep into the psyche of those writings, proved too tempting for a generation of females craving the exploits of troubadours, bards, minstrels, and poetic crooners; women filled most of the seats in his lecture hall.

His presentations came packaged in a handsome face, full head of salt and pepper hair, and a slim, trim body. His signature wardrobe was made up of worn jeans, a simple tee shirt and a black blazer. Ignoring even the worst weather, he often strolled into his classroom in his black flip flops. His humble approach to relationships, and his inclusive attitude towards persons of all persuasions, made him a much in demand invitee to all sorts of occasions. This kept him busy, and never lonely, even during holidays. Despite having no family in New York, he never spent a Christmas alone.

May of 2023 Gianluca was pushing fifty when he gave an out of character scathing lecture in response to comments made in his class by his students. The day's topic had focused on the quiet, subliminal power of women to influence the works of Italian Renaissance writers and artists. He spoke glowingly of Petrarch's Laura, Dante's Beatrice, and of Botticelli's Simonetta. In his lecture, he had transported his students to a time when the adoration of a particular woman had been the motivation for celebrated creations of literature and art. The spark that turned him sideways that day was a comment made by one of the women seated in the first row.

"Professor, I just don't get it. When did it all end? Men today just don't have it in them to feel that way about women. I can't imagine any man possessing that kind of motivation... at least not the men I know."

Gianluca pondered the comment for a moment, knowing how he would respond. Before doing so, he asked if the other women in the class felt the same way. All agreed. He looked down at his notes, flipped the pages of Dante's *La Vita Nova* on his desk, then looked up and jumped into his denunciation of the superficiality and selfishness of modern sensitivities.

"My dear Jeanine, in a liberated world, that interplay between a man and a woman, in a heterosexual relationship, let us be clear, is sadly improbable. The liberation movements that began in the 1960s, gaining purpose and clarity over the past sixty years, have decisively altered and redefined the expectations between a man and a woman. Can you deny that you consider yourself the equal of any man? Even greater, perhaps? Can you deny that you cater to your sexual needs as openly and personally as any man? If you desire the company of man in your bedroom, or for a weekend fling let's say, would you worry about what others may think? Would you be concerned with being labeled, of violating some norm? Of course not! Am I free to speak for every woman in this class?"

No one countered his theory, so he kept talking.

"Now, if men have come to accept this modern, liberated female, the easily available sexuality, the simplicity with which they can hook up, as your generation so conveniently defines it, what incentive is there in any male to bring himself to praise the beauty, the singular attraction… nay, the very essence, the soul of a woman when his actions and instincts are liberally guided by his penis? Why would any man want to work so hard as to write a sonnet, compose a poem in Dante's *terza rima,* or dedicate a work of art to any modern woman? Why? Can any of you give me a reason why any man would want to engage in the task of winning a woman's heart, when falling in love is so superfluous to what he really wants?

If getting laid or temporary companionship is the goal, if it is what both want equally, then there is no pressure on the part of the female to incentivize the male to first fall in love-whatever that may mean to each of us, and to commit to a romantic courtship. If the man does not believe himself in love, then there is no need to invent… namely, to compose or create something meant to be an extension of his feelings to praise the object of his passion. And if the female has no expectation of that display of affection because she is being guided by a liberated vagina, then my dear Jeanine your search for such a man will be fruitless, and please don't take this as a condemnation of your generation. If this is what you want, what you consider the better normal, then so be it… neither I nor any person or institution can stand in the way of what most of you would consider progress."

He paused to construct another argument.

"Can we still label a woman a slut who enjoys sex and has multiple partners? Can we still tolerate a dual set of standards: the virile, studly male, and the unchaste, immoral female? I don't see it. I socialize as much as any in this city, and it hasn't escaped me that nasty judgments are no longer made on those who deviate from traditional norms. There can't be, because it has become acceptable to ignore the norm, and to replace it with personalized standards… casting off the shackles of moralistic parameters imposed by institutions such as religions. Basically, society doesn't have the stomach or the power to impose a benchmark of behavior with a list of criticisms for those who refuse to abide.

While this may be a recent development, it has roots in the counterculture movements of the 1960s. Do any of the women in this hall consider themselves less than equal to any man due to an active sexual lifestyle? Anyone? Are sexually active women marginalized, ostracized, condemned to recant their transgressions with a life sentence in a convent, unqualified to be a bride? To don a scarlet letter? The answer to these questions would have been a strong yes as few as sixty years ago… no need to go all the way back to the Middle Ages. This isn't the first time we have experienced a measured shift in social principles. It has happened before, but only small vestiges survived. Human beings seem to retreat to more conservative behaviors when things get dangerously out of hand. I can think of the period following Vietnam when there was a hedonistic need to unload all the trauma of a very unpopular war. The free-falling experiences of the Studio 54 era, the explosion of drug usage, and decaying cities gave us the Ronald Regan years when America concerned itself once again with local economies, industry, love of country, and personal wealth; a return to conservative values as a correction to how far we had strayed from the center, from the nucleus. It is said that every revolution incites a counter-revolution. So, you may be the catalyst for another revolution, but will it survive? What action will you take, what course will you follow when you find yourselves at fifty with no significant other? Will you live happily alone, capable of confronting old age and death with no one by your side? Did you put off the thought so conveniently while you were enjoying life with no concern for a future you did not fear?"

His students remained momentarily stunned and silent. The lull was interrupted when one male student in the top row of the lecture hall stood up and loudly applauded. Gianluca was familiar with the outspoken Jason, so he challenged him to elaborate.

"Jason, you either mock me or you have found some common ground."

Jason kept his cool.

"Well, professor, I actually agree with much of your unproven thesis, but let me ask you-how many poems and sonnets have you written, and weren't those Renaissance passions more like obsessions?"

Gianluca smirked and quickly engaged.

"My good man, if those men had acted haphazardly and with little regard with their passions, then yes, we may characterize them as obsessions. An example of how this was avoided would be the passion Dante admits for Beatrice, if you recall, in *Vita Nova,* he has no problem at first professing an earthly, physical love for her which could have sickeningly turned into an obsession. Now recall what happens-he is overwhelmed by her honesty and purity, he stifles his carnal urge, and his passion turns spiritual. Ultimately, Beatrice becomes his connection to God and Heaven in the *Divine Comedy.* I find it amazing that he would sacrifice his temporal love to elevate a woman further beyond his grasp with divinity. That is bordering on emotional suicide! My God! He serenely anoints Beatrice with sainthood and abandons his crush. There is satisfaction, I believe, in having the woman you love all for yourself, but these men found a way to quantify their love for women they could not have.

Dante and his contemporaries in literature and art were aware of not crossing that fine line, for doing so would have betrayed their truth, and we would have inherited our Renaissance version of *Fifty Shades of Grey.* How sad a thought. Now to answer the other part of your question, I did write poems and letters to a girl I was sincerely in love with way back in high school. I thought her to be the most heavenly of creatures. I was smitten not only by her beauty, but by her whole being. Every smile, every word spoken, every movement, every glance was a biological work of art. However, she was the girlfriend of the best-looking guy in our school, and the best of the athletes... problem was, he was also one of my best friends, and a very likeable and humble person. I harbored my truth, I didn't cross the line, and I sent her those poems and letters incognito."

His top row nemesis wouldn't let up.

"So, Dante elevates Beatrice to something resembling a nun to fool himself into thinking she is so divine, so holy that she becomes untouchable. Excuse me for being so blunt, professor, but I think Dante had to find his best excuse to avoid the fact that he just didn't have what it took for Beatrice to notice him, you know, to consider him a potential lover. He then accepts the outcome, but he needs to manipulate the process, control the fiction to appease himself. It's like some guy who goes out to bars and clubs with co-workers or friends just to be around some woman he's crazy about who is completely out of his league. He comments on her beauty and how appealing she is to his guy friends, only to conclude that she's not worth it because a woman that amazing could never be faithful to one man. You see, he conveniently constructs his story to create the perfect reason in his mind why he shouldn't even try."

One of the girls sitting next to Jason backed him up.

"I agree professor, I think it was a major cop-out by Dante and he comes up this brilliant tribute that is nothing more than an excuse."

Morelli's chin sunk to his chest, and he closed his eyes in despair.

"You're killing me. You're applying a juvenile contemporary idiosyncrasy to a much more complex Renaissance reality. Your young man in the bar has every opportunity to act with a minimum of consequence if things go wrong. He can walk away, accept the outcome, and in a matter of minutes all is forgotten. Dante had to consider violating deeply established social norms. He would have been infringing on the sanctity of another man's woman, and the reputation of the female and her family, with the very real risk of being exiled from Florence, likely to forfeit his life in a duel or in the extreme, a victim of a homicide in which the perpetrator is exonerated for rightly defending his honor. When you consider those factors, it is no wonder to me that he boldly nurtures his love in the only manner available to him. I refute the notion that he chose to divinely elevate Beatrice as an excuse for his impotence, and instead I am convinced it is the enlightened decision of a deeply impassioned man to extend the lifeline of the love he shelters through his writings."

Another of the women in class, Sandra, sighed and prodded her teacher.

"Professor Morelli, do you think that these Renaissance men would have still produced their works if those women had been theirs and if they had gotten laid? Would you have written those poems and letters if that girl had been your girlfriend?"

Confidently, Morelli delivered his opinion.

"I must believe in the strongest way that those men and myself would have remained true to our feelings and continued to express our love as the relationship evolved. I mean, if you and the woman you love are together, then the spoken word becomes as powerful as the written word, it is still a manifestation of your feelings."

She kept him thinking.

"But can two people continue to love each other with the same powerful passion for an entire life? Isn't that a bit unnatural?"

"Perhaps it is, I can't say with certainty. I haven't had

the good fortune of being that deeply in love in my adulthood. I know that in that final year in high school, I could have loved Annmarie the rest of my life. It might be a bit naïve to think things would happen exactly as you envision them, but I would rather take my chances and venture down that road than to hesitate at every challenge. If I fail at making the proposal, then I would default to my thoughts and use my words to honor my feelings.

It's been said that we should allow ourselves to fall in love even if it dwells exclusively inside of us and causes us pain. The poets spoke of the spasms in love, of the sweet agony of having loved, and I agree that it comes with emotional risks, but that one can mitigate those risks by understanding the good in that pain. It's the feeling perhaps that one has at end of an intense two-hour game of basketball, an intense workout, or at the end of running a marathon. Yes, there is an abundance of soreness and aching, but there is also a deep sense of satisfaction that you endured the torture, and as your body regains its strength and heals, one can't deny the accomplishment. In the same sense, one's heart heals and there is fulfillment in knowing that the pain transforms itself into a memorable testimony of that love. I believe the message they were sending us down through the ages was one which places a high value on suffering for another. There are obvious religious undertones promoting the willingness to take on the most impossible of devotions, such as never having the woman you love, and despite that, to still squeeze a few drops of spiritual nectar from those afflictions… enough perhaps to stimulate one to leave an imprint in the form of poetry, literature, and art; in essence, to salvage the best of one's existence even in the depths of despair.

They could have given in to their depression, rotted away and died off. They chose, instead, to lift pen and brush not to pity their torment, but to celebrate the power those women had over them, and I think that was courageous and to be celebrated. In Christianity, particularly in Catholic teachings, to endure injury to advance the condition of others, is an undertaking rewarded by God. Therefore, God looks favorably on those who did not give in to their weaknesses. Think about it… Dante gets to stay in love with Beatrice, and he retains the good favor of God. There could be no greater happy ending: Dante experiences eternity in the company of Beatrice in Heaven.

Those events would find no appeal in a generation preoccupied with the here and now. There may be no value in focusing on the afterlife for most of you, but to that generation, it was the perfect alternative… the life to come being superior to the one on earth. Now excuse my expression, but that is fucking amazing!"

A less outspoken female found she needed to add another dimension to the discussions.

"That was intense. I understand exactly what you are saying, but I have found all those feelings very much more evident and honest in another woman. I have been in a long-term lesbian relationship, and I must say that two liberated vaginas work so much better together."

The others laughed and applauded approvingly.

"I mean, there is much less stress with very clear expectations. I find there are no *head* games if I may use that expression. No battle of the sexes, with less selfishness and a greater urge to cater to the needs of my lover. I find there is more romance, and a stronger commitment to make the other happy. This is not an attack on hetero people, nothing against the *dicks* here, but I confess I tried that, and no matter how *deep* my disappointment, I stayed friends with my male lovers. Turning to another woman for my emotional needs seemed so much more natural. I know this would have confused the crap out of your Renaissance poets, but I would like to think that they would have sided with love in any form."

Perplexed at first, Gianluca found his best response.

"Okay, I can appreciate the monkey wrench tossed into this, I can respect your situation, and I would want to agree with you, however, based on their deep religious indoctrination, our Renaissance men would have dwelt on the sinfulness of a homosexual relationship. If they had a friendship with the two lesbians, they may have cryptically expressed affections for them, but the heresy would have haunted them as well. Dante, for instance, would have had no choice but to place them somewhere in hell, most likely in one of the less tempestuous circles. I would think he would have attempted to treat them as he did *Paolo* and *Francesca*, but I'm not sure he would have gotten away with it. You are all familiar with the adulterous couple, and you recall how Dante may have been an admirer of their love, but he sadly meets them in the second circle populated with the lustful who forfeited reason to their illegitimate passions and sexual desires. Not sure Dante would have mentioned homosexuality outright, but I have to believe he would have treated it with compassion."

Morelli then noticed Tracey itching to get another comment in as she shook her head in disagreement. Not convinced with the argument he had made about courage and motivation to act, she insisted that Morelli give up more of his past.

"You speak of courage; now wouldn't it have been more courageous to win the female over completely? I mean, why not put your guts out there and just tell her face to face? Why did you give up on Annmarie?"

Morelli betrayed a bit of annoyance in his response.

"Tracey, your questions seem filled with the presumption that one should go out there and claim what they want. That sense of entitlement has always been one of my criticisms of your generation. Many of you walk into these classrooms with the notion that you are entitled to an "A" because you have self-evaluated long before you entered college, convinced that it's the only grade that can validate your genius.

Just because you profess love for another, it can hardly mean you are entitled to have that person. In the very least, I would have had to consider the feelings of my best friend, and the fact that Annmarie was securely involved with someone she already loved, even if it was a teen love that still had some maturing to do.

Here's what I have learned, and what I believe to be a better truth: there is no courage exhausted in a bold-faced affirmation of one's love for another. The bravest action is to confront yourself, peel away all the artificial layers of indoctrination, discover your most organic, quasi-primitive condition, and ignore the entitlements… deny yourselves what the system has taught you to demand. In the process you will learn to appreciate, even love the life that others project. If there are insurmountable obstacles to having the person, or to have your love rejected, then love the life, and not the person. I know that is asking much given that in our contemporary culture that option would be considered too unselfish."

His words became stingingly sarcastic.

"Why would you want to waste your time fantasizing about what you can't have when you can just move on to someone more available to feed your ego. I mean, you might end up writing the most beautiful sonnet ever to memorialize the power a woman had over you. Now why would you want to make that contribution to humanity?"

Jason stood up again and played into the professor's challenge.

"Fine, I think I get it. There's a woman in this class that I greatly admire, I mean borderline in love with, but I have seen her on campus with another guy. I can easily compose a poem or a sonnet, as you insist, to memorialize (waving his hand above his head as if to trivialize the notion) how she makes me feel. Now, do I give her what I write in person, do I email, do I drop it off incognito at her dorm room door, or do I publish my work with the hope that future generations will get a chance to read them with commentary from some professor who will be teaching the stuff in the year twenty-five hundred?"

Chuckling and whispers from his full class of twenty-six filled the hall as they eagerly anticipated Morelli's answer. He took a moment testing his response in his head hoping to avoid contradictions.

"Good try. It would be foolish to think that I could ask you to apply the same fatalistic process as a Renaissance poet. I can't imagine it would work the same way or that it would have any value. I am bestowing on you instead, the opportunity to change the narrative; to apply a modern standard that could be praised in the future for its own uniqueness, on its own merit. Write your poems and your sonnets and deliver them to the deserving female. Let us in on the reaction if you so desire, with no need to reveal the person. Will your attempt be successful, or will you be forced to retreat to your cave to commiserate with the ghosts of our friends from the past? Point being that you can still feel the sweet convulsions of love and find a way to reconcile should you be rejected. Then you will be on equal footing with the greatest of destitute lovers. Question is, will you continue to praise your love in prose and elevate her to some mystical platform to be admired by future generations? You must admit it makes for a timeless story about the tribulations of a bankrupt suitor; bringing sighs and tears to those who will read your passages. In my gentle opinion, I believe it to be a fate more interesting than those of men who realize, who conquer the object of their love. Sadly, my guess is you will confidently give up and move on, leaving little trace of your amorous excursion."

Jason became inquisitive as he amplified the discussion.

"So, have there not been stories of those famous writers who won over their love? I mean, stories of men who did have an affair with the woman of their dreams, even if the results were tragic? Aren't those just as interesting, just as powerful? I can think of Guinevere and Lancelot, for instance. It involved adultery, betrayal, and clearly, they had sex."

Morelli became more determined. "Where's the tragedy?".

"Professor, it obvious! King Arthur loses his wife's affections to one of his knights who has sworn loyalty to him."

"Fine, but these are tales where there is consummation, and most of these are narrated by an author, a third party. The resulting union of two bodies is the culmination of the energies spent, of all the talk and the courtship… and that's where it ends; they either die in each other's arms or they live happily ever after, as we are made to believe. The poets we are talking about lacked similar opportunities, and as such, spoke to us about the experience of bodies that never became one in their own melancholy words. So, people who have had unrealized loves in their lives make this deep connection to these works because they suggest a path to lessening their trauma in favor of singing the praises of a would-be lover. You may one day experience the same trauma by falling deeply in love with an impossible someone, but you can lessen it not by singing her praises, but by finding a replacement that will keep you busily involved, helping you to forget… and even if you don't feel the same intensity, you *have* moved on. Not sure if it's clear, but I can't imagine imposing on yourself the same emotional constraints as our Renaissance friends… there are other options, and contemporary writings mimicking those of the past may today be ridiculed, condemning the poor romantic to order a pepperoni pizza or a gallon of ice cream to help get over it. It just seems that we have gotten to a point where losing a lover is no big deal, and certainly nothing to write about."

Tracey reacted as if in a trance.

"Professor, excuse the expression, but that's fucked up!

I'm sad to say that you're right. I understand the differences between then and now. I understand what you mean by the liberated vagina… like, I really don't give a crap if my lover picked up and walked out on me. I would be somewhat hurt, but not because he doesn't love me anymore, but because maybe I did something to get him to leave. Still, I would get over it in a week or so, and then just kinda move on, you know, keep living my life. I don't think I could ever need someone so intensely to have me get sick over it. And I also want to say that these poets were all men. It seems that today a woman would write about an impossible love rather than a man; and I don't want the guys here to think I'm sexist or rude, but I just don't think men today care enough to fall in love and to have those kinds of emotions… I don't think they have it, at least based on the dates I have been on, or even the men I have spent a few months with. And you may be right about not having to work hard for a woman's affections because, once again, they are dealing with our liberated sexuality; you know, women that are ready and willing to hook up. I'm not sure what I prefer more: a romantic guy willing to court me and work a little harder for my affections, or being a liberated female who enjoys calling my own shots on dating and sex… I enjoy that freedom, and maybe today's women are also losing their need to be pursued and married. I'm in no rush right now, but I feel that as I get on in years, I would want something more traditional, some other person to share my life with and to grow old together. My parents have been married for twenty years and I still admire the love they have for each other and how caring they are… they have been each other's best friend since high school. I don't know… I get so confused about this shit."

Gianluca's reaction was already hanging on his lips.

"My dear girl, I think the confusion is as common today as it was in the fourteenth century, indeed throughout human history. Those poets and artists were probably much more confused about life considering the inability to make sense of the restrictions on their free spirits. They thought of life as a vast empty canvass or a book of blank pages ready to record experiences as they lived them, yet their creations could have been censored, even burned as heresy. They would have loved living in our century, even if for only a short time, but I'm not so sure they would have produced at the level they did. Freedom is double-edged… you can have uninhibited minds creating and inventing beyond even our imaginations, or it can stifle a mind that needs an impulse, a cataclysm to create. Our poets and artists had to work within constraints that would be unacceptable today, and I believe those restrictions fueled their desires to invent. Then again, who knows. We can only predict with so much certainty how things would have turned out. So, much of what I'm saying is pure conjecture, and knowing these geniuses as well as we do is still no guarantee we can factually construct their every decision."

As more students became involved in the discussions, another girl, in gothic attire, indigo-colored lips and nails, raised her hand to ask her professor about his future.

"Professor, I have two questions. Considering your age, have you planned for your future? I mean, not with money, but with companionship. I gathered from our discussions that you have never been married and have no children. Is it getting a bit late for you? And secondly, what about those who acted on their desires and hooked up and did the nasty, what happened to them?"

The others whispered a string of indecipherable comments as Gianluca dealt with the sharp intrusion into his personal life.

"Wow, you have me dead and buried. My dear Cassandra, your concern is well taken; it's a dilemma I have been dealing with. It hasn't escaped me that time is becoming my oppressor, but I have come to terms that I may be able to live out my years alone in the company of myself. I have dated, and have had steady relationships that lasted several years, but I succumb to my selfish interests like many urbanites. I mean, this city has been my constant companion, and it has served my needs as well as any woman could have… except for the physical intimacies, of course. I confess I have enjoyed the perks of our liberated world in that it makes no demands on us to settle down. In that way I'm no different than your generation."

He paused to gather his thoughts.

"Yet, in my heterosexual world I have yearned for an honest love affair, but I have no expectations that it will happen, nor am I easily swayed. It would take an exceptional woman, and I don't mean exceptional in beauty or personality, but one capable of defeating my self-worship, to break me down, and conquer me with all her virtues. I'm convinced no such person exists, at least not for me. Why would any woman want to take on that task? So, I live my days blissfully capitulating to the impossible. As for your second question, there were individuals back then who acted on their desires, some real, some fictional. In most cases things did not turn out well. Best example I can think of again is the fate of Paolo and Francesca in Dante's *Inferno Canto Five*. Dante enters the second circle of hell where he meets actual sinners. Remember, the lower the circle, the more serious the sin, and therefore the more intense the suffering. The souls in circle two are those who gave in to their carnal impulses and betrayed social and religious laws. While the sins are unforgiveable, Dante expresses a deep compassion for the two lovers, as if condoning their actions because he is such an admirer of true love; in fact, he faints at the thought of seeing them in hell, and to witness the depth of their misery. They are there because Francesca has committed adultery with Paolo, the brother of her deformed husband. Paolo has fornicated with a married woman... no good. This was really bad stuff back then. Paolo's brother kills them both when they are discovered. They necessarily end up in hell unwilling to have acted on conscience; they ignore the morality which would have kept them from sin, aware of their wrongdoing but did it anyway. Dante has no choice; he must place them in hell, or his work will be seen as a betrayal of Christian teachings and lose credibility. Since they are both killed in the act, neither has time to repent, to admit to their sins and express remorse. They were lovers in life, and they remain lovers in hell, but they are tossed around incessantly by furious winds never allowed to escape the torment. Think about this-they retain the intensity of their love for each other but lose the mortal powers they had to act on it. Imagine that kind of suffering for eternity. Remember, to the Renaissance mind, heaven and hell are eternal, whatever happens in those places goes on forever. So, here you have an example of two who did the nasty, as you put it, and are duly punished. Hell was a real place to them.

Manipulating your conscience from steering you on a righteous path increased your chances of sinfulness, and therefore a one-way ticket to hell."

She wanted to know more.

"Bottom line professor, the woman you describe for yourself doesn't exist, so you are not willing to compromise or consider a companion that falls a little short? Is there no room in your view for love to grow, for a woman to learn, to have the chance to kick your narcissistic ass?

As for Paolo and Francesca, I would have done the same. I would have consumed the affair if I felt that strongly about my lover. I would think that living the truth would appeal to God in any form. If God is the purest truth, then why wouldn't God validate the truth by rewarding the lovers and only punishing the murderer? Paolo's brother was guilty of rejecting the truth and living his own lie: the falsehood that he deserved Francesca. I'm so sick of God's hypocrisy, of how powerless he seems when human morality would have easily forgiven the two lovers. Why would God be so determined to enforce punishment on the truth? I don't get it."

The rough inquisition from Cassandra generated an uneasy abstraction that had him searching for some balance.

"That's a powerful statement-well said. But why leave something so profound to chance? I prefer to have my ego kicked around and trashed in a first encounter. If the spark is there after only a few dates, then your weakness is rewarded, and you can start planning a future together. As for the God thing, the very notion of a supreme, almighty being with the power to judge was meant to sort the good from the evil, and not truths from untruths. I don't think God gives out brownie points to those who live sinful truths. Paolo and Francesca may have been truthful to themselves in the acts they committed, but Dante is powerless to place them anywhere other than hell, and his deep tenderness and mercy for the lovers is not enough to displace the Christian dogma that demands condemnation. At least the first two circles of hell are described as much less hard core than the lower circles where punishments are much more in line with Medieval tortures."

As his frazzled voice dwindled to a whimper, he murmured his final thought as the period ended.

"In a more tribal setting we were meant to minimize our personal needs, abide by rules of mutual survival, and to live and produce for others."

The lecture hall had almost emptied when Cassandra approached him.

"You know, I'm not totally convinced that your Renaissance heroes were any more concerned about humanity than the average guy. I think they produced their works as a way of justifying their weaknesses, their lack of courage to go after what they really wanted out of life. Paolo and Francesca did just that. When Dante meets them, he may be showing sadness for them, but I also think he is beating himself up for not being more like them. I have to go, but I would love to talk to you more about this topic. We only have one class left, and I'm graduating in two weeks, so do you have time to meet. Do you know the Poet's Café' on Bleeker and Sullivan?"

"Yes, I spend hours there, you can imagine."

"Fine, how about tomorrow around six?"

He nodded hesitantly, captivated by the shadows that shrouded her eyes. She smiled and confirmed.

"Great, see you tomorrow."

As she disappeared down the hall, Gianluca leaned against his desk anticipating the difference of opinions that would probably characterize their encounter the following day. He couldn't help wondering about Cassandra's growing interest in the class. She had fulfilled the course requirements admirably, never missing a class, handing in all her work, receiving high grades. What confused him was her semester long silence in class. She hardly said a word, paying close attention to lectures and discussions. He kept the thought alive as he retreated to his apartment after picking up food at his favorite Korean take out. The following day he had no classes, but a full schedule of department meetings and an appointment with the university publisher's office to review an edited version of the first five chapters of his new book-*Insights into the Writings of Jane Austin*. The afternoon was spent researching at the university library. That evening he prepared to keep his appointment with Cassandra.

It was a short stroll to the café from his apartment. Cassandra was there early sitting at a small bistro table for two in a backroom corner. The eclectic décor included rows of books by famous poets stacked on bookshelves harnessed precariously to the stucco walls. Framed posters from the Poetry Foundation hung to fill open spaces, while visitors added their own graffiti poetry on tables, furniture, and any uncovered spaces on the walls. The atmosphere had a Beatnik quality to it, with Dylan and Joan Baez songs, and other folk artists from the fifties and sixties playing from tiny speakers dangling from ceiling brackets. Stacks of old books sat in bins for sale at a dollar each. Paintings by art majors sat lined up on the floor against the wall like file folders waiting for curious buyers. Morelli had purchased several in the past to decorate his loft apartment in Greenwich Village. Cassandra greeted him with a smile as she took one last drag of a joint before extinguishing it and tucking the unused half in her blazer pocket. As Morelli took his seat across from her, he noticed that much of her gothic makeup had been replaced by a more relaxed, preppie look. He also picked up on the school crest stitched on the right side of her blazer. He leaned over to read: Saint Catherine Academy for Girls.

"Is that your real high school blazer?

"Yep, it is my high school blazer, and yes, I was raised to be a good Catholic girl. I still wear it, but only to remind me of all the things I hated about my teenage past."

Perplexed, he asked why she had such ill feelings about her high school years.

"I fought my mother to keep me out of an all-girls Catholic high school, but she insisted and won. They were four miserable years that still haunt me."

"I know high school can be an issue for many, but I hardly hear talk of hating it. What got you so irritated?"

"The fucking hypocrisies. We wore conformist uniforms while they talked about free will. The girls all acted out their lies about chastity, and the make-believe role models they were supposed be, when in truth they were total bitches and sold out on their virginity as soon as they found a dick they liked. They did it so they wouldn't lose the guy to some other chick. The richer girls advertised their shit every day, and the super smart ones would freak out on you if they didn't get straight A's. I didn't match up on any level. I struggled with grades, my mother worked two jobs to pay the tuition, and girls like me had to wait in line for attention. The ones with the power couple parents, you know, lawyers, doctors, bank presidents, were treated with white gloves. The school knew that with those people it wasn't just about the tuition, but more so about the big money donations they would make to the school's endowment. I didn't have the money to start college right after high school, so I worked and here I am thirty-five and just now getting out of college."

"Yes, but why such resentment? Did you expect those girls to overcome their wealth and power privileges to create a more equitable environment? Did you truly think they would ever be that concerned with you, and wasn't it just another example of how things work? You must know, your experiences have been around for centuries, there's nothing new here. Equality is an impossible utopia. Some will always have more or want more than others, and they will find a way to get it. Humans are not capable of equality by nature and habitat. Our distant ancestors who first discovered that it was better to live in a cave than to brave the outdoor elements, developed means to keep that cave theirs. Those on the outside, without a cave, realizing it offered a better chance at survival, developed the means to take it away, to conquer it, even in a Machiavellian way. It was that human nature that kicked in and is still around because it evolved with us. Obviously, factoring in evolution, we keep creating the means to compete and dominate. Every attempt at creating more equitable societies will always have this time bomb built into it, and it is the reason why past attempts have failed. Forgive me, it's in my nature to lecture, I didn't mean to turn you off. Your mom's struggles have paid dividends. You seem to be well focused on doing something meaningful with your life. I gather your dad wasn't around".

She attempted a cold, indifferent response, but it was clear the topic carried some pain when she lost eye contact with Morelli.

"The fucker left when I was three. Saw him only on Christmases for a few minutes. Haven't seen him since I graduated from high school. He didn't show for that, and last I heard he was shacked up with a woman somewhere upstate with two kids. I don't think he ever wrote any poems to my mother. They never married, and she got pregnant when she was eighteen. The wimp couldn't handle the responsibilities, and he wasn't able to hold a job long enough to pay the rent. Mom moved back in with her parents. I was pretty much raised by my grandparents in the Bronx."

Morelli's compassion kicked in attributing his upbringing to good fortune. "I was a bit luckier. Problem is we can't choose our parents when we are born. Mine were very much in love. They had me early, and then concentrated on their work as professors in Italy. They spent much time researching and writing their books, but they never ignored me. They took teaching jobs at NYU, so they moved to New York when I was about to enter high school. I lived an eccentric existence in the company of friends my parents cultivated from the university. They eventually retired to their home in Padova. They enjoy a very bohemian life in a small cottage near the city. But this isn't the reason you wanted to meet. You had some need it seemed to follow up on something we discussed in class."

Cassandra leaned back on her chair, and turned away toward the large smokey window, her eyes tailgating each passing car. She remained silent, ignoring the café chatter. With her mind made up, she revealed how little her request to meet had to do with the class.

"What about the British accent?"

"I was dropped off at a boarding school in London from the time I started middle school. I was eleven. Throughout those years into high school, I came back to New York only during the summers. The accent came easy-I picked it up quickly because I liked it."

"Look, you're a lot like those poets, and I think you also lack the balls to say what you want. You prefer to clothe yourself in abstractions so that others can't define you. You live this shady existence somewhere between reality and the romanticism that shapes your views of relationships, and I think you refuse to side with either. Are you settling on the same fate as your poets? You would choose to deny yourself the pleasures of any relationship so you can pity yourself in some pathetic romantic delusion? Why are you so into loving the illusion instead of falling in love? You don't have to be in love to love, you know. It can be a process. You start with liking the person, finding common ground, doing shit you both enjoy, and then you grow into each other. You do share a certain kind of love in a relationship that doesn't initially set you on fire." She paused, scanned the room.

"I can't stand men like you, but I admit I find you weirdly appealing. It's like I have this urge to blow your mind in a wild fuck, but then I think I'm only feeding your arrogance. In the end what matters is that we satisfy our needs and curiosities... neither of us gets over on the other. Is that something you can deal with?"

Morelli sat dumbfounded, unable to find the words that would either express a moral displeasure to change the topic, or to keep the conversation alive, succumbing to her truth. He decided to follow her lead to see where it would take him.

"I'm not sure how to react. Part of me wants to walk away from the conversation, but I know that would be artificial and cowardly. You've shown the greater audacity, making me feel quite small. I want to disagree, but I can't deny some of the truth in what you say. I admit I would want to experience the same convulsions as my poets, and I understand the futility in that, but to take it to that level would be to push the human-to-human experience to its greatest climax... if I'm allowed to use that word around you. You see, what stimulation is there in achieving the conventional, to make a choice in a partner, marry, have children, pay off a mortgage, grow old and die? It is a mind-numbing path, dictated by norms and social expectations. I want to be challenged by the unconventional, the improbable... to be totally consumed in a mental and emotional battle with the promise of an alternate nature, something that guides us way beyond our human limitations. I would think something akin to a high from a strong hallucinogenic, but without the drug. A high driven exclusively by our own atoms. Shit, listen to me, I'm going off on stuff that just seems wacky to people. I'm so sorry… I should save this for my classes."

She had taken her shoes off while he juggled his thoughts and words. Her toes flirted with the inside of his leg in a feathery caress causing his next sentence to fall apart like a disbanded puzzle. He refused to panic, so he pulled a pen from the inside pocket of his blazer and started composing words on his napkin. She pushed aside her shoes and walked barefoot to the counter, returning with two double espressos and a small bowl of panna.

"Writing me a poem?" She asked sarcastically.

"That might come next, but right now I'm simply trying to record what I want to say, since your toes are making it extremely difficult to concentrate."

"Well then let me continue since I'm enjoying that side of you; weakened and confused."

Her toes picked up where they left off. She anticipated him pulling away, but his leg became a willing participant. She doubled down by pushing closer to his crotch pleasantly aware that it wasn't only his leg that had stiffened.

"Professor Morelli, if I didn't know any better, I would think you're 'growing' in love; you've responded so well to the stimulus... bravo!"

He moved his hand slowly below the table attempting to guide her foot away long enough to manage his erection, only to sense that touching her toes did more to prolong it.

"So, is this your big tease? Am I supposed to give in at this point and invite you back to my apartment? I wouldn't expect such a cliche move on your part; I thought you much less counterfeit than this."

She ran her hand over the top of her head brushing back the long midnight hewed strands, sighing as if bored with the professor's predictable reaction.

"Gianluca, your performance is the cliché. So predictable for a man, even one as worldly as you. I have no intention of fucking your brains out just for the sake of a fuck. How sad of you to think that I need to prove how good I am in bed. Men think that the goal of all premeditated actions is to feed one's sense of self-worth. I have no desire to prove how unconditionally I can conquer your penis... to have you capitulate, and then to unravel you, so you finally understand who you are. You see, I don't think you know who you truly are, and I have this weird need to challenge you till you acknowledge it. I'm convinced that the philosophies you advocate for in class are as weak as you are. That your kind of love is an invention, a false state of mind. That your willingness to eternally romance a woman that doesn't exist is the ultimate surrender, the ultimate cop out, and you can't continue to believe that what you teach should be an aspiration for others. You see, I think that you can shed all the bullshit, and fall in love with the sex and not necessarily the woman."

Perplexed, he asked why.

"Why is that so important to you? I think you miss the point. We have two avenues when it comes to the impossible: we can either make it possible or accept its impossibility. If making it possible is impossible, then we should romance the impossibility. I'm perfectly happy with that choice. Look, I have a need to romance what constitutes the greatest impossibility in my life. I choose to walk away from an improbable love not because I am too weak to try, but because I am convinced it will never be reciprocated, that circumstances will not allow her to share the same feeling for me. I refuse to drive my affliction into a dead end. I want to exhaust its intensity in praise of what is not mine. I think it's wrong of you to believe the aspiration to be delusional." She snapped.

"Holy shit, Gianluca! There it is again, that need to own a woman so you can love her. If you can't own her or make her yours, you have no right to love her, just let it go. How can you fucking love someone you haven't had in any capacity? I mean, if you never held hands, if you never took a bath together, if you never laid in bed naked, never discovered each other's bodies, each other's being, then how can you declare your love? Give me the chance to prove that you can have me, love me, love the moment, and still not be in love. I promise it will change your life. You can't wait until your dying day in the hope that you will have your Beatrice... look at what happened to Dante. He spent the rest of his life romancing someone he never had. Fuck, that path should be the least of two choices, and only when an alternative doesn't present itself. I'm your alternative."

She paused, sipped her coffee, and waited for a reaction. Nothing. She became irritated.

"Are you seriously going to avoid life? It's almost as if you are hoping to fall in love with a chick who doesn't know you, willing to piss away your days thinking you can recreate that artificial ideal from centuries ago. Your poets and artists have you captivated and brainwashed, and you are an enabler… you really want that… you fucking want to go through the same persecution, the same torture. So, if this magical female should cross your path, you will fall absolutely in love, she will even repay your affections, but you will be the ultimate dick and refuse to consume it just so you can place yourself on a par with your martyrs. How pathetically amazing that you've known this all along. You have no intentions of ever allowing any woman to mess up your sick plan. Worse yet, I can't believe that your debilitated mind makes me want to fuck you even more. I have this crazy urge to conquer your ass, and then you can go off in search of your shit. And what if you are incapable of leaving some footprint, some fossil of yourself for future generations to discuss you in a classroom. Then what? You will have pissed away the chance to fulfill yourself sharing a common destiny with someone, and no one will ever learn about it. You'll be a forgotten gravestone in some overpopulated cemetery."

She took a deep, exasperated breath, and angrily gave her ultimatum. "So, we need to test each other. Your place, a nice hotel, or a weekend in my favorite town Newport."

He covertly scanned the area around him wondering if anyone had listened in on her words. Secure in the fact that her voice had not risen above the chatter of others in the café, he lowered his eyelids, and in thought he begged himself to

suffocate his logic and to follow the scent laid down by
Cassandra.

When he came to: "You are inviting me into your bed.
Doesn't it bother you that I'm the guy teaching a class you're
enrolled in? That I'm fourteen years older, and that we seem to
have little in common? I've been to Newport. I would love to
experience it in your company, but I don't want to fuck, I have
such a hard time getting that word out."

She smiled, ran her foot up his leg one more time. "My
dear professor, I will spend the time between now and then
thinking of a way to change your mind."

He finally allowed the leg massage to relax his posture,
slumping further into his chair. "Fine, let's deal with your
obsession. I'm curious, doesn't the age difference bother you.
Is this a daddy thing?"

She sarcastically, almost angrily chuckled a bit louder.
"You know, fuck you! You just had to go down that road. I
don't have a daddy issue because I hardly know what it is to
have a real dad. I got over that many years ago. That was
totally fucked up! You're a project for me... an experiment.
You need to be your age, someone younger wouldn't work. I
need your stoicism, your patience, your maturity to carry this
out. Younger men would fight it. They would want to control,

or at least share control of the process, and therefore sabotage it. This is not a head game... I explained it. I need to know if subliminal love, the love that is forced to dwell in the subconscious is superior to the love that is consumed.

You challenged us to think in those terms, now I challenge you to prove it. Can you resist me in bed? And if you can, I need you to come clean. If you can't, then I need a reason that will leave no doubt in my mind that there was no love exchanged, that you felt no love in the act itself. You understand this has nothing to do with your orgasm, and nothing to do with being in love with me. It has all to do with control. Will you be able to keep your quest for the impossible separate from what is real, from the skin that touches yours, from the breasts you want to touch, from lips that fuse to yours generating those violent shivers as they peel away, and finally from a body that has offered itself unconditionally?"

Morelli held his own, refusing to surrender to the sexually charged monologue.

"I need to be assured that you will not forfeit your friendship, nor your company should your experiment fail. I would hate to think that a relationship could fall prey to a misunderstood weekend. Will you deny me that in the event things work out differently?"

"Gianluca, you think so little of me. I have known for months that I could enjoy your company in any capacity."

CHAPTER 2- *NEWPORT CONFESSIONS*

Newport surprised them both. Cassandra's quest to exploit Morelli's weaknesses was replaced with a growing respect for the professor's willpower. As she settled for easy, intelligent conversations during long strolls on Bellevue Avenue, he began to feel that tender, amorous pinch in the company of an accommodating female. Charmed by her casual sexuality in sheer peasant blouses plunging loosely over tight jeans reaching down three quarters leaving her ankles exposed, rooted in a pair of low-cut white sneakers with pink shoelaces, he remained amazed at how the gothic had been replaced with a mellow, suburban look, challenging his every attempt to ignore her femininity. He asked about the transformation. She replied that it was common for her to decide on a feeling, an emotion and to then dress it up. He found her reasoning refreshing, adding to the intensity of that pinch.

They dined on the Wharf, sipped cocktails on Thames Street, spent the evenings wrapped in a blanket, seated on one of the lawns lining Ocean Drive gazing out at Newport Harbor, finishing off a bottle of Pinot. They finally had the time to test each other's philosophies without the restrictions imposed by classroom academics and the pace of life in New York.

Gianluca's temperament grew sluggish as Cassandra's nature made successful intrusions beyond his rationality, striking at the very citadel that jealously guarded his meticulously fabricated notions of love.

"You know, it doesn't escape me that you might be enjoying this. You even got all tingly when my body got a little close. It's not like you pulled away. Let's see how much of this you can handle."

He was so focused on her words... he hardly sensed her hand hidden under the blanket caressing the inside of his leg until it reached a startled crotch.

"So, how would Dante have reacted had he been sitting here with Beatrice? Would he have stifled himself, denied his penis the pleasures of a loving fondle or two? I know, he would have pulled away, appalled that one so divine as she could act on her impulses, on her own desires. Are you about to pull away? Will you leave me empty handed?" She giggled at her last remark.

He couldn't resist a spontaneous smile. It calmed the waters a bit, as he abandoned the power to change the course of things. She backed off fearful of instigating an embarrassment, returning to the inside of his leg with soft, slow strokes, granting him a well-earned recess. There was no panic-Gianluca was not a fifty-year-old virgin dealing with the trauma of an initiation. It was, however, his first experience with a woman so in control of her flirtation, and sexual courtship. His liberated mind was having a tough conservative time letting go of traditional practices that had escaped the scrutiny of the contemporary sterilization of male-female relations. It was not in him to initiate, but once a woman was comfortable, he found she welcomed his traditional courtship. Gianluca had never made a move without consent. That approach had him waiting patiently beyond first dates, genuinely willing to enjoy a woman's company, easily dealing with any impromptu sexual craving.

When they retreated to their hotel room late that Friday night, she invited him to shower with her. He hesitated, but finally gave in. Turning him on came easy as she suds him up with her juniper and patchouli shower gel. Not long into her slippery and playful stroking, she sensed his growing discomfort. He was hardly responding to the kind of manipulation that would have sent most men over the edge, victims of an experienced woman. He wrapped himself in the towel she handed him, and slipped under the covers, ignoring the droplets trickling onto his face from the thick strands of wet hair. Cassandra followed, dropping her towel as she leaned against the mattress. Her damp skin caused him a slight shiver as she shoelaced her legs into his… beguilingly pivoting her still wet breasts gently into his chest. He sighed as one who had found a peaceful place in the arms of a moist embrace.

"Gianluca, I want to apologize for mouthing off about the whole sex thing, and for being insensitive using the word-*fuck*. Now I understand that for you it can't be just about a fuck. It takes you to a more primitive place that you are uncomfortable with. Being here in your arms is good, it's pure, no deception. Feel free to change your mind about the sex, and if it means more to you, make love to me. I'm not used to this, but I can't deny it has a hold on me. I came to Newport to prove you wrong about love, now I'm feeling it's me that is learning a deeper lesson."

Gianluca lifted her face and looked into her eyes. "You made the challenge, I said nothing. Remember, you did agree to not abandon the friendship or our time together should your experiment falter. I believe it won't because you have summoned my affections with your stubborn, in your face strength."

His fingers combed away strands of soggy hair that clung to her lips. She said nothing anticipating more intimacy. "Forgive me if I disappoint beyond wanting to feel your skin. I may be a fool, still I don't want to forfeit the chance of keeping you in my life after the sex is over. All too often something has gone lost the morning after. There have been times when I regretted it."

He paused as thoughts bounced around in his head. "You're right, I've lost sight of my place and time. Living the past has its traps, and I believe I have fallen for one. Here's the crazy part: I go back to their books and those pages I have flipped so many times, and I am transported, I leave the present wanting to feel their passions, their anxieties, the futility of catering to their sentiments, and ultimately the pain of having lost. I imagine myself living in a dangerous world, of being exposed or discovered, of living in denial, unable to exercise freedoms we take for granted. I feel that the love we wish to express for someone can only be immense if it overcomes those constraints. I don't see it today; I don't see the obstacles. I see only open doors through which we pass with ease denying ourselves nothing it seems… and in the process dimming the value of life itself. Cassandra, how can we arrive at the purest truth about ourselves if we have never been confronted with meaningful struggles? Where is the truth in a world that denies us almost nothing? What I found in the poets was not the power to overcome, but the power to accept. In overcoming one still finds a way to have what is desired. In acceptance, one learns to live without… no self-pity, no commiseration, no need for condolences, only the glory of having submitted to the inevitable. My poets would say: I have suffered my circumstance, I have accepted, and I have the power to memorialize it, to love in the deepest sense that which is denied me."

As much as she cared for his feelings, Cassandra couldn't help calling out his delusion.

"Gianluca, you run the risk of taking all this to your grave... what satisfaction would there be in that? You can avoid all the trauma, the torture and still take the difficult path to love. You may fall deeply for a woman who may not share the same, but you can spend your days convincing her otherwise. That could be the toughest thing you've ever done, but you could end up together rather than eulogizing her the rest of your life. Shit, what could be more rewarding than to touch, to kiss, to make love to a person rather than some fantasy that lives in your head! You've created a prison for yourself, and I'm sorry, but you seem stupidly comfortable in it.

Maybe I don't share the same passion for the way you interpret love, but I know my delusions and I refuse to cater to them. Time dedicated to fantasies is time lost. If I'm going to fantasize about someone, I'm going to make every attempt to turn it real. If it turns to shit, I'll give up and get it out of my system. For me it's not worth keeping the hope alive. I'm certainly not going to dedicate a life to constantly recalling what could have been... com'on Gianluca... what a waste for a person like you who understands what it takes to love."

As she caressed his face, he found no words. There was more he wanted to say, but the intensity of the discussion weighed on his senses, stealing away what little energy he had left to pick the arguments that would keep him inspired. She dwelt on his quiet body, pitying what she believed was a man caught in a tempest, incapable of freeing himself from the ghosts of his beloved poets. What Cassandra described as delusions, Gianluca had spent a lifetime protecting as reasonable obsessions. He was handsome, she thought, even as he slept. He had already beguiled her with his quiet sexuality. He didn't put it out there like many men, he simply wore it like an old, shabby pair of jeans. That look had always appealed to her, and it sent a message that he had a hold on his male ego... that his masculinity was of a gracious, reserved quality that made her want to cuddle up more, to cradle her head into his chest, trying to decipher what he sheltered so studiously in his beating heart. She wondered if she had fallen in love with him or his image. There was no need to provide an answer. The time shared with such a man was what she had imagined sitting there in his classes, plotting for opportunities to be alone with him, captivated by the lectures, the topics, his easy, likeable appearance, his willingness to expose his convictions. She recalled how difficult it had been to avoid seeing him beyond his title. The approaching graduation, the end of the semester had forced her hand. Now she was where she wanted to be, sedated in the moment, studying his face, running her finger over his five o'clock shadow, inhaling all of him, aware that sequels could be rare.

She thought of how the mere length of a semester listening to his teachings, observing his mannerisms, and paying attention to his conversations could offer enough to advance her affections. Her final reflection before joining him in sleep was to wonder if there would be happiness in a life together; if there would be true companionship, and sincere love that would endure. She imagined them living under one roof, a child or two, with blissful pizza nights, beach vacations, taco Tuesdays, and parent-teacher conferences. She giggled quietly, rebuffing the images, chiding herself for being so silly, all the time acknowledging that Gianluca had been the only man to ever get her to think that way.

The following day getting out of bed was delayed till late morning. Gianluca came to with a curious face. She thought him awkward, almost comical in his inability to say what was on his mind.

"You seem lost, like something doesn't add up. Are you confused?"

He looked around, jostled the covers to reveal his naked body. Moving his hand towards her side of the bed, it brushed up against her breasts. In his version of a panic, he tried to recall what had transpired that night. Remembering little, he debated if he should return for a second feel.

"Last night, did we..., I mean did you, did I..., you know... did something happen? I apologize for not recalling, I think I fell asleep."

She couldn't help taking advantage of his confusion.

"Well, my experience has been that most men fall into a deep sleep after a powerful orgasm. Come, you can touch."

She struggled to masquerade her smile as she gently pulled his hand back to where she wanted it. In that weak moment, he debated the truthfulness of Cassandra's words.

"Please forgive me if I was harsh in any way. It must have been the wine; I probably drank more than I'm used to. I am ashamed to admit, I remember nothing of... well, of anything we did or didn't do. Tell me, please tell me I wasn't rude."

"You were a perfect gentleman, fast asleep before you could lay a finger on any of me. Yes, we showered together, got into an oversized king bed, in a romantic inn, finished off a bottle of wine under a full moon on a clear, dark sky, carpeted with countless stars, and… you fell asleep. My dear professor, I can't say this has ever happened. I mean, I think I have an appealing body, and I confess I have been sexually active exclusively with older, sexy males. You have the added attraction of being a romantic, which is rare. So, what did I do to make you check out? I made no suggestions, except for being naked, and I made no moves beyond a touch or two. I have a strong feeling you're not gay, so I couldn't come up with an explanation that would rock me to sleep. I did enjoy watching your eyes twitch, your lips pucker up as you slept, and I deciphered the sighs that have given me an idea of where your dreams were taking you. I wonder, was it me you were making love to? I hope so."

He had argued himself into a corner, with little left to explain why he wasn't guided by his more erotic instincts. He thought himself a fool as Cassandra rolled out of bed and stood facing him.

"Come, I'm taking a shower, join me. I'm starving, and

I wanted to try that breakfast place The Mokka House. It has that eclectic outdoor pavilion with those funky tables and chairs, and all those statues and driftwood carvings... did you notice?"

He accepted her invitation as he held her from behind, around her waist while she tested the water. He leaned his face into her neck captivated once again by the earthy scent of her unblemished skin. She had become much more seductive in her patient approach, granting him a chance to reform his emotions, while she delicately controlled her urges. His student had untangled him in a manner he least expected. Gianluca had the self-control he needed to keep to his doctrine on relationships, but Cassandra had breached it enough to have him break down in the shower, losing himself in the pleasures she demanded and those she bestowed.

The walk down to Thames Street on a perfect Newport day gave him the time to urge his thoughts back to the brilliance of her body and how completely she owned his. His fondness kept pace with their short journey into the downtown which added to his willingness to romance Cassandra's flawless company. Waiting for his order of lattes and buttered croissants, he gazed back as she adjusted her necklace, in the shadows of artistically arranged regalia that included mermaids and whales of all sizes, art deco water fountains, and vintage tin signs advertising fishing trips, bait, and boat sales. She toured the grounds, touching and softly running her fingers along the smooth surfaces of the ceramic and iron sculptures. The sight stressing how the weekend had gone from the improbable to a warm delight. Cassandra kept to the behavior she had adopted, and in between bites and sips, she spoke only of life yet to come.

"I'm thinking of going into teaching. I enjoy working with young kids. I spent time as an aide in a Catholic elementary school in the Bronx. I found it pleasing, funny, and rewarding. There were tough days as well and dealing with parents was a constant issue. I want children one day. I feel they add to the value of life. It's not just leaving a part of you behind in an offspring, but it's also an extension of who I am. I see myself living on, becoming almost immortal in my child. It's like without one we just cease to exist, practically nameless, faceless, to be totally forgotten. I can't handle that. What about you, what plans do you have?"

Gianluca hardly hesitated feeling easy about the topic.

"I have decided to retire from NYU at the end of the fall semester. New York no longer feels like an inviting place to call home. The changes have become almost unbearable. I know we are done with the pandemic, but the attitudes, the cautions, the physical and emotional sores are still there, and I'm convinced they are here to stay. They call it the new normal. That term can be applied to so many episodes throughout history. This isn't the first time we have transitioned to a new normal. I'm just not good with it. I enjoy the company of genuine people, transparent and honest in their friendships. I don't see that it's possible in the short term. Perhaps years from now the humanity will return. I'm not willing to wait."

Cassandra became saddened by his judgement.

"Shit, it seems you're running away. Why such pessimism with New York? I know we've taken a beating, but to call it quits over a hardship experienced by so many is kind of extreme. Look, it gets to me too sometimes, but I don't want to give up, walk away as if it's the only option left. Besides, how are we supposed to carry on a long-distance friendship? Texting and emails are not good enough. I doubt you would enjoy that. A Renaissance mind would reject all that. Where would you go? What place would be able to hold your interest as well as New York?"

He gave a tired response.

"I have been planning since last year. I can depend on a decent pension… now I'm sounding old, and I have some friends who took well to life in Florida. I'm being influenced by cliches, but the chance of missing out on the cold, and dirty snow winters on the streets of lower Manhattan, seemed too inviting to reject. I've only been there once for a few days. It lacks something, not sure what."

She couldn't resist a little sharp sarcasm.

"So, we have the summer and fall to get tired of each other. You know the population is mostly older people. Are you going to live in one of those retirement communities for people over fifty? If I should visit, I wouldn't be able to stay with you... you would be violating an age rule, I can't hide my age. Imagine the dirty looks I would get, especially from the grandmothers who wanted you all to themselves. You could show off a trophy mistress attached to your arm, with everyone thinking-what a stud. My goodness, we would have to stay in a hotel. I'm not convinced you need Florida just yet. What about us? We have this very cool friendship going, we seem to enjoy the company, with no expectations of anything more than that, and now you're on your way south, to have the sun set on your wimpy ass? Is it a definite?"

He leaned forward with his arms on the table and hands cradling his latte.

"Wimpy ass? If I were a wimp, I'd stay, afraid of making changes. I can't stay in New York. It has shaped my views of just about everything. I need something radically different; a new perspective, a place where people spend their days at a completely different pace. I feel the stagnation, and I can't ignore it. Away from the classroom would give me the time to write. I have written three books mostly on research, but I still want to do something original... an historical novel perhaps. I could rework the relationship between *Dante* and *Beatrice* or *Paolo* and *Francesca*. I feel like I've been living in a fog; losing sight of the past, blind to what's to come. Mostly my fault for not being aware of my own evolution as things around me changed. One finds comfort in the predictability of a good life, and then the festering creeps up on you, thirty years go by, and you've petrified like an ancient fossil, a creature that lived as intended, never leaving its natural habitat. Don't you ever feel like time keeps stalking you, prodding you to migrate, to make changes... I don't know, to discover another you in a different place?" She gave him a puzzled look.

"I'm having a tough enough time trying to figure myself out ten years older than everyone else in your class. I came to this so late. The only thing that makes me feel better is that I struggled less than the others. I think I was more in control of myself, and the work came easier to me. I did do well in your class... you gave me an *A* on all my papers. Now had we done this first, I would have had to drop your class... I would have been wondering if the grades were legit. So, can you give your decision to get out of New York some more thought? They say long distance marriages work great, but long-distance friendships are soon forgotten."

That Saturday afternoon, the only way she could shelter from the chilly wind that whistled through the open spaces of the Amazing Grace harbor cruise was to fit as much of her body into his. She folded arms, legs and head into a fetal bubble and found a way to fit it into his chest. She kept her hands warm by stretching and disfiguring her long sleeves enough to cover them. As his gaze followed the outline of the Newport coast, ignoring the mega yachts anchored within inches of each other, he felt overwhelmed by her frailty. He wondered about his poets and of how they would have dealt with the chance to sense the vulnerability of a woman. Love may not have been nipping at his heart, but he admitted that there was something glorious in having Cassandra so selfishly his. He hung on, his arms tightening around her as if some hideous cuckoo clock kept reminding him to preserve every inconceivable minute. He had to admit that her experiment had succeeded. She got him to submit to the moment, to the time granted by a complicit destiny. He found himself doing just that as she dozed off, melting further into his squeeze, her glossed lips bristling in the rays of the setting sun.

The path back to the hotel took them along Memorial Boulevard and Easton's Beach, where they rolled up their jeans to test the water, and to admire the second half of the sun disappear on the horizon.

"You know, you took a short nap on the boat. You drooled, and your snoring had everyone looking at us. I had to hold your jaw shut, and I wiped your chin with my sleeve... I looked but couldn't find a napkin or paper towel anywhere. Then your head dropped into my lap, face down. I tried lifting it, but again, I was helplessly inept."

The look on her face was part shock, part comical. "No freakin way! So, what did you do? Did you get me up?"

"I couldn't. A sleeping head is like four time its normal weight. I could only lift it a few inches, no more. I let you lay there comfy on top of my... you know... my uh..."

"Your dick? You just let me lay there with my face on your dick and balls while everyone looked on?"

"Well, I didn't want to disturb you... you kept moving around, rotating as if on a pillow... a perfect angel. I had to fight back my excitement while remaining as unruffled as possible. There was a woman across from us who couldn't help a supportive chuckle assuring me it was all good."

Cassandra looked at him baffled. "Gianluca, you allowed me to put on a show. I can't believe you didn't find a way to stop me. You loved every minute. What a shit you are. Is the story true or are you messing with me? You're lying! You made it up, I can tell by the look on your face."

"Not quite... I let you be. I had to let you prove your experiment, and I did enjoy it. You were right in many ways. You've turned me into an old fool pushing some silly, obsolete notion of love from the past... I'm starting to see it."

"Absolutely not! That was never my intention. I don't want you to reject all that is precious about the past. I admire those lonely hearts, and their courage. I just thought your infatuation was a bit extreme, and I confess, blind to the beauty of experiencing a woman's affections, a woman willing to share herself. It's also selfish on your part since a deserving woman would miss out on all your passion. Today it's all about satisfying sexual hungers, and rarely does a woman get to be the object of devotion. You've given me a taste of that devotion, and I am addicted. Now, if I didn't drag your stubborn ass up here, you would have remained oblivious, and I would have been left wondering. You see, we are in the moment, we share the same place and time, and we are practically obligated to make it happen, to grant each other the encounter... we are gifts to our desires, and you can't keep pissing that away. Come on Gianluca, I get your dedication to something greater than all this but save it for when you find the woman you want to canonize."

The weekend in Newport had been enough to steer them away from a trivial affair and toward a ripening best friend bond. Cassandra was becoming the woman you didn't fall in love with for fear of changing her. He was unfamiliar with this creature who could mouth off criticisms or praise with no filter, who allowed her mood to define her, and who could coach a man's heart out of its refuge and into a state of delirium. He was intrigued at the instant equity-as if the sexes had been marginalized. She could be the female confidant as well as a bar buddy just hanging out, bitching about all kinds of shit. She made no further incursions into his heart except to reassure him that he would never lose her friendship. She pressured him to stay in New York, but Gianluca was determined to move his life in a different direction.

CHAPTER 3- *Moonstruck*

New York would put up a good fight for his affections. There were days when Gianluca was determined to leave, buttressed by all the slippery reasons he could crowd into his conniving mind. Then there were days when he would criticize those reasons as false and misleading. Cassandra only added to the agitation by refusing to let up on her attempts to steer him towards staying. That summer the two had grown accustomed to spending their free time together.

Gianluca was the typical urbanite preoccupied with works of art, literature, gastronomy, and museum visits. Cassandra had grown up across from the stadium and the fields of Pelham Bay in the northeast corner of the Bronx. She was a regular on one of the softball teams that competed in the Pelham Summer League. She still lived in the same house she shared with her mother. In her teens she worked at Auggie's City Island Bait and Tackle, and fishing for stripe bass and blue fish was still a passionate hobby.

While Gianluca busied himself completing his work on Jane Austen, she spent the weekdays, except for Fridays, running fishing excursions out of New Rochelle. She had inherited a thirty-five-foot Scout fishing boat from her mother's brother who had taught her everything about fishing the waters of Long Island Sound. The windfall earnings supplemented her medical billing job. She would steal away any time she could during those hours on the water prepping for the Graduate Record Exam. She was playing catch up in school so starting her master's degree had taken on some urgency. Her goal was to end up in an elementary school classroom as a teacher. She loved children, and the volunteer work she performed at the local Catholic grade school helped with the career choice.

She tried to get him on her boat, but Gianluca's fear of the water, inability to swim, and his weak stomach kept him landlocked. He would do the beaches of Maine and the mountains of Vermont on weekend trips where they perfected their liaisons in a comfortable blend of playful platonic and sexual provocations. It worked because the romance had been neatly set aside. They adopted the prevailing cultural trend that allowed for liberties in relationships and falling in love was not one of them. A step in that direction would have altered the neat blueprint.

They spent the long July fourth weekend in a small bed and breakfast in the Mad River Valley of Vermont. After a satisfying meal that first morning, which included several cups of Vermont's finest coffee, as noted on the table literature,

Cassandra succeeded in getting Gianluca into a two-person kayak. He had known nothing of her plan at first, so he resisted like a child who had just figured out that the lollipop jar sitting on the desk of the pediatrician's office was merely a distraction to getting his first shot. Once the reality set in, Gianluca practically cried. A river didn't scare him as much as the ocean, but he still feared drowning even in five feet of water. He hoped to use dangerous conditions as an excuse to drop out, but the Mad River was not living up to its name on a windless, cool July day with a string of cotton candy clouds drifting off beyond the peaks of the Berkshires in the distance.

"Gianluca, are you fucking kidding me? You can't get out, we're about to drift into the current. Stop being such a wimp, just sit, I'll do the paddling. It's only an hour to the end of the course. I'll go slow. Open your eyes! The river is beautiful and there's so much to see. I don't believe this… you are so embarrassing! Look at those two kids in the kayak by themselves… you don't see them complaining. Look at me!… holy shit, Gianluca, look at me! I'll make sure you won't drown. Fine, you can wear the helmet, but you'll look like a total doo fuss… oh my god, if you could only see yourself."

Her laughter filled the air around the launching dock to which Gianluca paid no attention, preoccupied with trying to fish out his stray paddle from the water.

"Holy crap, you freakin lost your paddle and we haven't moved an inch yet."

He finally composed himself when Cassandra reached behind her and grabbed his balls threatening to squeeze harder if he didn't calm down. Paralyzed, he settled into his role as a terror-stricken passenger.

The meandering cruise down the Mad River turned into an unexpected delight. Seated behind Cassandra and doing little of the work, he took the time to focus on his companion's engaging nature. He never felt compelled to act merely to please her, and she never asked for more than his company. When it became physical, it was two friends satisfying each other's sexual desires rather than love making. Her silence, and the soothing sound of the moving waters sent his mind off on a journey of its own. He wondered if the concept of a soul mate had more to do with compatibility than love. He thought of how completely unselfish she had been in tolerating his fascination with antiquated philosophies on love that contradicted her modern sensitivities. She had set it aside to enjoy the simplicities of a friendship unencumbered by unreasonable expectations.

While he initially resisted understanding her choice to enjoy the moment, and not the long-term plans, the appeal of such an existence began to take hold. It was a matter of stepping down from the lofty standards he had adopted with his exposure to his poets. He remained intrigued at the shifting norms that were factoring out the need to be in love to make love. Cassandra had made a point of that in Newport. But weren't these new norms disregarding the nature of humans to associate physical intimacy with strong emotional ones? How can sex be meaningful without love, he wondered. How could love not be the main ingredient in love making? Wouldn't that be primitive and ignorant? Weren't humans more than that; that all the literary and artistic creations were testimony to the genius of his species, and that it would naturally apply to interactions.

The troubadours had introduced that formula a thousand years back, and it detoured humans further from the carnality that had characterized earlier generations. Not that love hadn't existed prior to that, but the writings of the lyrical poets had mainstreamed heterosexual love in the form of damsels, princesses, and knights. Much of it may have been fictional, but hadn't fiction influenced much of human behavior? He argued that we were obligated to use nothing less than that same intensity and passionate commitment to relationships. But what if certain individuals were incapable of such conclusions? What if that standard couldn't be met?

Would humans be doomed to no interactions? Can it be taught that sex is meaningless if not practiced in partnership with love? Would that be denying our more basic survival instincts to simply procreate with any willing partner? Then why the modern contradictions where the emphasis has been placed on personal gratification, and that sex is simply another form of entertainment? Is that wrong? Is it wrong to do what he and Cassandra were doing? Was there love in their actions? Did he *love* Cassandra, or was he *in love* with her?

The difference to him was stark: If he loved Cassandra, then he loved the person, her being, her complete existence. If he was in love with her, then it was for what she represented for him... in love with the character, the personality, the traits that had him seeking out her company, her companionship. Was it more significant to tell a woman-I love you, than-I'm in love with you-or was it all semantics? He tried instructing himself out of his bewilderment, when he noticed that Cassandra had steered the kayak toward the disembarkation pier. Shutting down his thoughts relieved him of the mental exhaustion. His final tribulation came when he needed her help to pull himself out of the kayak.

That evening they chose a small bar and grill in town for dinner and drinks. The chilly mountain air offered the best reason to claim that small, corner table near the fireplace.

With her characteristic spunk, she ordered two Moscow Mules. He looked at her puzzled, not familiar with the drink. He was about to miss his usual glass of Chianti.

"Moscow Mule?"

"Yep, and you're gonna love it…"

With one sip he shook his head in disbelief that she had added one more item to the things she taught him to enjoy. He leaned across the table to touch her hand.

"I'm stunned by the way you nurture us. You find joy and purpose everywhere, and you have this mystical way of extracting valuable human experiences in the simplest actions. To consume a bottle of wine with you is to journey to the vineyard; to stroll along a tree lined street on a perfect summer day is to understand the purpose of a sidewalk; to navigate a river cutting through the majesty of mother nature's beauty in a flimsy vessel built for two is to fathom the worth of melting mountain snow. I can offer no greater praise for who you are. To you, life is this fabric of woven events, each elevating the human adventure. I'm beginning to understand your formula. Amazingly, it neutralizes the bad, the ills of life, and you pave the way for the good to happen. I mean, I never would have gotten into that kayak without your insistence, and I was able to find the good in that. I never would have sat on the lawn on

Ocean Drive in Newport to feel the pulse of your heart, the mist of the ocean waves gently spritzing my skin, and the absolute glory of a setting sun spotlighting the sailboats anchored in the harbor. Yet, all this confuses me further. Is this love? I mean, am I in love with you or do I love you? I feel so off balance."

She smirked, swallowed a mouthful of her mule.

"First, thank you for all those kind descriptions of how I make you feel. I've never thought of myself that way, but it makes me happy to know that I totally fucked up your head. You don't love me; therefore, you are not in love with me, Gianluca... and why are you asking me the same question in two different ways?"

"I thought about it today on the river. Being in love with someone is not the same as loving someone. If I said to you-I love you-, it would be different than saying-I'm in love with you-. Not sure you understand what I'm saying."

"My dear professor, I know you better than you know yourself. So, you may be in love with me, but you don't love me. In fact, I won't let you love me. We are fucking in love with each other, and you can stay in love for as long as you like, I can do this forever, but you are not allowed to love me. I don't want to be the one you love, it'll never work." She pushed him away. "Just because you find a way to manipulate what goes through that delusional brain of yours, doesn't mean you suddenly get these epiphanies about wanting or needing to love me. I'm fine with the way things are, it's the best two like us can ever expect from the other, so why ruin it? In your mind we could be making love, in my mind we are fucking. I didn't want to use that word, but that's what it is. You get to make love; I get to fuck. You need to stroke your head; I need to stroke my vagina… and I'm loving it because you are a beautiful man, sincere, clean, gentle, you pay attention to what a woman wants, and when I point you in the right direction, you never fail to please me. I won't allow myself to love you because it would go nowhere. I don't want that heartache. I'm with a man I know I can love, but our destinies won't tolerate it. Now, if you can't handle all this, we may need to rethink this relationship, or maybe we need to just end it." She loved him, but she couldn't own up to it. The option was to keep him in her life, and she was good with that.

A gust of wind rushed through the open window sending chills across her neck. She pulled her chair closer to the fireplace only to notice that she had attracted an audience that seemed more intrigued than disturbed. She telegraphed her apologies before returning to her place. She toned the volume down to an exasperated whisper.

"Why do you need to add anything deeper into this? Don't try justifying what we do with an emotional explanation. We agreed that we wouldn't go down that road. You piss me off, but it is fucking hard to hate you, so I find myself making excuses for you. Like, if you started in with me right now, you know, like touching me or you got naked in bed... I wouldn't be turned on! I would tell you to fuck off, and I would either read my book or text my mother."

He wore his remorse like a tired, overused Covid mask highlighted by the shadows of the flickering flames dancing around his face. The distortions from the special effects painted an eerie, depressed appearance. He felt he had crossed a line which he would struggle to fix. Cassandra wouldn't allow him that torture.

"Fine, so now you feel all bummed out. That wasn't my intention, and you know that whenever I feel uncomfortable with you, it doesn't last more than a few minutes. What are you having? I'm in the mood for a burger and some greasy fries. You got me feeling all raunchy like a college kid in the university cafeteria craving some sloppy food. If I gain weight, I'll blame your dumb ass."

She sneered as she hid her face behind the laminated menu.

"I can't imagine you ever getting chubby. I'm going to have the same thing. I'm not a fan of hamburgers, but you got me craving one… and who can resist a plate of greasy fries." She chose a bottle of Tempranillo off the wine list.

"You can have a glass; I'm drinking the rest of the bottle. I want to catch a little buzz before going back to the room. You got me pissed off enough that the only way I can get back at you is to punish you with the most torturous fu.., I mean love making. We're taking a shower, and there is no way I'm going to allow you to fall asleep… that's why you can only have one glass. I don't need some jellyfish dick in bed with me tonight… I'm going to make you reach the peaks of the Berkshires without taking a step… you wait." She changed the topic.

"When we're done with this weekend, I'm going to take some time off. I have to get ready for my graduate school exams, start my master's, get a full-time job, take evening classes, and do something with this life before I catch up to your elderly ass."

He hardly had time to put on a face. "Fifty is not old. I'm told it's the new forty… whatever that means. If I'm too old for you, why are you here with me? You don't seem to mind the older mind, the older body, the older wisdom. You even mentioned several times that you couldn't have had the same with someone your age. I guess I have some old ass assets you seem to like."

She pulled him further away from his safe zone.

"I meant old like in getting old, like getting too old to get married, start a family, settle down with people you love… that kind of old. I mean, don't you worry about that? Don't you ever wake up in the middle of the night thinking-I'm alone? Look, it may not be the ideal for everyone, but as much as I love my freedom, my independence… I'd be willing to sacrifice that for a good, long-term relationship-it doesn't have to be marriage, just a loving commitment to staying together, to see each other through till death. Gianluca, I dread the notion of being alone, of getting to an age when no one wants you. You know, when your old friends start dying around you, and those that aren't dead can't even get out of bed. It's all fine now… it can never be fine forty years from now. Seriously, it scares me, and it should scare you too."

He studied her words in quiet meditation. "Should I truly fear being alone? I can choose to live my life in the company of no one, live it as I please, sacrifice nothing to the needs, expectations, or habits of another human being, and then either have the appropriate social services care for my debilitated body or simply die. There is no immortality, and if death is inevitable, then why not welcome it at the end of a life lived as one chooses. I think choosing a solitary personal existence that happens to be fulfilling is the trade off when death comes calling. One must be completely convinced it is a decision made with no regrets. Having regrets as life wanes would be the ultimate self-betrayal., you…"

She cut him off with her usual scorn.

"Do you need people in your life?"

He seemed stunned. "Of course."

She came right back at him. "Then no fucking way will you get to that final, lonely chapter in your life with no regrets. You don't know yourself as well as you think. I don't care how self-absorbed you are in thinking that your myopic, little world is the perfect way to spend your God-given time, your regrets will consume you in your final days. How can you let that happen? How can you blissfully keep doing this, already fifty years old, and think you could still attract and keep the friendship of people willing to tolerate your selfish ass. You're still attractive now… twenty years from now there's no way I'd get into a shower with you."

He had nothing meaningful left to say, so he became

defensive.

"So, what am I supposed to do. Ask you to marry me, move into a house in the suburbs, have two kids and a dog, a minivan in the driveway, and live happily ever after? You just said twenty years from now you wouldn't shower with me... I would then be a fool thinking it would last until my dying day. That's what bothers me about committing."

She put her drink down, and this time she refused to whisper.

"You know, each time I forgive your narrow-minded, selfish bullshit, I try convincing myself to let you slide deeper into your pathetic emptiness. Then the pity overcomes me, and I ignore my rage, and I tell myself there are worse things in life. Now you have gone a step further-one I thought you weren't capable of. You have hurt me so deeply with your latest remark. I never once hinted that I had those expectations because I know well enough that you are incapable of being that person. You have made it annoyingly and abundantly clear, repeatedly, that you could never live that kind of life, and that's why I choose to fuck you, and not make love to you. That's what women fear the most... falling for a man who has no clue. Our defense mechanism kicks in, and we masquerade our feelings, so we don't get hurt. In fact, I would have known better, and I would have killed the relationship after that first night at the Poet's Cafe if I thought I was falling in love with you. Yes, I found you amazingly attractive, your British accent, wanting to sleep with you, and I fantasized about the sex, but I also wanted just your company. Falling in love was never in the cards. Gianluca, you don't have it in you to love a woman so unconditionally... it would take something cataclysmic. As much as I wanted you to be the different one, the standout, I have come to terms with the fact that you are one of many. You just have a lot more class; that's all that sets you apart from the shit out there."

She paused to catch her breath and to deal with her lie, then she broke down as tears cut skinny canyons into her cheeks.

"I don't get it. Most men just want to get laid, and then you roll along, and you don't want any of that, but you have no intention of committing, there's no in between. I would shower with you even a hundred years from now... true love has no limitations... I would even take care of your sloppy ass. Fuck, Gianluca, you are so dense... you know what, just forget everything I just said... it's like I'm dragging a lifeless body into a relationship."

She raised the dinner napkin to cradle and cover her

face, muffling the sounds escaping her mouth, wiping the flow from her nose. Bewildered, he had no clue what to say. Not once had Gianluca sat across from a woman unloading an emotional tsunami on him. He had never seen a woman cry. He initially thought it silly, and immature, but this was Cassandra, the woman that used the word-*fuck*-as part of her daily vocabulary; the woman who was in control of her moods, could drink a bottle of wine while wrapped in a blanket, fondling his penis, seated on the lawn along Ocean Drive in Newport; the woman who could invite him to shower with her, spiritually arouse his desires, and shut herself down at the first sign of his discomfort without the slightest lament. There was no way this could be a superficial wound.

The summer of 2023 offered Gianluca enough reasons to stay in New York. Cassandra had inspired him to redefine his relationship to women, to accept the value of living moments rather than spend his days constructing an uncertain future, and to allow sex a life of its own. In the past, his choice would have been to deflect the detour, but Cassandra had all the right ingredients to change his course. He thought of her as a force capable of altering an unbending habitat. An unlikely woman had pierced his bubble, and in his weakened state, he let some air escape.

Her influence had waned after the Wild River weekend.

She has all the right excuses to keep her distance. September sent him back to his teaching schedule, and the research to finally get his book published. He kept busy, but Cassandra popped into his thoughts constantly. He called often to leave messages. She ignored them.

Anger had nothing to do with it; it was all about the disappointment in having to toss Gianluca into the useless male garbage bin. She had once considered him the one that stood apart, the man who possessed the impulses that a good woman would want to reward. She had even considered a life with this man, and she already loved much about him, envisioning years of happiness. Still, she resisted falling prey to her strong feelings; she loved him, but she was giving up.

She had begun to think of marriage as an obsolete institution, based on his lectures about the liberated female. It stressed her, but Gianluca could have been right all along about living life alone. If marriage no longer had any appeal, if individuals have become so selfishly concerned with their own needs, then why give marriage any importance? He's right, she thought… live your solitary life filled with years of catering to your personal whims, fuck the rest of the world. You can invite people in when you find them to your liking, dump them when you can't stand their faces.

She thought her analysis was legitimate, but she dreaded the idea of becoming one of those. Maybe a traditional marriage could still work with the right person... but where to find this person? Did he even exist? Gianluca came close, very close-even perfect if he hadn't concluded that marriage would condemn him to a predictable, mundane existence. He had smothered the benefits under the weight of his convictions, and she dared not waste more of her energies believing he could be reformed.

She stayed out of his way. He tried to get back in. Nothing was clicking, and she had already moved on with an old boyfriend who walked back into her life when he dropped off his six-year-old at Saint Bart's Elementary in the Bronx where she had taken a position as an elementary grade teacher. He and the boy's mother had never married. He had full custody of his son when the courts decided that as an absentee parent who had abandoned the home, the mother was in no condition to care for a child. Cassandra and Ritchie lost their virginity to each other on their prom night and remained a couple until he moved to Long Island to live with his divorced mother. This was their first encounter in almost twenty years. Around Thanksgiving, they were dating, and having his son in her class, and both suddenly in her life, gave her a feel for what it would be like to have a family. Adam had started to treat her like a mother. She spent weekends in Ritchie's house and made weekday visits to have dinner or help Adam with homework. By Christmas they were on solid footing, and he invited her to move in.

That first day of December she received a text from Gianluca that he had resigned his position and would be leaving for Florida the second Saturday of the month. She tried toughing it out, but when the remorse set it, having abandoned him so completely, she promised herself to call him. Ritchie and Adam had given her reasons to keep putting it off. Never seeing him again was too much punishment. She gave in and called him. They agreed to meet at the Poet's Cafe one last time. It was the Friday night before he was to set his GPS for points south. She wore her anxiety like a heavy winter coat as they approached the corner table of their first date. She ordered a mocha cappuccino.

"So, you gonna order the same thing I'm having?" "Yes, you always ordered for me." She smiled as if to make fun. "It was one of the things I found cute about you. You were so easy when it came to stuff like this." She paused to take a sip. "You're leaving tomorrow, right? This is really gonna happen. You know, I stayed away because you hurt me. I dealt with your negative shit about marriage, and settling down, and about a life with someone, but you never wanted to consider the good in that, you never gave it a chance. You just dismissed it in such a way that it exposed your ugly side. Why couldn't you care a little for my feelings about it, and that it was perfectly natural for me to want a future that included a person I cared for, and that it would be doing what human beings have done for centuries… I mean, even your parents found each other, married, are still together and created you… why do you find that so unappealing? Look, this is not an attempt to get you to think of me that way. I have moved on… that's what everyone does these days… move on, and it was such a relief to get away from all your bad vibes, from all the shit about the perfect woman, the perfect love affair, the one you weren't meant to have. Get over it, Gianluca… there is no perfect anything. Most people settle for the least set of imperfections in others… now that is the closest you will ever come to perfection-a woman who has the minimum imperfections that you could appreciate enough to want to make a life together. And if you can't understand that she would be your best opportunity in the years you have left to give lasting value to your existence, well then you need to prepare for a time to come when you will question your past."

He was troubled not so much by her words, but the harshness of her delivery. He detected the undeniable truth when words were spoken so forcefully, and it bothered him.

"Tough words… so, misery is in my future. I'm sorry, I'm sorry for not having those values. I can imagine the pathetic ending, the selfish ending, the lonely ending… somewhere in New York or Florida, eventually in a home for wayward seniors, in a wheelchair, being fed by some beautiful aide. You're right, it's the worse possible way to end it all for someone like me, but I don't know how to change that, how to keep it from happening without the compromise you talk about. Even you were unwilling to compromise when you decided on me. You didn't like much of what was out there, but for some reason you're making it perfectly clear that I am good enough."

She stayed quiet for a dozen seconds debating the impact of what she was about to say.

"This is what I can't stand about you, and it keeps getting in the way. I am compromising, and I'm not afraid to admit it, because I want more than just me. I know you have it in you to love me, because I would give you every reason to do so. I have avoided feeling strongly about anything in my life for all the usual fears. I don't want the occasional boyfriend, the weekend lover, the asshole you meet at a wedding or in some bar. Yet, I don't want to give in to loneliness, I don't want to leave more of my life to chance. You don't care that we belong together, you ignore it like it will never matter to you. Does it matter to you that I'm dating an old boyfriend who has a six-year-old son in my class; that I took a full-time position at St. Bart's elementary in the Bronx teaching first graders; that I love the job, and that I'm a fucking great woman full of love and passion to share? Does any of it matter at all? Are you alive?"

She became weak knowing he would soon create a void that would depress her. She held on while he subliminally pummeled himself, acknowledging his insensitivity. It may not have been intended, but it was too late to explain it away.

"I can't excuse my detachment. I never meant to hurt you or to disregard your feelings. I have been so blinded by my own conditioning that it sometimes turns me into a monolith... cold, hard, and removed from what makes others happy. I hope you can open your heart again, to have me remain a part of you. I can't imagine becoming an old fart without you telling me to wipe the saliva from my chin or to blow my nose."

"Yeh, well you already have some shit dangling from the side of your mouth."

In a panic he pulled his napkin to his lips to deal with the embarrassment. She laughed.

"Just kidding, but it's probably what you'll hear from

me when you do have hairs growing from your nostrils, and eyebrows that can be combed. I might be able to visit once or twice a year to straighten out your sad ass."

"You seem to have settled down with this old boyfriend. How's that going?" She became upbeat.

"I'm not counting my chickens just yet, but I am really happy with Ritchie and his son Adam. The boy is a sweetheart, and Ritchie has been a lot of fun. It's like an instant family, and I get to feel what it's like. I know someone like you may think it silly, but I get a chance to kinda try it out."

"Do you like it that much?"

She gave it some thought. "You know, I do. I'm sharing my time with two people who want to be with me. Something as simple as going out for a pizza becomes an intimate experience."

"What happened to the mother?"

"Ritchie never married her. She took off about two years ago and hasn't been seen since. She did call for Adam's birthday and Christmas, and she's living with some guy in Connecticut."

"Do you think she'll ever want to get back into Adam's

life?"

"Don't know, but I can handle it. I love Adam, but not like a mother, and I know to keep it that way... at least for my feelings towards him."

"Well, I'm happy for you. I wish I could come to terms with my stubbornness one day to be as settled as you. You did the right thing distancing yourself from me. I would have kept getting in the way of your happiness. I can only hope that your predictions about old age are not entirely true, and that loneliness will not corrupt my spirit. You put a scare in me about being alone, but I'm going to take it as far as I can before I turn to shit. When I do, you'll have to come down to Florida to drag my ass into that home for dying seniors. You'll be the only person who would still know me."

She smirked. "My dear, sweet Gianluca, I have no doubt that you will find your *Beatrice*, your golden girl. She will be real, you two will have each other to love and enjoy, and you will never write your infamous poems and sonnets to the lover that never was. It is the best I could wish for you-that you will never have to deal with the impossible, that whoever is fortunate enough to have your love, will fulfill you. Please be good to yourself, you still have time. I grant you my love if you will accept it. I hope that you'll take at least that much of me with you." She struggled getting through her last sentence, wiping away her tears with both hands.

He sat quietly, gazing into her eyes, searching for the right words. "I'm destined to live the fool's life. You tried steering me away from myself, and I squandered it for what may turn out to be pathetic, elusive expectations. If to be alone is to become destitute, then I accept what I deserve. I often stop to think that my happiest days have been with you. I have taken so much for granted, ignoring the passage of time, and mortality itself." He paused, searching for more words. "I understand your happiness with your new family. It is so typically unselfish of you to make two more people happy."

They ran through a summary of the events that characterized their unconventional bond. Cassandra poked fun at all his idiosyncrasies. Laughing, they put any stray moments to rest, dismissed reasons that could have damaged the friendship… making facial promises to nurture their peculiar kind of love. That last evening in New York, that small table at the Poet's Cafe became a fixture easily summoned when nostalgias came calling. He would stick to his decision to leave; Cassandra would devote herself to her fledgling family.

CHAPTER 4- *GO SOUTH*

While valiantly retaining the appeal of an iconic American city, New York had been battered by the Covid 19 Virus into a social and political misfit with sad stories of people dying alone in hospitals without the comfort of loved ones, and of zombie survivors forced to turn inward, with mouths and noses hidden behind stale surgical masks. Flocks of muted beings went about their business robotically keeping six feet away from others as instructed by ominous floor stickies, wondering whether an apocalypse was living up to a biblical prophecy.

Gianluca Morelli would not be the first to leave the city behind. Many had already given up on the fading promises and hopes, and much the way his Renaissance heroes were compelled to leave behind the alleys and the piazzas of Florence for the hills of the Tuscan countryside during the Plague, he planned a similar exodus. The good professor couldn't help making the ironic, yet very real connection to the topics he covered in his syllabus. This new pestilence had bridged the gap across time pushing Gianluca away from the only life he had known. Leaving New York was the lone plan, anything else would work itself out as it happened. He departed at the end of the fall semester that second week in

December. The university provost would soon receive his resignation with shock but respected Gianluca's decision. He gave up his apartment and furnishings to a colleague in his department, he loaded a few boxes with the personal items he cherished into the trunk of his Alfa Romeo Giulia and started his trek southward. The morning of December 9, 2023, as he crossed the George Washington bridge, he questioned his mistakes, miscalculations, whether his motivation for leaving was sincere, and if he appreciated the world beyond New York enough to become a part of it.

As he looked back at the Manhattan skyline along the West Side Drive with the inevitable nostalgia suffered by a native New Yorker, he reminded himself of how deceiving the sight could be. The allure of his city had called out to countless people seeking whatever it was they imagined it could offer. It may have been an opportunity for a better life for a newly arrived immigrant, the prospect of fame and fortune for an aspiring Broadway actor from the Midwest, or an entrepreneur seeking new fortunes. To the lucky ones, New York had kept its promises. There were also the disappointments cemented onto the faces of waiters and servers stuck at those jobs when the theaters failed to call; of those toiling at manual labors for long hours for little more than subsistence pay; and those who had wagered and lost it all on Wall Street. Gianluca was aware of the lack of sympathy for the dead-end stories in the big city. Any person on a subway car, people crossing paths on a crowded street, driving a city bus, or patrolling in a squad car could have been a portrait of regrets and what ifs.

He would have invited the usual reflection on his own existence had his affections for New York not waned. He thought of how exhausted he had become investing so much compassion and self-control with every liberal social demand. Had he contributed to a better humanity? Had he enhanced the lives of others? Had he furthered the cause of human respect, love, and tolerance? The long hours on the road offered time to reflect, and as often was the case, the conversation would remain in his head; talking to himself was the only place the truth overwhelmed him and where he could curse like a New Yorker.

"The pandemic contradicted so many of my perceptions. If things went well, people had no problem playing the game. The bloated discussions, the pretentious parties, the privileged gatherings, even my department meetings were full of condescending snobbishness masquerading as social correctness. Then Covid came along exposing all the hypocrisies, and the suppressed fears we kept tucked away so conveniently because there was no reality check, no real challenge to the manufactured lives. We hid away in our apartments, tuned into the news stations all day and night, aligned our thinking with patronizing, pontificating politicians, and shunned others, often suspicious of any unusual behavior or appearance. This is so fucked up, listen to me, I was one of them. I spoke the words people wanted to hear, I expressed opinions that paralleled theirs, I licked their asses just to feel connected. If I had been such a believer, so convinced it was all good, would I be so critical now that I'm leaving? Could it have been so superficial, so artificial? Why did I submit so easily? Shit... was I so insecure, so unsure of myself, so afraid to contradict, to question, to call them out. I've been such a wimp, such a dick."

He took a deep breath as he re-focused back to the road and the signs that kept him on Interstate 95 South. As the New York skyline across the Hudson blurred to his left, his mood turned to the failed relationships, and how he had been betrayed by his emotions.

"There were the times when I deceitfully set aside my beliefs and entered relationships for the wrong reasons. I should have known that Charlotte was bisexual. I thought I was in love with a woman who was in love with a woman... how sad. Then there was Adela, the Latina who worked at the university bookstore who turned me inside out. Sex with her was never easy, never equitable. She was in complete control. How could I not fall in love with a such a woman? I turned it into a head game. Any other man would have set it aside and just enjoyed her. Not me, I had to find fault in something that was purely hedonistic and erotic... who the fuck does that? I spent precious hours attempting to apply some awkward logic, some warped philosophy to two naked bodies on a bed. How disappointing that must have been for her. That last time in my apartment, she laughed and shook her head in disbelief to my nauseating and frustrating conversation. She slowly walked out dragging herself to the staircase, refusing to wait for the elevator.

She left her job, and our paths never crossed again. Like her sexuality, her detachment was decisive and without contrition. I was too dense to even suffer my own pathetic behavior. I pissed away a willing companion, a breathtaking seducer, and a rare female friend.

You knew there was a policy that professors were not supposed to date their students, but Tanya was impossible to avoid. I loved the flirtations, her beauty, her cappuccino skin color. I would have given in immediately. I became so weak around her. I still can't get over how difficult it was to concentrate on her words each time she came up to discuss something after class, and how I kept the brilliance of her eyes and the pillowy lips stored away in that part of one's mind dedicated to the memory of things uncommonly beautiful. I think it was sometime during the middle of her last semester that neither of us could resist any longer. It started with cups of coffee, then dinners, then nights together.

It was a mistake to invite her to move in. The difference in age started weighing on both of us. Maybe some small, remote college town upstate would have given us a bit more time together, but New York wouldn't allow us to tolerate it. There were too many distractions, too many temptations, with little need to depend on anyone for company or affections. The seminars and symposiums I attended were simply too academic, too clinical. Then showing up with her attached to my arm still caused people to whisper. I ignored it as best I could, but those assholes still made me uncomfortable, and it showed. Tanya picked up on it each time-that's when I knew it wouldn't last. She left a short note she was leaving for California without a hint. She had once mentioned going out there to work on her master's at UCLA... I think I would have understood. Then again, I was being a shit for letting the relationship become superficial, a routine with no prospects.

I wonder if she was in love with me. Did she want me to commit, tell her I loved her, talk about marriage, children? I was never good at unraveling what was inside a woman's head... it was easier to make believe I cared, or I understood. We all got caught up in using each other. How did I get that way? We chose to ignore our pathetic existence... we had neutralized the pain, set aside our values, and repelled criticisms. We honed it to perfection because no one was going to admit to any harm, no one wanted to be labeled a victim, since doing so would diminish your social worth, and not many wanted to live in limbo in a place like New York. That was exactly the way I lived. I did all that crap, maybe aware of it, maybe not... I don't know. Maybe I knew all along, but conveniently smothered it. What a prick, I shouldn't have been able to pass judgment. I thought myself so above others, so better at defining life, at feeling snug in my hollow omnipotence only because I could practice it in a classroom full of needy twits. Why should I be amazed? It was expected that at some point I would find my own sanctimonious spot in the twilight zone. Look at me now, running away when it all started falling apart, when the power of the unexpected, the improbable, easily trashed all our collective intelligences, philosophies, theories, creations... reprocessing us into piles of stunned and perplexed freaks incapable of marshaling our own humanity to mitigate our insecurities. It was much easier to abandon and hide than to confront and console. All we could see were shadows, and half covered faces with exposed, solitary eyes that begged to remain incognito, insisting on complacency, and the resolve to avoid contact. Can I blame myself for leaving?"

He paused, sipped on his caramel macchiato, bothered by the suffocating industrial landscape along the turnpike. He considered himself lucky he didn't live in New Jersey.

"Then Cassandra happened. If I ever thought of myself capable of being a total fuck up, then I proved it with Cassandra. She did everything right, I did so much wrong. She cared enough to tolerate my shit. While the other women never cared enough to be hurt by my carelessness, Cassandra found a way to ignore it, even turn it silly and innocuous. Yet, my arrogance still managed to mess up a good thing. I'm not sure I could ever love a woman enough to imagine the rest of my life without her, and with Cassandra I was too much of a coward to consider it because I was afraid that she was *that* woman."

It was the loneliest he had ever been. Talking to his head was his only option. There was much to sort out, and those solitary hours fixated on the painfully dreary highway offered the excuse to think about things he could once blissfully ignore. It could have been a reckoning, an act of contrition to admit to his poor behavior or begging forgiveness from people no longer in his life just to make himself feel better.

That first day he drove through all of Virginia when he

couldn't stop yawning. The four hundred miles to the border with North Carolina took him little more than seven hours. He exited the highway at the town of Euphoria, driving through the downtown along Main Street, at the end of which he came to a newer looking Holiday Inn. The clerk was very kind, offering him a free upgrade to a suite. He didn't think it necessary given that he was only staying one night, but graciously accepted, recalling the stereotype about southern hospitality. The suite was a regular room with a sofa and a desk in a small living room area… not much of a suite, he thought. At the concession in the lobby, he had purchased some fruit, nuts and two bottles of water. He hadn't given hunger much thought during the trip, failing to stop for food. In bed, he checked his Google maps to follow the outline of Route 95 all the way to the South Florida west coast. He changed his destination to Naples, an area where some friends had settled. He had phone numbers and addresses promising he would network with them for guidance. The images along main street Euphoria tickled his curiosity, so he looked up information on the town.

"Population is just under six thousand, it was chartered in 1967, but its history goes all the way back to the establishment of the first colonies. It claims to be the southern gateway to Virginia and that it is the midway point between

New York and Disney. I can't begrudge people for their choice of where to live, but I could never imagine myself in a place like this. I guess one's preoccupation with just living, surviving, gives them enough things to do and worry about. Then again, there must be some joy, some payoff, some small-town advantage that I just don't see. How many times can you stroll the six or seven blocks of Main Street? How many times can you eat at the Huddle House where they advertise *Any Meal Any Time*, and when does greeting the same people day in, day out, get old? Not fair of me to use my value system to pass judgement, I should know better. Maybe I'm just afraid of what I'm witnessing-this America beyond my natural habitat... one that is so unfamiliar. This place depresses me. I do hope Florida has something more to offer. I'm trying hard not to be a snob. New York may have its faults, but one can't deny the daily, almost minute by minute excitement of a world class city. It offers so much, yet it isn't for everyone, I know, and many could even hate it."

He had given his mind a good workout between the driving and absorbing the culture shock of a small town in Virginia. That morning he rose early wanting to make sure he would reach south Florida by the end of the day. He couldn't resist the allure of the Huddle House, so he decided to have some breakfast there before taking off. The menu was an assembly of the most unusual food combinations. The photo displays added a level of wickedness to the enormity of the portions. He tried to make out the beginning or the end of the giant, shapeless *Prime Rib Tips Stuffed Hash Browns. The Southern Smothered Biscuit Platter* was piled several inches high with every breakfast food imaginable and topped with a pale, milky colored cream sauce. It seemed built for two or more people, but the guy seated at a table to his left was tackling one alone. He ordered a cup of coffee, set aside the menu, and asked the waitress for two egg whites.

She asked for clarity. "You want just the whites of the eggs, leave out the yokes? You sure? There ain't much left to eat without the yokes."

"Well, let's make it three whites then. I'll also have two slices of multigrain toast."

"We have white and wheat toast."

"Wheat, I guess."

"Any sides with that delicious breakfast?"

"What do you suggest?"

"I was playing with you on that delicious breakfast thing, don't take it seriously. You ain't from around here...

you from New York?"

"Yes, is it that obvious?"

"Yep, I can tell mostly from the way you talk, but also because of the egg white thing... no one from around here would ever order just the whites. This is mostly a farming and livestock community, so people load up on a big breakfast to get them through the day usually all the way to dinner time. No time for lunch. You should try the grits. Our cook Marcus makes them nice and creamy... people love them."

"Well then, let's go with the grits... can't wait."

As he sat calculating the hours to his destination, he was distracted by the amount of chatter, the incessant good morning greetings, the playful comments about a local's new haircut; the Christmas decorations on Main Street; the sad record of the high school varsity football team with a no-win season for the first time ever; and the positive vibes about the town's new female mayor. The vision that struck him the most was the family style relationship between blacks and whites. They ate together, laughed it up together, shared personal stories about spouses and kids, cows and horses, the fading pandemic, and the coming holidays. What he witnessed allowed him to better understand that in New York the dynamic between the races appeared to be more superficial, more tenuous, more concerned with not offending or coming off as racists. It also dawned on him that despite seeing mostly the same neighborhood faces at the diner every morning in New York for his coffee, there were no good mornings, no chatter about local issues, no casual greetings, and the only person talking at the counter (in Arabic) was Anibal, the owner.

In Euphoria he was surprised by the fluidity of race relations. He thought that in that restaurant people had truly become color blind. It appeared a more natural integration rather than a forced desegregation. It defied the notion that the south was more racist, more segregated. There was an extended family feel and the Huddle House had become a gathering place to bring it together-a daily reunion as a reminder of the commonality of life that bound them. Alice delivered his order asking if he would like a refill on the coffee.

"Yes, please. Alice, can I ask you… is it like this every day in here? I mean, is it always this friendly and happy? I also noticed that everyone knows each other by name, and it's like one huge family."

"My, my… you're not used to this. Yes, it is like this every day, and we would have it no other way. The folks in these parts have learned to live together as family because they have so much in common. Once you peel away the differences, you lose sight of them, and everyone becomes just another person working hard to survive… and that deserves respect. So, yes, this happens each morning, and I thank the good Lord for it. What's your name?"

"Gianluca."

"Well, John Luk, I love this life. It may not be fancy, I don't get to live the big city glitz, and I couldn't imagine doing this kind of work in New York-I'd be living in a shelter on the money I would make. I have a nice little house all my own… you may find it hard to understand that this is a good life, but I can't imagine any other."

He smiled and showed appreciation for her words. "You know, I really do understand the appeal in a small-town support system where all of you recognize the common ground. I'm amazed at all the energy, and the goodwill remarks… it's as if a bunch of good friends hadn't seen each other in years. You show your gratitude living another day, no matter what it is that motivates you, and you come into a place like this as a reminder that life is good and precious. I can't say the same for New York. I mean, people are friendly, there's the occasional-good morning, but one must guess at how genuine it is, and it lacks this kind of enthusiasm… people just don't get to know each other as intimately as here. Except for good, long-term friends, people stay out of each other's way. Here you have a natural need to be *in* each other's way. I must say I like it… there's a sincere humanity that seems to brighten your days."

She filled his coffee cup agreeing with much of what he had said.

"Well now, we do have our bad days, but they don't last. Around here we use each other's good company to keep all the nasty stuff in check. I could have a miserable day with paying bills, making ends meet, having a hard time finding a stray chicken, or needing to change a furnace on its last legs… then I get to work, and it's like a drug that gets you to forget your problems even if just for a few hours. I love these people, I love my job, I have a good boss who pays me well, and I even have health benefits. Can I get you something else?"

"I'm good, I'll take a check, and I want to thank you for the talk and your kind company."

"Oh please, it's what we do. Are you leaving us today?" "Yes, I retired from my position at New York University after twenty years of teaching, and I'm meeting up with some snowbirds who decided to move to South Florida. I'm planning to make it my new home."

"Well, you have a safe trip, and I do hope it all works out for you. Come back and visit anytime, you'll always get a free refill."

Back on 95 South, he was expecting to arrive in Orlando late that evening. He had always wanted to do Disney as a child. He figured that even as an adult, he might get back in touch with that kid that matured too early... the one he lost contact with years ago. He attended an all-boys Jesuit high school in London from October to May, retuning to New York to spend his summers in Manhattan. His British accent was a point of attraction at his parents' social gatherings that kept him in the company of mostly adults. He thought about those years when his mother would return to Padova each August to teach Italian to foreigners. She spoke several languages and enjoyed reconnecting with her hometown. His father spent each August doing research in New York and in Washington at the Library of Congress. The weeks in the nation's capital gave Gianluca time to explore the Smithsonian which he argued at the time was better than lounging around the apartment in New York.

"I always wondered whether Mom and Pop missed each other when she left for Padova. She must have gone at least ten years in a row... I can hardly remember a summer when she was home. Pop didn't seem to mind one bit. I never recall him sad or depressed. Then again, they treated each other more like roommates than husband and wife. They even had two twin beds in their bedroom. I never gave it much thought, I just got used to it. There was this kind of mutual respect version of love they shared. There were never any arguments, no fights, no question of finances… It was a very peaceful existence. They both cooked… food was never abundant, but good. I did a ton of summer readings in the evenings before an hour or so of television. They read near the fireplace in the living room, each seated snugly in their own oversized recliners. They came up for air at times to make the other aware of a literary discovery or a newer interpretation of an obscure Italian poet. The Renaissance, Romanticism and the Enlightenment all had a place in that same living room. There were books everywhere. The shelves had run out of space years earlier, and then piles of books started appearing like totem poles in any uninhabited space on the floor. The large nineteenth century desk was littered with manuscripts that somehow turned into published essays and books. I came to think of it as organized chaos… chaos yes, but organized in their minds. I wonder how they ever found the time to have me. Now that I think of it, I never saw a photo of mom pregnant, or of me as a baby in a crib or the typical naked baby photos. There were several as an adolescent, a teenager, birthdays, and graduations. Shit, I have never seen photos of their marriage. I'm not sure they even exist. I bet they were never married. They met while teaching, had a little something for each other, and in those days, marriage would have been a common next step except for bohemians like them. They had me believing they were lovers as teenagers. Fuck! After all these years it took hours alone in a car to have me figure out that maybe they never married. That could be the reason why Mom still used her maiden name *Gemma Trevisan*. I know that it is common for Italian women to keep their names, but I would think she would have at least hyphenated. This is all very freaky. I shouldn't be surprised when I think of how unconventional our lives were. Does it really matter if they were or weren't Mr. and Mrs. Matteo Morelli? I mean, they still spent a life together. Maybe never being married but living together is the key to avoiding a divorce. Next time I'm in in Padova, I may find out more.

Still, during those years I never felt like I was missing out on much. I was okay with just being with myself. In high school I was on my own. My buddies always insisted on staying out of our dorms until curfew. Those were my best years. We were a bunch of carefree preppies dressed in jackets and ties, money in our pockets, and the entire city of London as our playground… amazing! We strolled with kaleidoscopic crowds; read accounts of those imprisoned in the Tower of

London; got into trouble trying to get the Queen's Guards to laugh; rubbed elbows with the bums and the uber rich, and we wondered who the mystery passenger might be in the Jaguar limousines with dark tinted windows. I can't recall any bouts with boredom. As we grew older, we moved on to clubs and concerts, and the emerging internet craze. For some it was hetero, for others it was gay, for others still it was a work in progress. We were all pure. There was no indoctrinating language, no religious fanaticism, none of us aspiring politicians.

While showing concern for the direction our lives took, our parents refused to live their lives through us. We could have fucked it up with all the freedom we had, but for some reason, and I can't figure why, we found a way to stay out of real trouble. Except for some pot, drugs were hardly an interest. Sex was always a topic, even for the girls. By my last year many claimed to have lost their virginity since oral sex qualified. Still, no one was fooled. We knew who had succeeded for real, those who may have, and those who had no chance. There were some who had to talk about it, and those who shunned it, but the rare teen pregnancy caught much attention. The girls all banded together, with abortions scheduled and performed in one day. Parents knew nothing, and that was better since they were Catholics. No one ever got into trouble.

I'm still amazed the girls were able to keep everything a secret. All the other topics were fair game, but pregnancies got the easy silent treatment. I guess they all figured it could happen to any of them, so investing in tight lips, despite the temptation to talk, was smart."

"God, those houses are so close to the highway. How do those people tolerate it? I guess you can get used to anything. I remember when I stayed with Aunt Rose in the Bronx one summer, a block away from the elevated train. I hated the noise, but everyone in her family hardly noticed it."

He turned his attention back to the road.

"Amazing how the landscape changes so completely the further south you drive. This stretch of 95 is pleasant, much greener than the areas around Washington and Northern Virginia. This is small town country. Who knows how many there are with miniscule populations like Euphoria where people know everyone's business. This is where the entire town shows up for Friday night high school football games; where people look forward to county fairs each summer; where you marry your prom date; where grandmothers still make apple pies from scratch, and probably where there is some famous spot teens park to make out. I remember watching the movie Pleasantville a few years back. There's got to be a dozen

Pleasantvilles from here to Florida."

After a short stop just outside Savannah, the blue and white winter sky had become dark with those heavy clouds that reminded him of the ones that showed up to dump a few inches of snow on New York.

"Shit, it's starting to rain… is that hail?"

Hail, the size of gumballs began pelting everything in sight, some ricocheting off the Giulia and onto the highway. Traffic came to a complete stop as he spied police cruisers flashing their blue and red emergency lights. Cars were stopped, lined up parking lot style as far down 95 as he could see. His GPS offered limited information, but the red outline of what appeared to be a major accident some miles down the road, made it clear he was going nowhere. When he finally pulled up to one of the state troopers, the news got worse. It was a multi car and tractor trailer pile up about fifteen miles ahead of him. The trooper gave a bleak assessment based on his experience; it would take hours before traffic returned to normal. He suggested exiting at the town of Kingswick to spend the night if he wasn't in a hurry. Gianluca took the advice and drove onto route 341. Ten miles later he was in downtown Kingswick. He pulled into the parking lot of the Lover's Oak Inn at the far end of the town. The nineteenth

century Victorian building was invitingly decorated for the
Christmas season, and Gianluca could tell, as he walked into
the lobby, the place was a class act that had retained all its
historic charm. The bar with its long counter in what would
have been a large living room, already hosted a nice crowd.
Christmas music played in the background, and the pleasant
chatter of people greeting others and those checking in filled
the cavernous lobby. After a friendly greeting, the clerk at the
front desk offered a king room with a view of the town.
Gianluca signed on for two nights and was handed a Victorian
skeleton key attached to a brass tag in the shape of an oak
stamped with a short history of the tree and the neighborhood.
Folklore had made the spot famous as a place where lovers met
to pledge their devotion or to make marriage proposals. He
appreciated the attachment to traditions that made a place
more inviting, and a better understanding of the inn's name.
His room had a large king bed and floor to ceiling windows
that looked onto the small square built around that famous
tree. The entire district was lit up for Christmas adding a
luminescence in the late afternoon twilight to a town that was
already full of energy. I've arrived in *Pleasantville*, he thought,
as a sarcastic smile owned his expression.

CHAPTER 5- *HOSPITALITY AND GOD*

Gianluca had no intentions of staying beyond two nights. The weather had turned nasty and unpredictable for an area unaccustomed to winter storms. A squall had deposited a blanket of large flakes on the town. He thought the image of the bulky, snow-covered branches of the lover's oak with the inn in the background would have made perfect subjects for a Norman Rockwell painting. When he looked down on the square, he was instantly reminded of the snowy street scene in the movie *It's a Wonderful Life*. He had made a habit of watching it each year during the Christmas season with a soft spot for the older black and white version.

After a long, hot shower, he ventured down to the bar for a drink and to ask about a place for a dinner good enough to have him forget the bad food he nibbled during the ride. The bartender, Ernie, asked if he was from out of town while he poured him the glass of Chianti.

"Staying at the Inn?"

"Yes, for a couple of nights. On my way to Florida. I just retired from my teaching position in New York."

"You may be staying longer from the looks of things. The forecast is not good for these parts. They're saying snow, but mostly ice for several days, especially along 95. See, we're not equipped for this kind of weather like up north. I think we have only four salting trucks for the entire county."

"I'm here because of the pile-up on 95 about fifteen miles south of your exit. The trooper suggested getting off and staying in Kingswick. He made it sound like things wouldn't get back to normal for quite a while."

"He wasn't lying. Pile ups on 95 can keep people stuck in their cars for hours. Sounds like it was another bad one. They'll probably cover it on the news tonight."

"Please to meet you, Ernie." Squinting to decipher the name tag. "Are you a local? Maybe you know of a place with some good food?"

"Not born local, came here back in 1990 from Jersey and I never left. I did most of my bartending in the casinos. The money was good, but I got tired of the atmosphere, and listening to gamblers tell stories of how they just missed hitting it big... too depressing, I had to get out."

"Seems like you found a happier life down here."

"Look, the money is not the same, but you don't need as much of it. The people are good to you, it doesn't get too cold in the winters, and the summers start in the spring and end in the fall. There are flowers and colors everywhere you look, and the days are long and lazy... you think you're going to live forever."

Ernie then greeted a man who had just pulled up on a stool next to Gianluca. "Good evening, Clarence, the usual?"

"Yes, please."

"Clarence, this here is professor... sorry, didn't get your name."

"Gianluca Morelli."

"Yes, Professor Morelli from New York. Professor, this is Doctor Clarence Hightower, he runs Georgia Maritime College."

The two men spoke at length about their experiences in higher education. They compared notes and found there were more similarities than differences. Gianluca learned that Dr. Hightower was the first black provost of the college, after being its first black male to graduate way back in '68 and of his tenure as the first black male professor.

"Well, you must be quite the celebrity around here. You have had many *firsts*... impressive. I'm guessing you are from the area."

"Born and raised just outside of town."

Ernie couldn't hold back his admiration.

"Clarence here was also mayor of Kingswick for a term, still coaches the high school baseball team, and worked with Jimmy Carter when he was governor of Georgia. He is loved by the entire town."

Clarence smiled insisting on a slight correction.

"Now, Ernie, there are a handful of my neighbors not entirely in love with me. Professor Morelli, in the south we have a saying: '*Better a bad harvest than a bad neighbor*'. I have a bad one right next door. I keep telling myself to be patient, the son of a bitch might move."

"Call me Gianluca, please. Listen, in New York if you stand in the hallway of our apartment buildings, within minutes you'll know who is getting divorced, who is moving, who is still in love, who did the cheating, and who is taking a beating. Uber Eats, Doordash or the pizza delivery guy will give you an idea of what's for dinner. This goes on every day with amazing regularity. I would think in a house you have more places to escape the bad neighbor thing."

Clarence smiled.

"You could say it is one of the perks of small-town life… don't hate us. I have a cozy room I built as an extension with huge windows that look out on my garden and a thin stream that runs through my property. I call it the bunker, a place I can escape to, to get away from all the noise and confusion. I've done my most productive thinking there. Best of all, it's on the complete opposite side of my nasty neighbor's house… I can't see him; he can't see me… beautiful!"

"I have no choice but to envy you. The only place I could call a refuge in New York was the University library. No garden, no stream… a small plant on the librarian's desk was all the nature we could hope for."

"Are you transiting to another destination, or will you stick around for a while?"

"I ended up in Kingswick purely by chance off 95 that was clogged for miles because of a hideous accident. I don't regret one bit having done so. This may be a small town, but it seems to have a big heart. Everyone has been cordial and accommodating. New Yorkers are by nature friendly, but not intimately friendly. You can get directions, and an *excuse me* every so often, but you can also get pushed onto the subway tracks by a panhandler despite the five-dollar bill you gave him. The oddity for an outsider would be to question the surreal harmony that gets a place like New York up and working each day when the instinct would be to just get away. I'm one of those who invoked that instinct to leave. So, to answer your question, I was on my way to south-west Florida when Kingswick asked me to pay a visit. I have friends who migrated there and are living seemingly happy lives based on their reports. I haven't visited enough to develop an opinion. I gave NYU twenty years of service. Then the pandemic stripped New York of its glitter. The city that never sleeps became the city that couldn't get out of bed. I admit becoming disenchanted, and in need of a change. I know what I'm running from, but I'm not sure of the reason, and I'm not certain of the change I'm looking for... a bit of a vagabond."

"What did you teach at NYU? And what about that British accent?"

"Literature of the Renaissance, Enlightenment and the Romantic Period. All my early education was at a Jesuit boarding school in London... my summers in New York. "

"Well, perhaps I can help with that change you speak of. We have a position we need to fill in our humanities department. Your disciplines are not represented presently, so we have no courses with those titles. One of the suggestions made by the members of the department was to attract a professor capable of filling the need, rather than have some take on an added teaching assignment. I confess none of our people would have your expertise. Would you be interested in laying some roots in our community. The stipend can't possibly match your NYU income, but the cost of living around here is much less of a burden. You can't ask for more change than this, and I bet you may come to like it. I don't know if you're still publishing, but this is an idyllic place to get your writing done. No rush, think about it. Stay an extra day or two if you're not yet expected in Florida."

Gianluca sat stunned by the frequency with which things were happening. The accident, getting off the exit, driving into Kingswick, finding the inn, and then by chance meeting Clarence with a job offer.

"I will give it some thought. Leaving New York had all to do with leaving the city, not leaving my work. Teaching has been a passion. I'm tempted to think it's something I should still be doing."

"Can I entice you to meet with the department? No need for an interview, simply a few minutes for introductions, and the chance to have your questions answered. By the way, if you haven't had dinner, we have a wonderful Italian restaurant. I would think someone named Gianluca wouldn't let the opportunity pass him up. It's a ten-minute ride to my side of town called Golden Isles and Saint Simon Island."

The hungry professor jumped on the invitation despite some hesitations about the quality of Italian food in south-east Georgia. He promised himself not to be a stuck-up New Yorker, and to remain humble in his interactions with the locals. He also enjoyed Clarence's company and was eager to learn more about the town. Before leaving, Ernie confirmed with Dr. Hightower that he would go by his place on Saturday as promised to pick up the things he was donating to the local Catholic church.

"I'll be by around ten. You said everything is in the garage."

"Yes, it's all there. I'll help you load up."

"Great, Tom and Jason are also coming by to help with the furniture."

"Perfect, that will give me a chance to talk to your boys about college, and I can also go over that liquor license application for you."

"Much appreciated, Clarence. See you Saturday."

Clarence pointed out some of the landmarks during the ride. Moments later a skeptical Gianluca stood before *Massimo's Real Italian Restaurant.*

Massimo had purchased the industrial style building twenty years earlier, made appealing upgrades over the years, and added an outdoor patio which had become a popular foodie destination and watering hole for locals and visitors. Clarence had nothing but praise for the menu. There was little on it he hadn't tasted and admitted to eating there several days a week. Gianluca took notice of the waitress who led them to a table near a window that looked out on Bay Street and the East Kingswick River Marina. She cordially greeted Clarence.

"Good evening, Dr. Hightower, we have your favorite *spaghetti alla carbonara* special tonight if you're in the mood. Bottle of Chianti?"

"Yes, perfect. My dear you know me so well."

"Fine, and I have a bone to pick with one of my professors. Can I come by your office tomorrow so I can deliver my grievance?"

"Come by anytime you're free, I'll be all ears. Professor, this is Leylah, stepdaughter of the proprietor Massimo Brunetti and daughter of his lovely wife Emma. This here is professor Gianluca Morelli our lost soul from New York."

"Pleased to meet you Professor, I do hope you have a fair grading system where you teach. Where in New York?"

"New York University, Humanities Department. I teach European Literature… well I did. I decided to retire, and I was on my way to Florida when I was forced off the highway because of an accident. Your Italian pronunciation is so perfect… have you studied the language?"

"I have studied my stepfather all these years… learned the language arguing with him. I'll be right back with your wine." She yelled out to her father to alert him about Clarence.

"C'è il dottore Hightower qui stasera. Vieni a salutarlo." *"Doctor Hightower is here this evening. Come greet him."*

He wasn't only floored by her perfect Italian, but her beauty, the darker skin, and the African American features. He tried masking his reaction when Clarence picked up on the bewilderment.

"Her mother Emma was able to work a few hours a day for Massimo while her husband battled a brain tumor. Poor man was in and out of a hospital bed for several years. Leylah was in her first year at Maritime when things got worse. She gave up her college years taking care of her father during the day, while her mother tried to make ends meet. She dropped out and took a night position at Home Depot.

Leylah's mom is black, and her dad was white. Their daughter is their masterpiece. She is beautiful, intelligent, well spoken, determined, and the best of people. When Emma came to work for Massimo, he gave them the apartment above the restaurant rent free. That was a huge help. Massimo and Emma fell in love and married four years ago… it was a wonderful day, there must have been over one hundred guests right here

Eventually Leylah started working here as well. She's the one who now runs the place. She kept taking courses part time, and she's about to get her degree. Emma also learned some Italian. She and Massimo are so perfect together… pillars of the community. I believe Leylah is in her mid-thirties. She sings in the choir and volunteers at church, she delivers donated food from Massimo's to the local charities, and she's a regular in the group that entertains the youngsters at the children's hospital in Savannah.

She and Massimo are close. She calls him *pop*. I know she studied in Florence for a semester in sophomore year, and she spent last summer with Massimo's relatives in Italy. You seem a bit taken by such a creature."

Gianluca was caught off guard by his remark.

"I apologize for being so obvious, but there is something so likeable about her. Her Italian is impeccable, the pronunciation almost native, and there's a spunk to her that begs an argument; the kind you love having with someone undeniably capable of putting you in your place. Her beauty is indescribable, so natural, so easy, and casual. Nothing artificial, nothing that doesn't belong. I'm struggling... I mean where does one find the words? Clarence, please forgive me if I'm being insensitive in my reaction."

"By no means, my Yankee friend. Your reaction is more a testament to one being deeply affected by his teachings. You're a troubadour, a product of your studies. A woman like Leylah can generate many reactions, yours happens to be an appropriate one. You've been smitten by a southern belle... you may not survive this."

Clarence barely got his last remark in when Leylah returned with the bottle of Chianti. She filled their glasses halfway and asked what Gianluca would like to order. "Professor, have you decided?" His response came late as he was taken by the smoothness of her voice, and the fleshy wetness of her full lips.

"Si, allora, vorrei anch'io un piatto di spaghetti alla carbonara, con pomodori e mozzarella fresca."

Gianluca used his Italian to be friendly and to hint at some common ground. He ordered the same as Clarence with a side of tomatoes and fresh mozzarella. Leylah took his order without acknowledging the Italian. Sensing a flirtation, she came off rude. "I'll place your order, but it will be a while. We are a bit backed up... been busy tonight."

Back in the kitchen she dealt with the frustration of meeting another self-absorbed, pompous professor. She then reminded her father to visit their table.

Clarence was greeted with Massimo's signature hug, a dimple-to-dimple smile and a promise to send out a piece of his famous ricotta pie for dessert. Gianluca was introduced and the two started a lively conversation in Italian. Massimo spoke briefly of his journey from a small town south of the city of Bologna first to New Jersey to work in his uncle's restaurant on the boardwalk in Wildwood, to eventually take a job in Atlanta on an invitation from a friend.

In time, he started vacationing on the Georgia coast. At the entrance to Saint Simon Island, he came upon this shuttered building that once produced textiles. It had been claimed by the city when tax bills went unpaid for many years. Massimo's bid to purchase it with a variance to build a restaurant was accepted as part of the city's effort to rehabilitate property eye sores to keep the tourists coming. He admitted to having the best of lives owning his own American dream and doing the work he loves. Gianluca promised to return to spend more time with him… he was charmed by his story, and he wanted to know more. After meeting Massimo, there would be no question in his mind about the goodness of his food. The carbonara did not disappoint, rivaling the upscale places in Manhattan.

Gianluca returned his attention to Clarence and the budding friendship begun at the bar. "For a Jersey guy, Ernie seems to have made the adjustment quite well."

"Yes, he's a good man, as are most of the people around here. We have a small Catholic community that worships at the Church of St. Brendon, patron saint of sailors. There is also a K through eighth elementary school popular with all denominations. The Irish came about a hundred and fifty years ago mostly from County Wexford as fishermen and sailors working for thriving industries out of the Port of Savannah. They also settled along the coast on Saint Simon Island and Kingswick. Saint Brendan's dates to eighteen seventy-five. All our churches find the need for donations at some point when money is running low. We all make sure nothing goes under. We are much like any eco-system... we can't afford the loss any one specie that would alter our world. Everyone chips in. It can be donations, money, labor for a new roof, plumbing, food... anything that guarantees we all happily see the light of another day. Ernie is a member of the church, he's a great advocate and has the ear of many at the bar. He got me to donate all my stuff while I was sipping on my rum and coke. He loads his pickup and before you know it, the school has new books, an extra table or two, laptops, boxes of pencils, you name it. He even got the town to donate a complete playground they were replacing in Oceanside Park. Most of us are Evangelicals and Baptists, but like I said, we have a need to see to the wellbeing of everyone in this town. I can't imagine having a drink without Ernie's good company."

"I have always wondered about the relationship between religion and these small southern towns. What am I missing?"

"More than religion, it's about having God on your side. See, down here, God is just one of us. Folks think of him, or her, as some of the feminists at the college insist, as the go to person when things get a bit out of hand. When you consider the turbulence during a century and a half since the Civil War, peace and a good life have been elusive commodities. To many southerners God is the common denominator. If people can't find good enough reasons to get along, to respect one another, finding God in a church with a good preacher, a good sermon, good gospel music... well, you can't come away from that experience without loving your neighbor or in the very least wanting to practice your compassion for others.

Religion and God have gotten over the segregation of the past, our churches are full of folks from all walks of life. For those who have come to terms, there's no desegregation in the south, only a natural integration spearheaded by a God convinced that good must triumph. If you want to witness all this goodness for an hour, come to service on Sunday at the Coastal Georgia Baptist Church. Sermons are uplifting, people find comfort spending a peaceful hour in good company, and you get to hear Leylah sing. She is the lead in the choir. She plays several instruments including the harp... I mean, who plays the harp anymore. In her hands you would think you're crossing the pearly gates. I call it *goosebump Sunday.* Talk about being touched by the finger of God. Her voice is angelic, and you are instantly transported to some heavenly place. It's less about religion and more about a weekly reminder of the feelings that bring us together."

It was a moment that forced the New Yorker away from

the comforts of his entrenched opinions. He could have ignored the God talk, but Clarence wasn't some religious fanatic, he was a scholarly and grounded man who explained his religion as the synthesis of humanity and spirituality. After the first Sunday at church, Gianluca became a regular.

"Amazing... I came to the same conclusion during my one-night stop in Virginia. In a town called Euphoria, I witnessed exactly what you're talking about... there was this easy, fluid integration and not some mandated desegregation. You give it a whole new dimension. I'm used to thinking of different versions of God depending on the religion. Your focus is on what God represents, and not the image. In that sense, if God is the embodiment of goodness, then that becomes the prevailing theme, and that feeling permeates the community. I can see that in the interactions... you can feel the sincere goodness that motivates relationships. You're saying I can expect that just about anywhere in this town?"

Clarence smiled, closed his eyes, and shook his head.

"We have our share of detractors, but we keep working on those few who need to see the light. Best of all, people see it as God's work, and they get involved. You have those who will criticize it as fanatical, but they are wrong because they haven't lived it. It works. It's a form of social security when social security wasn't even a concept. Folks around here have been taking care of each other for generations. Look, there are many like Leylah who could be spending her days selfishly planning her future. Instead, she dedicates time in the care of others in day care centers, senior citizen homes and soup kitchens. Does God have anything to do with that? I like to think there's something divine at work. I've had my hesitations, some doubts, and almost lost faith completely when I lost my wife, Amelia. I didn't blame the cancer, I blamed God. But then, when I'm on my boat on a glorious summer day bobbing around without a care, feeding the seagulls, with my sweet thoughts of Amelia keeping me company, I look up at the sky and I think-God's spreading some of that love. I'm surrounded by perfection, and I must believe it doesn't just happen.

I eventually apologized to God with the understanding that even he is doing his best. If all of nature is his creation, then he is right in letting it take its course. It took its course with Amelia... it takes its course on those perfect days. God wants us to find the good even in the bad. It's how we survive as a species. I found pure goodness in my wife, and it's that goodness that allows me to minimize death, to make it insignificant... I refuse to let death gloat... to let it define us. She lives on, but death dies. You can probably guess that my words are influenced by *John Donne...* one of my favorite poets. I read the poem *Death Be Not Proud* in my eulogy."

"Yes, yes... of course, also one of my favorites! I know his works by heart. I have used that poem in my classes. I always get a 'wow' reaction from my students. *'Death, thou art slave to fate, chance, kings, and desperate men, and dost with poison, war, and sickness dwell, and poppy or charms can make us sleep as well and better than thy stroke; why swell'st thou then? One short sleep past, we wake eternally, and death shall be no more; death, thou shalt die'.*

What an amazing tribute, giving your wife the power to defeat death. I think Donne was on a quest to grant the soul dominance over death... in essence, death can't kill it... death shall be no more because the soul wills it. Amelia's soul gets to censure death, degrade, and disgrace it. That alone should give you reason to keep her alive."

"Couldn't have said it better. Gianluca, it is something we all need to come to terms with. You see, I can't fathom not seeing Amelia again, not being with her in some capacity. Donne says after death we wake eternally, well it's that awakening that motivates me... that is the one promise I will hold God to. If his truth floats, then he must come through for us, he must make good on eternal life after death. I have invested all of me in that promise… and I choose to live as such so that I may be worthy. Doing good, caring for others, for this community… living that commitment every day of my life in the hope of once again looking into my wife's eyes, caressing her face, holding her hand, losing myself in all of her like when we were teenagers. We fell in love in high school, and we never lost that love."

He paused, taking a minute to sadly consider the alternative, wiping away the dampness in his eyes.

"In the end, even if it turns out to be a fool's dream, I will happily play the fool if it keeps the hope alive. Hope is the only prescription my dear friend… nothing else can fix my heart."

"That level of pain is what scares me. To love another so powerfully, and for so long a time, sets you up for the greatest agony one could endure. How do you go on living? I mean, if you still live in the same house, every inch is a memory. Clarence, I have avoided loving anyone the same way to save myself from your kind of pain. Listening to you talk about it, I can only consider myself a coward."

"Sincerely, I may have taken the same route had I known, but now that I find myself believing there is no way I would have forfeited the chance of being one with Amelia. I'll take the pain, which is great, but I had her love which was and still is much greater. She keeps the hurt far from my heart. Look, you may lose the person, but you never lose the spirit, and she keeps reminding me that there is still so much to live for, to carry on, to keep her burning in me so that her flame is never spent… especially for the boys. Gianluca, to be human is to confront these ordeals. Best part is that we are equipped to deal with them if we allow those we have loved to guide us. These may be my words, but it's Amelia's gospel I'm quoting. Have no fears when it involves true love… that's what she would say."

He may have been a thousand miles from Manhattan, but the likeable southern town took him in like a wayward son. His background in historic literature and its connection to social attitudes opened a window onto a place like Kingswick. Just as other locations on the planet and in times past, humans collecting to form a community will spark the creation of a culture particular to it. He knew that the common denominator had been the need to survive and the dependency it fostered among its inhabitants. It may also have been true of a large urban monster like New York, but he felt that the interactions to survive were based on formalities, the legalities of labor, contracts, lease agreements, and goods and services.

In Kingswick he presupposed an informal cooperation

of lending, borrowing, gifting in time of need, helping, exchanging freshly baked foods, leaning on God as one of the neighbors. He saw it as an older America having evolved with a handful of modifications, still vetting the traditions that remained beneficial to many. He was looking beyond the stereotype, thinking he had encountered a more organic humanity, and he was liking it.

"You mentioned your boys?"

"I have two in their thirties... one is a lawyer in Atlanta, the other is a physical therapist with the Atlanta Braves... no complaints. They worked hard, dealt with their mother's death, and are my two shining stars. When Amelia died, the boys and the good people of this town got me through the depression, and the unrelenting apathy to do nothing. It took almost two years for my wife to die. The breast cancer had been festering for years, then it invaded the rest of her body. We tried every possible therapy... the most the doctors could do was to give me some more time with her. She closed her eyes for the last time in my arms, on our bed, in our home."

His story turned Gianluca mournful in a way he had never experienced.

"Clarence, the sadness takes me beyond a broken heart... I'm so sorry for all you endured."

"I've moved on, but never been interested in another woman. I have enough to keep me busy. The boys visit often. I have a smaller house on St. Simon Island right on the ocean. I love to fish, read, and I am still writing and publishing essays, mostly on the state of higher education. I think of Amelia often in a good way, not in some sad, nostalgic way. The thoughts of her, images of her face, her smile get me through the day… keep me happy. People would think I'm losing it, but when I'm out on the water on a perfect day, I answer all her questions on how I'm doing, the boys, and Saint Simon gossip."

Gianluca found it easy to relate.

"I never did find the right one. Completely my fault. I'm too difficult, not good at compromising."

"Well, my compromise was easy, and it paved the way to be blessed with Amelia's goodness and her unique love. I consider myself the most fortunate of men for having learned the art of getting along. I gave of myself haphazardly early in our relationship… didn't think she would ever consider me. She rewarded me by becoming my wife, and then gifted me the best years of her life. Nothing more precious on this good earth than a woman's unconditional love. You should try it."

The sun was about to set in the western sky, it's rays still shimmering on the calm waters of the Kingswick River.

Gianluca agreed to meet with Clarence and the Humanities Department the following day. Back at the inn he stopped for a nightcap at the bar. Ernie was happy to see him.

"Welcome back, professor. How was dinner? As good as New York?"

"Freakin' great, as we would say in Manhattan. I had a wonderful meal at Massimo's, great food, cool atmosphere, and I met Massimo... what a pleasant man. I also met his daughter Leylah."

"You got that right, professor. Massimo is all around good, and Leylah... she comes here for a quiet drink almost every Friday after the rush hours at the restaurant-just to get away. Let's just say that God was having an exceptional day when he created her... top of his game... his Mona Lisa moment. People never seen anyone more beautiful, but don't fall in love, she will disappoint you."

Gianluca tried brushing it off after clumsily exposing his interest in her, but Ernie eased him through it.

"You got that sparkle in your eyes when you mention her... you ain't the first, you definitely won't be the last who won't be able to stop thinking of her. She's had that effect on men, and even a few women. When so many guys asked her to the prom, she decided to go alone. They voted her prom queen; she declined and gave the award to her friend Sandy, one of the autistic girls… the entire school applauded. She's had several marriage proposals from men and women… ignored them all. We had an executive here from Disney Studios for a one-day conference… he stayed a whole week because of Leylah; ate at Massimo's every day. He left completely defeated, a total wreck. A photographer from Vogue magazine was down here taking background shots when she met Leylah. Never seen a woman so in love with another woman. Leylah was friendly, had a few drinks with her, even took her through the nature preserve and the inlets for her photos. When the Vogue lady realized her girl was a dead end, her only choice was to go back to New York a bit bummed out.

I had dinner once at Massimo's. It was a quiet evening; the place was almost empty. Leylah sat at one of the tables, looked like she was doing work for school. I was curious, so I asked what she was reading. She said she was doing a research paper for one of her classes on her hero *Jane Austen*. I had no clue who she was. She showed me two of the books written by this Jane lady back in the 1800s. She explained she was her hero because Jane refused to be any man's woman. It seems that Ms. Austen wrote about happy ever after endings about men and women falling in love, but she refused to have the same ending for herself. According to her, Jane never married, found a way to earn her own money writing in a time when women weren't allowed to publish. She became famous but she died practically poor. See, to me that says everything about Leylah. Usually, a story about some lady writer two hundred years back wouldn't interest me but coming from her it was a story I never forgot. I even read one of the books." He reached down below the counter and pulled out a copy of *Pride and Prejudice*.

The more Gianluca learned, the more he likened Leylah to one of his Renaissance women: an imposing character, a romantic at heart, a tame ego, a casual motivator, and the unique beauty to unleash a tempest in the hearts of men. In a giddy way, he thought, this woman had given him the best reason yet to stay. Teaching at Georgia Maritime would be the excuse; Leylah would be the inspiration.

He notified the front desk that he would extend his stay for another week. In his room he brought himself back into balance after feeling the discomfort of becoming infatuated listening to Ernie talk about Leylah.

"I'm being so idiotic about this Leylah thing. I've liked women, enjoyed their company, but I have never felt this foolish delirium. I didn't make assumptions about a woman choosing me as a companion or lover. I usually just let things happen. Now I'm trying to stop my mind from devising reasons for staying, questioning whether it would be awkward to eat at Massimo's every day, and stifling this juvenile hope of meeting up with her by chance strolling down Main Street. How do I handle this? I mean, she is the kind who keeps you fixated as you rudely ignore the company of others, deaf to all their chatter. The one you sneak a stare at for as long as you can, shifting your glance just in time before she catches you. At the restaurant I couldn't wait for her to come gliding back into the dining room with her little pad, her beautiful black curls bouncing like dozens of mini-Slinkys with every step she took, and the impromptu smile that greeted the regulars. You want to be around her to marvel at her nature, and what appears to be a sincere, graceful soul, pure and full of goodness... fuck, listen to me, I'm describing Dante's *Beatrice*... there must be something seriously wrong with me. This is totally nuts. She is so beyond me and anything I represent. But then, what am I looking for? A relationship? Am I in love with a woman I just met? Stop being a dickhead... you don't know her; she could be a total mess. No way, she has been around Massimo all these years, and Ernie's descriptions were so sincere... why would he embellish her? I'm freaking out... I need to get some sleep.

I'll talk to Cassandra. She'll say I'm out of my fucking

head, I can hear her voice cursing me out that I'm not capable of falling in love with a real woman. That I've already settled for the impossible female who, in her words, lives in my fucked-up fantasies. Maybe I should just leave. I'll thank Clarence for the offer, and I'll get back on 95 and get my ass to Florida. I'll be safe there. I don't want to end up a loser like the Vogue woman and the Disney guy."

He squeezed out one last string of restless thoughts before finally giving in to the mental exhaustion. Once again, he had been victimized by a delinquent brain soaked with anxieties.

"Gianluca, please, just fall asleep, shut it down."

CAPTER 5-*HE'S FROM NEW YORK*

"**L**eylah, I was going to sign up for the Intro to Renaissance Literature class, but no one has ever heard of this professor."

"What's his name?"

"Some Italian name, Gianluca Morelli."

"Holy shih tzu, I know him, he's from New York. He taught at NYU. I met him at the restaurant, he came off so full of himself… tried to flirt with me in Italian… such a turn off. I thought he said he had retired and was on his way to Florida. Dr. Hightower was with him; he must have convinced him to stay and take a position."

"Old, young… what's he look like?"

"Around fifty, looks younger. Handsome, pleasant face, appealing if he kept his mouth shut. Best part is that British accent… it would be sexier on another man."

"That's good enough for me… I'm signing up just to see if he can handle a little southern heat. You should sign up; we can work on him together. Don't you still need another course to fill your English requirement?"

"No, but I can use the course for my history requirement. Look, Claire, I'm not sure we need to tolerate him an entire semester. I'm not one to take bullshit courses for an easy *A*, but I'm tempted to take Collingworth's class on

Shakespeare… everyone gets an *A*. I wouldn't mind a lazy spring semester so I can start planning where to do my master's."

"Com'on, you should take him just to see what it's like being in a class with a guy who has taught at NYU. Look, Georgia Maritime is a small, commuter college. We don't even have dorms. The professors here are mostly adjuncts. I'm signing up, I'm curious."

"Fine, maybe you're right. It could also give me some clues of what to expect if I go away to Atlanta, or God forbid, New York."

Gianluca signed on as an Associate Professor. He submitted copies of his course titles and descriptions the week before he met with the department. At his informal orientation everyone got a chance to exchange greetings. One of the female professors bypassed all the formalities asking if she could sit in on some of his classes. She spoke slowly, rolling out words that had been fermenting for decades in a barrel of feminine moonshine.

"Professor Moerellee, did I properly pronounce your surname? And what a lovely name, *Janlukaw*- I have never once come across that one." She *twanged* the Italian name into submission. "It is such a pretty sounding name… please forgive me for the weakness in my pronunciation. Now I realize this request may violate some vague protocol, but would it cause your little old heart anxiety if I were to sit in on some of your classes? My expertise is in Popular Culture and American Literature. When I find the time, I catch up on our European cousin. I admit, however, that I could use some guidance in how to show them greater appreciation."

Gianluca nervously scanned for reactions... there were none. He then realized the awkward silence sheltered hidden opinions.

"Yes, of course, if there are no objections from the department or from Dr. Hightower."

The others knew to stay out of it. Clarence looked at him indicating he had none, then introduced his colleague.

"Professor Morelli, this is Dr. Catherine Davies, acting chair. Our previous chair decided to retire at the end of the fall semester. Her interest in sitting in on your classes is purely academic, we have a tradition of not conducting formal observations, except for adjuncts. You bring a whole new set of offerings to the department... we are excited and I know certain students will be. The course titles and descriptions you handed in were posted yesterday. Students will be able to look them over online."

A luncheon of southern favorites was served in the faculty lounge where Gianluca had a chance to engage in friendly conversations. Clarence had retreated to his office where he had asked to meet with Catherine Davies. He wasted no time taking on Catherine on a familiar topic.

"Catherine, I can tell he is your type, and your flirtation didn't go unnoticed. Your ex is still reeling over the divorce, and he hasn't left you alone. You haven't helped the situation much by keeping him dangling like a catfish on your hook. I allowed you two to stay on in the department against my better judgement. I should have asked one of you to resign... I find myself regretting it now. I don't see this ending well if you follow your instincts with Dr. Morelli. He is a good-looking man with a very endearing character. He has no experience with southern women... not difficult to see. I have had excellent conversations with him, and in a short time I have come to know him intimately. He is sincere and genuine, and I would hate to see those traits undermined. If we were having this conversation in New York, you would have gotten Me Too, Me three and Me four after my ass. Down here we have an understanding that we get in each other's business to set things straight with no one else involved. Let's practice what we do best. I'm appealing to your Southern sense of decency... your ex will not be able to handle it, and his reactions could stupid. I want Morelli to like it here, and we may get to hold on to him for a few years. Given the budget for the position, we can certainly do no better."

Catherine leaned back in her chair, crossed her legs,

and shifted her eyes away from Clarence to refocus on the mid-December winds nipping at the shiny, deep green leaves of the magnolias.

"My darling Clarence, while I can appreciate your concerns for our new man, my intentions are my business, unless you want to exercise your power, however late, to rid yourself of me. The guy is fair game for any woman. He is a fresh face, different from all the philistines around here, and that fucking British accent... are you kidding me? You're right, he is a man whose company I would enjoy. I promise to go easy, to let him ripen a bit. Women like me live very lonely lives in Kingswick, unless you like sitting on a stool in one of our classy bars being hit on by a three-hundred-pound ball of drunken blubber who smells like a freshly slaughtered pig. Or maybe I should settle for one of our drooling, emasculated, pseudo professors in button down striped shirts tucked into oversized khakis, and sheepskin moccasins, masquerading as intellectuals.

Paul has been my ex for quite some time, so he needs to learn to deal with his psychosis, his delusions. I intend to live as I am, and to attract the company of a man when I feel the need. Clarence, no offense, but if I were not pushing forty-five, I probably would have toned it down a bit. I have some uninvited wrinkles in places I thought would have held out at least until the Falcons won a Super Bowl, but they just crawled up on me overnight, and I'm not happy. If I wait for that Super Bowl trophy, no man will be able to find a smooth patch of skin anywhere on this body. I still have something left, and I aim to use it. He came to the meeting dressed in a tie, and an Armani suit in that very masculine, trim body. He smelled good enough to brush up against, hoping that some of his scent would rub off on me and give me something to dream about. I don't need to know much more about him. He gave off these little signals, quick bursts of hormonal energy, and this may be too much information, but my body absorbed them like one of those heavy-duty paper towels. Sweetheart, we've known each other for almost two decades… I have my needs. I'll be as discreet as possible, but I'm going to want that man in my bed. Are we done?"

Clarence rubbed his eyes, unleashed a heavy sigh, and laid his head on his desk. Catherine got up, returned to the gathering to sip on another glass of wine, and to spy the mannerisms of the unsuspecting Morelli.

CHAPTER 6- *PREDICTABLY UNPREDICTABLE*

It wasn't NYU, but the small coastal campus had a New England fishing village feel to it. It was built around two nineteenth century Victorian mansions donated to the county by prominent Savannah families who once used them as summer homes. They housed the college administration, and on the second floor of Mercer House, Gianluca walked into his new office. It was larger than he anticipated, with an ornate Victorian desk, plenty of storage space, fine framed prints on the walls, and two oversized windows that looked out on Saint Simon's Bay. The view was enough to give him a good feeling about his decision. The place was growing on him, and the unaccustomed kindness and attention had a strong family feel to it... the kind that reminded him of what was missing in his life.

Another week was added to his stay at the Inn while he looked for a place to live. Clarence wasn't the best at real estate, so he handed him off to Massimo who had purchased two more buildings over the years, and he had an empty apartment in one of them. It was close to the campus, and the pleasant stroll to work made it an easy choice. The rent was a quarter what he paid in New York, it was around double the size, and it had a terrace. The furnishings were new and appealing. The kitchen and bathroom had been recently updated. All was good when he felt his phone vibrating in the inside pocket of his blazer... it was Cassandra.

"Hi, I was thinking of you. I was going to call. I have some story to tell you. I never made it to Florida."

"Well, I also have a story to tell you. You go first."

"No way, how are things in New York."

Cassandra had already decided to deliver her remarks surgically and with no remorse. "Gianluca, I'm pregnant, almost four months pregnant."

His immediate reaction was to congratulate her thinking it had something to do with Ritchie. The four months remark stopped him from uttering a word. He thought about it and did the math.

"The baby is mine."

Cassandra's response came from her gut, full of nervous energy, spitting out words at the speed of light.

"Yes, and I'm not going to make up some bullshit story... I did it on purpose. I'm not afraid to tell you the truth. You have a child coming. How do I explain this? I wanted the baby, and I don't want you to take any responsibility except if something should happen to me. I know this is turning out like some warped Hallmark movie. I wasn't certain about us, and I wanted to be a mother. You were the only man I had ever known that could be a good husband and father. I let go of the husband thing, but the baby had to happen. I used you Gianluca, I certainly did, so hate me all you want. I know it was wrong, but it was a fault I was willing to commit. Go ahead, be as angry as you want, let it all out. Maybe afterwards you'll come to accept it and let me be a happy mother to our child. Please go on with your life as if it hadn't happened... I know it's easy and shallow of me to speak these words, but I took the chance of telling you because you have a good heart, and I don't want to raise this child constantly hiding the truth. I have no doubt this will be a beautiful, healthy, and amazing human being... so let me love it with no remorse"

Gianluca slumped into his sofa to do some hard thinking.

"I don't suppose it's necessary to do a paternity test."

"Gianluca, please!"

"Fine, I don't know what to think right now. I'm just confused, a little off balance. I had some news to tell you, now I'm not sure I want to share it."

"I was hoping this wouldn't turn you off. Why can't you talk to me?"

"The pregnancy takes the steam out of my situation. I was sidetracked in Georgia because of a massive accident on 95. I got off the highway and decided to spend a night in a town called Kingswick. I took a room at an inn where I met a man named Clarence Hightower who happened to be the provost at the local college. He runs Georgia Maritime on nearby Saint

Simon Island. We spoke, became friendly and he ended up offering me a position in his humanities department. I didn't take it seriously at first, convinced I was still heading to Florida. Then I started liking the place and the people. I extended my stay for a week, and I finally gave in and accepted the job. I was excited to tell you and to find out how you were doing. Now it seems trivial compared to your news."

"I don't know how to make you understand. I would like you to be fine with the baby. You can get over the deceit, I want you to be happy knowing that you granted me a beautiful gift. You probably think I'm being a total bitch about this, but you were the perfect choice."

"So, I should be pleased to know that I was your personal sperm bank? Wait, so when we met at the Poet's Cafe in December, how did I not notice? Why didn't you tell me?"

"Shit, Gianluca, if I had said something you would have thought I was using that as an excuse to have you stay. I wasn't going to let that get in the way of your decision to leave. You had given up your apartment, resigned from NYU, and notified all your friends in Florida that you were on your way. You're a good man, and there was a chance you would have changed everything thinking you were then obligated to give up your plans. There's no way I would have wanted that for you, so I said nothing. I don't need an unhappy, resentful man in this baby's life. You left, and I was good... for you, and for me. I could have lied and said it was some other man's child, keeping you in the dark forever.

Gianluca, this baby had to happen from the moment I walked into your class. I loved being there for the material, but also because of you. I learned to like everything about you-your passion for teaching, the way you took the topic of love to a whole new place, and your sweet mannerisms. The first time we met at the Poet's Cafe I was already in love, and I took a chance you might feel the same. I then understood that wasn't going to happen. Eventually, it didn't matter anymore, it was just good to be with you. The trips, the sex, our conversations, your goofy idiosyncrasies... I looked forward to all of it. Yes, I may have lived with some disappointments, but knowing you would one day leave New York, and exit from my life, well... I plotted, but it wasn't meant to be calculated, selfish or hurtful. I wanted a child, Gianluca, but I also wanted to keep a part of you... you can see I got both."

She paused, wondering about his silence.

"I need your blessings. I need you to make me feel right with you because I already feel right with me. I regret the way it happened, but I don't regret the outcome."

He pulled the phone away from his ear, tried to find a reason to feel slighted, to think himself a victim, or in the extreme, angry. It all seemed silly and useless.

"You're the only person I know who can pull that off and

still have me love the way you manipulate me. When is the baby due?"

"Around May 24th give or take a day."

"The semester ends May 19. I'd like to be there when you give birth."

Cassandra said nothing.

"Hello? Cassandra, you still there? Hello?"

"I'm still here, I just had a moment. I almost can't believe you said you wanted to be here... that would make me so happy."

"Fine, I'll fly up around the 20th. How is it going with Ritchie? You two still together?"

"Yes, and he knows about the baby, and he is good with it. Because of the pregnancy I moved back in with my mother. We are making plans... not yet sure where it will go. We talked about it. We're getting older and having a solid family life is something we both want. I'm already working on my master's. I want to get done by next year and apply for a position in the public schools. Gianluca, I feel like good things are finally happening, things that are real, the kind you can touch. With your blessings it couldn't be more perfect."

"Well then, I will be there to welcome this child. I'll text you my address at the college, and my office phone number."

He paused, gave Cassandra and the baby one more thought.

"Hey, I am truly happy for you, and in an odd way I'm feeling good about this. My only concern is what part I will play in the baby's life. We can discuss more when I come up."

"You are the father, and I would think this child would want to experience the best in a father. Distances will not matter if your heart is nearby. You are the best of men, and you will prove it over and over in this baby's life."

He summarized the conversation with a quiet smile knowing it was a Cassandra decision he might have been able to predict with some contempt. Instead, he was forced to admire her unpredictable nature once more. It had defined their relationship, and he had always been in awe of it. Still, despite the offer by Cassandra to release him of any obligation, he realized that the prospect of fatherhood now offered an excuse to abandon the Leylah courtship. He was overcome with a bittersweet sense of relief.

CHAPTER 7-*GONE WITH THE WIND*

The following week he walked into his first class loaded up with a stack of syllabi, his bag, and a knot in his stomach. It wasn't the lecture hall he had been accustomed to back at NYU. The smallish room was equipped with a large conference table and seating for about twenty. With five minutes till the start of class he counted only five students. At NYU his classes maxed out each semester. By the time things got going, however, he had standing room only. The seats were all taken, leaving two students to lean up against the back wall. He hadn't dwelt on any of the faces, concerned with finding two more chairs. He then scanned the room, and as he attempted to introduce himself, the words got stuck in some dead-end spot in his head when he made eye contact with Leylah. He greeted her with a smile and a quick, quirky hand gesture. She ignored it hoping he would just continue with his intro.

"Welcome, I'm Dr. Gianluca Morelli." He always pronounced his name as if checking into a hotel in Milan. "I'm sure you recognize me as the new guy on the block. This was not a position I had applied for. In fact, I was on my way to Florida after taking an early retirement from NYU. A nasty accident on route 95 detoured me into your quaint town where I met Dr. Hightower. We became instant friends, and during dinner at your famous Massimo's restaurant, he asked if I would be interested in filling a position in humanities. It was a bit of a tug of war with myself... in the end I chose to stay. I picked up the British accent during twelve years of boarding school in London-I thought I'd get that out since everyone is always puzzled by it. It's not the accent people expect with a name like Gianluca Morelli. I taught at NYU for twenty years. I was born in Italy, then came to America with my parents who had been invited to teach at NYU. They are professors who have now retired to their hometown of Padova.

So, Manhattan had been my home all these years. Laying new roots here has involved a pleasurable dose of culture shock. Three weeks have passed since my arrival, I have settled into an apartment nearby, and Massimo's has kept me from having to cook. Go ahead and make fun of my accent, and anything else about me you find awkward... I'll be the first to laugh. I hope to keep you engaged in the material. I try not to lecture; I urge you to do as much talking as I will. I encourage participation, insights, input. No observation or opinion will go unappreciated, so speak up, get involved, feel free to argue with me. The title of the course is *Gender Roles and Social Norms in the Literature of the Renaissance.* We may be going back in time about eight centuries, but you would be amazed at how contemporary the issues are. My hope is to instill an understanding of those norms as they applied to that time, to feel for the rebelliousness of those who produced some of the most intriguing literature ever, and to bridge the time gap to the present. I will introduce you to poets, troubadours, and their lovers. Best part, we will investigate the motivations that led to their writings... what was it about that society, the women, and the passions of these men. I hope to have you come to love the literature, the characters, and the genius in their words."

He spent the remainder of the period reviewing the syllabus, introducing the text, and answering questions. As the students filed out at the end of class, he was greeted by Claire, Leylah's friend. "Professor Morelli, hi, I'm Claire. I was skeptical, but after your introduction I am now looking forward to your class." Leylah stood nearby waiting. She was removed enough to stay out of the conversation. Gianluca sensed the less than friendly posture. He decided to say hello and left it at that.

Meanwhile, Catherine Davies made good on her promise, attending his very first class. She was an elegant woman winning her battle with ageing. Her first marriage lasted a year... she was eighteen. Learning came easy to her, and just before her thirtieth birthday she had earned her doctorate at Emory University. Her second marriage to Paul Considine, a department colleague, was running out of steam after four years. She probably knew better, but the thought of pushing fifty had her stumble into another suffocating marriage. Catherine found the right affair irresistible... and being married was never an impediment. Gianluca was over-qualified.

He had all the right ingredients, and as a Yankee, he was practically a foreigner which added to the intrigue... she knew exactly how to handle the outsider.

Early into the spring semester she started sitting in on more of his classes. She kept quiet despite wanting to participate in the discussions. The students didn't make much of it, accustomed to having professors sitting amongst them. They did, however, notice the way she doted over him after class. Several sessions in, she decided on some private time with him in his office.

"Dr. Morelli, forgive me for disturbing you... is this a bad time?"

"No, please, come in."

"I'm sure you have noticed my attendance in your classes. I thought I'd come by to discuss. Your introduction to the history and the demographics that contributed to the birth of Renaissance literature was fascinating. So many dismiss the historical factors when it comes to literature as if it is a product of spontaneous generation. I have always disagreed. I believe so many ingredients are present that condition the works."

"Yes, my first book dealt with that topic. I'm a firm believer that literature develops hand in hand with the growth of communities, towns, cities, and nations. It is affected by traditions that get passed along by generations. That's historical, not spontaneous. There may be enhancements, modifications that are unplanned, but to me those are not the foundations of literature."

"Dr. Morelli, this may be forward of me, but I find myself captivated by the passion you put into your teaching. Would you like to meet for a casual interlude away from the campus? Dinner at Massimo's? No pressure... feel free to refuse."

"Massimo's has kept me nourished while I try to find a normal pace to life. I do enjoy the atmosphere and the food."

"Well then, this Friday around seven?"

"That's fine, thank you for the invitation."

"Dr. Morelli... or may I call you John Loocaw... I look forward to a pleasant evening in your good company."

Later that afternoon he sat in his office delaying his trip home to get his head around the events reorganizing his life. He was soon to become a father, Florida was history, and he had introduced himself to a new class of students in a small Georgia town. Catherine Davies was coming on a bit strong, and despite feeling the need to fall in with his new colleagues, he was searching for a way to cool her down. He thought of the funny way she pronounced his name, and of how she reminded him of *Scarlett O'Hara* in *Gone with the Wind*. If she was cut from that same cloth, he figured he would need some advice from Clarence. He thought of how Leylah reminded him of *Melanie* in the film. In the description that Clarence had given, Leylah was less concerned with her femininity, while compassionate about the condition of others. He couldn't help the comparisons since the characters had somehow conditioned his images of southern women. He considered his views were perhaps stereotypical, but he knew that would fade with time.

With several hours till his next class, he walked back to Mercer House. On his way in, he caught Hightower's attention who waved him into his office.

"How was your first class?"

"Went well. It looked to be thin on numbers, but about a minute before class it swelled to over twenty... pleasantly surprised, I prefer a full class. They seemed a bit distant not knowing me, an unfamiliar face on campus... like who is this guy from New York. They enjoyed my short personal history. I noticed a few -oops, wrong class- reactions once they got a look at the syllabus. I suspect there will be some attrition. I'm used to it, happened at NYU as well. You'll have those sincerely interested in the topic, and those looking for an easy way to a decent grade. My syllabus won't satisfy that population... I'm guessing they'll drop the class."

"The going rate for the tougher classes is about sixty percent retention... let's see how you do."

"Clarence, can you give me a few minutes to pick your

brain?"

"Of course, have a seat. Cup of coffee?"

"A bottle of water would work. I was asked to dinner by Dr. Davies."

Clarence couldn't help the interruption.

"My goodness, already? When she puts herself in motion, there's no stopping her. I thought she'd give you a month at least. Here's my best advice. Keep it superficial, platonic... we do have a college code of conduct which discourages dating among faculty and with students, but we have never enforced it. You can talk about keeping people apart, but it gets complicated when you can't uniformly impose it. Getting into the personal lives of people creates too much hostility. A college campus becomes an uneasy place when there are many hard feelings hovering about. I've had to ride that fine line many times. Things have worked out, but that bomb is always ticking, and my fear is that I won't always be able to defuse it."

He then took one his deep sighs, leaned back and interlocked his fingers on the back of his neck.

"Catherine, Catherine... what to do about my dear Catherine. Best thing about her is that she loses interest quickly if things are not to her liking, which ultimately makes her harmless. She enjoys being in control, and with men there must be a challenge; it can't come easy. Her men have usually been strong minded until she turns them into wimps. Now this is all strictly confidential… it dies in this office. If she should ever find out I prepped you in any way, she will lose what little filter she has, and only God knows how long the firestorm will last. She has a dedicated following among the students, and a very casual way about her in class, but you always know who's in charge. I'm one of those who enjoys her classes. No question about her teaching skills. If you have accepted the invitation, show up. Avoid flirtatious talk if you can. She will dump you if she can't get you to engage romantically. If you find yourself in her bed, it's already too late, she will come back for seconds… she'll consider you property until you declare yourself to someone else. Look, all this is mostly comical, and don't expect a serious backlash should things not go her way. As I said, she will lose interest, and move on."

Gianluca rolled his eyes unable to control a befuddled smile. He thought he understood the advice, but he hadn't absorbed the blueprint.

"Fine, I need to make some adjustments. I'm assuming she's not married." "She was, to Paul Considine." "The Paul in our department? Are they divorced?"

"They married years back, but it didn't work out; divorced after only four years. One other caution now that we are on the topic. Paul still has feelings for her, and it's noticeable. He's weak, and she knows it, so she gives him the attention he craves. It feeds her ego, and his hopes. Not sure how he will react if she markets herself. There's no doubt she will try. You'll have to find a delicate way around it. I can't suggest a plan… I have no experience with stuff like that. Look, I'm sorry if apprehensions are creeping into taking us on; I do hope you won't change your mind. With some luck she'll move on to other hobbies."

Learning about Paul made him instantly uncomfortable. It was too late to get out of the dinner date, so he left it alone, but at least now he had a better idea of how to handle her. He turned his attention to his new class and the presence of Leylah. He thought about her distant, cold attitude towards him, trying to understand what would have her act that way. Her beauty made a statement no matter her attitude… there was no escaping it. Alone in his apartment, he began considering the variables.

"I can't imagine someone that beautiful having any faults. Yet, there must be something about her that is unlikeable… it can't be that she is perfectly flawless in looks and character. It's just that her face, her skin, the way she moves about the restaurant, her interactions with people… so appealing. The way she looks in those leggings, her Maritime hoodie, that casual elegance even in everyday clothes. It amazes me that she can be all that, so modest, yet sexy, almost sexual in a way, without promoting it. She's so purely feminine... my god, how can one not want to love her? You need to control yourself; you will say all the wrong things, or you'll act like a schoolboy fool, and make no impression at all... just an encounter soon forgotten. I'm going to have a tough time of it in class. I can't dwell on her. If I make eye contact, I need to move on quickly. Listen to me, I'm assuming she would have no interest in me. I know, she's a student... but she is in her thirties, just like Cassandra. Is it fair to let a classroom get in the way of a relationship? I'm being totally asinine. Cassandra was right... I want to feel love, and be loved, but I have it scripted all wrong. There is too much about her that makes me..." He paused realizing the obvious. "I've grown weak giving in to real love, and I have no clue how to deal with it. If she only had a fiancé, engaged to be married, then I could walk away. She could then be the women I never knew... keep it impossible and fantasize my way into a solitary existence, content to glorify her in volumes of literature. What is wrong with me... is that what I really want? To follow in the footsteps of my poets had been easy when I was not the protagonist. The passion was artificial, adopted. Now the passion is real, magnified to the same level of those spirits who spent their lives celebrating a creature never to be theirs.

Cassandra insisted that love needs to be tried, it needs a life of its own with no interruptions, and that one had to understand and accept the challenge, and to prepare earnestly. She would say you don't climb Everest in shorts, a tee shirt, and flip flops. I know she would laugh her ass off if I said that I have met my "Everest"… she would think me corny and call me an asshole, and that I either go for it, or waste away, pen in hand, hunched over the pages of regret. I've gotta stop this, I could end up talking to myself all night."

Before falling asleep his thoughts returned to the movie and Scarlett's pathetic relationships with Ashley and Rhett. Ashley was too wimpy, so she lost interest. Rhett understood that Scarlett needed a challenge, a man who wouldn't fall so easily. She couldn't manipulate Rhett; he was too much like her. Catherine Davies had all the same "Scarlett" traits it seemed, so using the movie as a guide, and being more like Ashley was probably what Clarence meant when he said she would lose interest. Leylah had a passion for matching her soul to those of others. There was something, it seemed, clear to Gianluca that she embodied all the goodness in a woman without neglecting any of her feminine qualities.

CHAPTER 8-*THE STRENGTH TO BEAR HER SMILE*

On a cool and rainy Monday morning, Gianluca sat in his office reviewing his notes prepping for his next class. The syllabus topic was *Renaissance Women and the Question of Divinity*. He would use Dante's encounter with Beatrice at the entrance to heaven in Canto XXIII of the Paradiso to make his point. Later that day he stood in front of a full class dominated by women. He casually introduced the topic.

"Imagine the Blessed Virgin Mary; the virgin who gave birth to Jesus as the ultimate female role model. You may respectfully reject the notion, but in Dante's world it was a very real standard. Women, at least those of the aristocracy and the merchant classes, were indoctrinated from childhood by family and the church in the virtues of virginity. They were excused from conceiving through divine intervention to make certain none would ever believe herself to be the equal of Mary. We also need to consider the purpose of intercourse. There was no absolute proof that the Church promoted intercourse only for making babies, but when one considers the powerful symbolism of divine intervention, it's no wonder there would arise a certain disdain for recreational sex. In a village setting or small parishes, local priests could easily insist on the avoidance of pleasure to mothers and their daughters, linking it to sin. The closest, therefore, mortal women could get to divine intervention would be to avoid foreplay, and orgasms; allow for a very tame penis to penetrate quickly, and ejaculate with the hope of a sanctified pregnancy. Questions or reactions?"

Immediately, several arms shot into the air eager to comment. Gianluca couldn't help himself.

"Yes, Leylah, you appear agitated."

"Excuse me, but I am. My feeling is that the men of the Renaissance, both fathers and priests used their power to control not only a woman's life, but also her clitoris. It seems the husband was entitled to his orgasm and the trajectory of his ejaculation, even if it only lasted several seconds... nothing much has changed by the way ... while the female was taught to avoid pleasure, and perhaps even deny it if she was secretly enjoying an orgasm of her own. Here's where I'm confused... you are making a point of how laymen and priests conspired to subdue, mold, and define the sexuality of women with the pathetic excuse of divinity. I don't believe it was sincere. I think it was manipulative so that men could safeguard the virginity of women for those who would become their husbands, and to avoid pleasure of her own to keep her chaste. In the extreme, we still witness female castration in parts of the world for the same reason. I'm sure most men made a playground of the wife's body, and they were under no obligation to avoid pleasure. I'm sorry professor, but I find nothing romantic in social conditions that played into the selfish needs of men. I also think Dante lucked out because Beatrice died young... she was still beautiful. What if she had grown old, gotten fat with four kids? Would he have still used her as his subject, or would he have opted for a woman still in her prime? See, there are so many variables that Dante would have not allowed to influence his writings... he was going to write his fiction no matter... any beautiful young chick would have done."

He expected the feminist backlash, but it had never been accompanied by such a powerful argument.

"Okay, I can appreciate your sensitivity to the topic, but romanticism wasn't meant to be a part of the bedroom activity. Certainly, there were men in love with their wives, but we know little of that truth because many of those men had no reason to expose their love in prose... doing so would have been the equivalent of putting your love life on display on Facebook. You ran the risk of ruining your reputation, even losing your place in society.

The romanticism becomes a dominant ingredient in the experiences of those men who had no chance of having the women they desired. So, when Dante dedicates most of his writings to a very married Beatrice, he does so because it is the only way available to him to love the woman... he allows himself to romanticize the Beatrice who would be his. In the end he conveniently makes her divine... in a sense still a blessed virgin to him, and when he finally meets her in heaven, she comes to him in the image of a pure and blinding light, a divinity for whom he lacks the substance to even bear her smile. He is not yet worthy of her presence; he hasn't quite earned it.

So, when we deal with the idea of divinity in the Renaissance woman, the focus is on those men who were doomed, as Dante was, to express a love unrealized, unfulfilled, and in a last, desperate manifestation, the object of that love is anointed and given a place among the holy. Now some might say it's a convenient cop-out... like saying if I can't have her, no one can. She instantly becomes a protégé of the mother of Christ... angelic, pious, and untouchable. It would be unfair of us to apply a modern feminist admonition to the actions of twelfth and thirteenth century men. The conventional thinking at the time was that men and women suffered their conditions, not abuses. Survival depended on each playing still primitive roles.

The modern woman is mostly a product of the post-World War II era. So, judging the Renaissance man with modern values developed over the past seventy years or so would dismiss the realities of the past, and deny us the humanity in the writings of the great poets. We shouldn't ignore the reality of those social norms and passing negative judgments on them is the easy thing to do.

In this course I'd like you to sideline those criticisms so that we may appreciate the catalysts that drove those individuals to create masterpieces of literature. I would think that any of us would invite a powerful attraction to another person to motivate us to act or just to feel the tingle, the impulse. Who knows, the result may be a life-long companionship or another contribution to great literature. Either outcome, I suppose, would elevate us."

As he gazed back into Leylah's eyes, she appeared unconvinced. He pushed her for a reaction.

"I'm sorry, but I think your explanation only adds fuel to the crap those men employed in seeking their own fame. It really pisses me off when professors like you anoint the views of others that you agree with. Because you're convinced it was fine to glorify muzzled women, you build a complete curriculum around that belief and then you teach your gospel like it's a revelation. I reject your fake romanticism, your fiction, and the fake ideals that men used to further their own shit. I mean, even Dante needs to make Beatrice holy before he can praise her. What if she was a floozy? What if she had cheated on her husband, but no one found out? What if she secretly had a lesbian affair with one of the maids or a best friend? That doesn't matter to Dante because he cares only to present us with his version of this woman... and that is incredibly self-serving. He molds her, makes her famous and in the process gains eternity for himself... how fucking convenient at the expense of a woman... sorry for cursing."

Two girls sitting across the table gave her a standing

ovation. Gianluca smiled knowing he had successfully instigated reactions that kept his class fresh and interesting.

With minutes left in the period, he ended his class with a final remark. "Yes, but what does it matter whatever else she may have been if Dante writes only about his initial impulse? If we fall in love at first sight when we know so little about the person, what importance is there in what lies beyond that? Yes, we may fall out of love later, but if there is no later, we are left only with that first inclination, and for Dante and his generation, that was all he could hope for.

Well, I'll take a day or two to think about whether I deserved the thrashing. Along those lines, I have written college level instructional books, but I have yet to feel that elusive spark from that one individual that would allow my heart to own my pen and send me off into literary immortality. Just think of the improbability of two such individuals finding each other.

See you in three days. I have some short assignments posted on the portal, please check them out."

As the class emptied, he awkwardly tried to get Leylah's attention by playing down her attitude and asking about the week's special at Massimo's. Still fuming, she answered as she marched towards the door.

"I didn't make the menu this week, my mom did, ask her when you come in."

She followed Claire into the hall. Gianluca leaned up

against his desk, squinting his annoyance at his juvenile attempt at a conversation, when he noticed Leylah break off from her friend to join Paul Considine as they exited Mercer. He followed their progress along the path that led to the campus cafeteria. Curiosity got the better of him, so he decided to casually stroll in the same direction. In the large dining hall, he noticed the two sitting at a table with cups of coffee, engaged in a lively conversation. Leylah smiled frequently and seemed genuinely involved. He stayed out of sight wondering if the conversation had to do with Paul's course. He remembered Leylah mentioning she was also enrolled in his class on *Nineteenth Century American Literature*. Judging from their body language, their encounter had little to do with academics. He walked back to his office bewildered.

"Could it be those two are involved? I need to leave this alone... mind my business. He is a good-looking man, has a friendly way about him, probably in his mid-forties, and she's in her thirties, so what's the big deal? I'm looking for impediments to the relationship because I like her... I would be the ultimate hypocrite if it were me sitting across from her. I can't compete with a man from the area who has had several years to make an impression on her; I just got here. Maybe Leylah is his way to get over Catherine... weird... I didn't think she would give a man that much attention."

That evening Gianluca was at Massimo's promising to spare Leylah his infatuations. She had given him no reason to think she would even want his friendship, and that was enough to stifle his emotions. He sat at his favorite table near the window that faced the beaches of Saint Simon Island. It reminded him of the evenings on Bowen's Wharf in Newport. In that instant he felt a deep nostalgia for Cassandra's company. It was sad to think he had taken those hours for granted, selfishly mired in his fantasy to join the ranks of his hero poets. He was shaken out of his trance when Leylah approached to rattle off the day's specials.

"Hi, you asked about the specials in class today. This is what we have: chicken parm with a side of ziti, and a glass of Chianti, fourteen ninety-five; shrimp scampi with a side of capellini and a glass of Pinot Grigio, sixteen fifty, and finally, our famous meat lasagna with a glass of Montepulciano thirteen fifty."

He asked no questions, making up his mind quickly to go with the lasagna. She soon returned with a glass of water and his Montepulciano. As he took a sip of wine, Massimo had a few minutes on a slow evening to greet him.

"Ciao *professore*, good to see you again."

He detected a slight accent still giving him a foreign appeal.

"Massimo, your place has become an extension of my

home. It makes no sense for me to cook when your food is so good, and affordable."

"So, you have taken the position at the college. I'm happy for our community. Dr. Hightower tells me you are a scholar of Italian literature."

"Dr. Hightower is being too kind. I have my parents to thank for my passion. They are both retired professors from NYU as well. They retired to their hometown of Padova. They started their careers at the University of Bologna."

"*Dio mio, il mondo diventa sempre più piccolo!* (My God, the world keeps getting smaller). I worked at the University in Bologna as a cook before coming to America. I knew many of the professors there. They came to me when they had special requests. The work was enjoyable, the money was barely enough to live on."

Massimo's story came to an abrupt stop when he recalled Gianluca's last name.

"Is your father's name Matteo?"

"Yes, Matteo."

"My goodness, Doctor Matteo Morelli I knew him in Bologna. He was a professor there when I worked in the kitchen. I didn't know him as well as some of the others, but he was always a gentleman. What about your mom, did she teach there as well?"

"Yes, they met at the University as young professors.

They dated secretly, and then married in Padova before accepting positions at NYU. "

"What is your mother's name?"

"Gemma, her maiden name is Trevisan. Did you know her as well?"

Massimo paused as if trying to recall.

"No, I don't think we met... I do not remember the name. You know, there were so many professors. Well, you enjoy your dinner. I make sure to send you a slice of the ricotta pie."

Massimo ended the conversation abruptly, and somewhat nervously. Gianluca gave it no particular attention as his eyes followed Leylah darting around the large dining room delivering and taking orders, amazed by her work ethic.

Talking to his head again: "Incredible that she dedicates herself to this work when she could be focused entirely on her life. She is as rare as everyone describes her. There's so much genuine goodness in her. God, it's so difficult not to want to get to know her better. I wonder what it is about Paul Considine she finds attractive. Maybe I'm exaggerating the relationship... it could be that it is a very friendly, platonic thing. It didn't look that way in the campus center. This is getting stupid; I should have gotten back on the highway for Florida... I never would have met her."

He looked down at a page in his notebook to see where he left off in class forcing his mind to reset. Moments later

Leylah dropped off a basket of bread and some dipping oil, hardly stopping at his table. Once again, he sensed her rudeness. This time it bothered him. He didn't think his actions had come close to offending her, yet there had to be something about him that turned her sideways. When she returned with his lasagna, he had to ask.

"Leylah, I know you are super busy, but can you sit for a few seconds?"

"Actually, I was going to wait for you to finish your dinner to talk to you about the next assignment."

He quickly abandoned the intended confrontation in asking her to sit. Her need to discuss a course topic softened him enough to improvise a new reason for his invitation.

"Funny, but I had a similar reason in asking you to sit with me. I was taken by your analysis of men and the divinity of women. It seems you truly believe it was exclusively to guarantee a woman's virginity for a future husband. You completely reject the chance that for some men it was the only way left to them to romanticize the forbidden woman? What do you think of someone like Dante, in his day, comparing Beatrice with the untouchable Virgin Mary? He had no chance with her; he knew it, accepted it, but memorialized his feelings in the writings he dedicated to her. Why do you reject that?"

"I don't reject it outright, and I'm a bit pissed that you characterized my opinions in class as feminist. I think that's a sick modern-day habit for men to diminish the worth of what a woman has to say by labeling it as feminist. It was purely a woman's reaction based on historical evidence. Do you deny that men used their powers to force virginity on women, and that the church was complicit? I don't see how any of the poets of that period could seriously consider their writings to be organically romantic if they saw their women as untouchables, I mean they were real, but not real. You can respect a nun, respect the notion of a Blessed Virgin, but can you really be in love with images? Don't take this the wrong way, but I get the feeling that you are looking for the same excuse where you can claim to love a woman that you can't have. You show such passion for these Renaissance hopeless romantics that you maybe wish to be one of them? Look, I'm sorry, I don't mean to offend... I don't know you well enough to have said those things... I take it back."

He wanted her to keep talking. He gave her lips and her mannerisms as much attention as her words. It was a first experience with her softer side, and he thanked himself for not calling out her rudeness. He likened her thoughts of him to Cassandra's. They had pretty much come to the same conclusions, and it gave him pause to again think of how obvious he had become.

"I take no offense, it's not the first time I have been

accused of pandering to the past. I got caught up in it when I was a teenager, and I fell in love with the whole notion of being in love, real or imagined. I have always held that the greatest human act is to show unconditional love for people, and particularly for one person. We can love the world, but if the stars align and we get to meet that one individual that completes our human experience, then life has truly been generous. I do hope that my sentiments will not keep you from giving your opinion and from enjoying the course. So, speak up, express your feelings, your thoughts, and I can handle a few critiques on my character… it will force me to grow up."

Her rant lost steam after he admitted his fault.

"I'm sure your lasagna is ready; I'll bring it out."

Leylah's image kept him company during the walk back to his apartment. He recalled how Dante described Beatrice's face as a "*light too bright to behold*", and that it took work on his part to earn the right to look at her. Leylah gave off the same light. Not blinding but illuminating and inviting. His good feelings were driven by a giddy admission that she now seemed approachable. It took but a fragment of her to spark the emotions he had kept under control; all of her would have him capitulate completely. Still, he turned defeatist when the hurdles in his head started exploding like land mines.

"What if she thinks me a complete fool for even trying. I

can see me stupidly misjudging her kindness and friendship for something more. I don't think I could live it down. The embarrassment would kick my ass all the way to Florida. Then there's the age difference. It may not be an issue... a thirteen-year difference seems like much, but I don't think it is when the man is older. I mean, I think I look good, not old for my age. I never feel out of place at gatherings meant for a younger crowd... I don't know... I'm so fucking confused."

He could manipulate all the best possible outcomes, but there would be no easy path to Leylah's affections. He sensed a destiny like his poets. What once was his sought-after literary pinnacle as a lover without a lover, had become a fate he would now choose to avoid. Like the winds reshaping the dunes on Saint Simon beach, Leylah had become the author editing Gianluca's life.

CHAPTER 9 -*INTERSECTIONS AND GHOSTS*

Gianluca came to think of his encounters with women as intersections. The haphazard meeting of souls either by chance or by design. He had intersected with Cassandra it seemed by design. The relationship had a history to it, a timeline with a tangible start. It took time for Cassandra to consider her affections eventually acting on her feelings as her arousals for her professor demanded an outlet. Catherine Davies and Leylah had come upon him by chance. He didn't see much of a design in his detour into Kingswick, finally giving fate some credit for how things were developing. Diminishing the importance of outcomes, he chose to participate.

Dinner with Catherine Davies would have been more intimate had it not taken place at Massimo's. Gianluca followed the advice volunteered by Clarence, keeping the encounter superficial and formal at first. It seemed to be working until Leylah delivered food and doses of antipathy towards his date. The poor attitude was noticeable, but Gianluca had no clue until Catherine offered an explanation.

"It might have been better to have someone else work this table. I'm not one of her favorites. She took my class two semester back and spent most of it arguing with me. I wasn't going to let her set the tone, and I found much of what she said to be irrelevant to the course topics. She filed a grade grievance-

I gave her a B minus. At the time my ex-Paul, was the grievance arbiter. He offered to recuse himself, but I insisted he stay on to decide. We went through two sessions and boy did she play the victim, insisting that the grade had something to do with me disliking her. I've been at this long enough to know how to keep my feelings about a student tucked away until I can drown them with a good bottle of wine. I respectfully shut down her opinions only because she stood firm... in every class! I started thinking there was something about me that got her madder than a mule chewing on bumblebees. Twice she left class early and never returned. I did ask for a one on one, but she refused. Paul ruled in her favor, no surprise there, and the two became close friends. Probably closer than Paul should have."

"I saw them in the campus center... they did seem very much involved."

"Paul and I ran out of romance early in our marriage. I think it all had to do more with just growing older and accusing ourselves of being wedded to our jobs. Time creeps up on you, that little bit of panic sets in, and you do something foolish like get married. We didn't leave off well-he hangs on thinking there's still a spark. I hold no grudges; we'll have coffee and even dinner at Massimo's occasionally. Leylah has more than what it takes to draw a man's attention away from what would otherwise occupy his dick. She's naturally a kind person, yet still naïve about men. She thinks she can have a friendly, intelligent relationship with Paul. He is a good-looking man, has a humble, kind way about him, so I can see her attraction. I felt the same, until he became too attached, too needy, and an emotional burden. Nothing I did could ease his mind, calm his soul. I had to get out of the marriage, and as you can tell, I have moved on to feed my reputation of hunting down men like you. I'm sure Clarence and others have already cautioned you, so let me tell you what I've told them-my best years may be behind me, but I plan to use and enjoy what I have left. I'm not looking for long term, deep commitments... too late for all that. I'd like just some steady companionship, you know, sharing a night out, a few drinks, cuddling, some good sex... and ease myself into my wrinkles until there's no sex or passion left... nothing more."

Her final comment caught Leylah's attention as she worked a nearby table, and the roll of her eyes didn't escape Gianluca. He then took Catherine's opening to the frank discussion to make his feelings known.

"I have had my share of good friends which may be the reason why I never married. The campus culture provides for enough human contact, so you contentedly overlook the need for more intimacy. In fact, you end up avoiding it. Not sure if you agree."

"Like I said, my marriage was a freak exception. Many in our profession never married or are divorced. It's a weird existence I admit, but I would find any other predictable and boring. I apologize for the distraction; I should have suggested another restaurant. Perhaps we can end this on a more comfortable note back at my place. I have a great bottle of Grappa I purchased in a small Italian alpine town, and I bake a mean apple pie. Took one out of the oven just last night. I promise no games, just a friendly nightcap."

He accepted the invitation; secure she was being sincere. She was a beautiful woman who had aged into a very appealing package of sexuality and class. He admitted to a mild weakness around her, and her casual interaction at the dinner table was a bit of a turn on. Months had passed since his last night with Cassandra, so he cautioned himself to resist the temptation. Catherine found a way to delay their exit from the restaurant long enough to make sure Leylah caught sight of her harnessing her hands to Gianluca's arm. The "Scarlett" in Dr. Catherine Davies was making an impromptu appearance. She had known for the past year of Paul's flirtations with Leylah, and despite having no interest in a reconciliation, she held a pestering disdain for the local beauty. The good professor from New York remained mostly oblivious to the thorny feud, fooled by the cosmetic civility.

Catherine was too much to handle. She got what she wanted that night. Gianluca had no chance. Her sudden, but well-rehearsed seductions kept him initially a shriveled, unsuspecting spectator. He finally surrendered when she swept aside his requests to slow down. It was a timeless, three act play in which she dominated as the main character, her mouth rhythmically churning him into a lump of exhausted molecules, sighing to the pulsating sensation of a bittersweet sore, then slowly relenting, falling asleep to the sound of seagulls laughing at him.

The morning after regrets were inevitable. He awoke, fixated on the ceiling, aware of where he was as his brain pushed the instant replay button. He cringed as Catherine, still sleeping, rolled her naked body towards him, her breasts lounging on his chest. It was a sunny Saturday morning, and as much as he wanted to get up, shower and leave, the view of the sun targeting the waters of Saint Simon from the large bedroom windows of her beachfront single level cape was enough to ease him back into the pulpous mattress. That it was Catherine's naked body still turning him on, mattered little. He was romancing the moment, recalling Cassandra's instruction as he gently ran his fingers across his colleague's back. She responded by caressing his chest, stroking the dozen or so hairs as she drowsily summoned her promise to make him a southern breakfast. Gianluca slipped into his boxers, used the blanket to cover the rest of him before ungracefully stepping onto the deck, slumping into one of the sling chairs. It was an unusually warm April morning. The shimmering waters of the bay kept his attention as he flirted with one more reason why he didn't regret making Kingswick his new home. Leaning back, and lifting his feet to the wood railing, he lowered his eyelids to ignore the sun, almost dozing off when a voice called out to him.

"Good morning professor Morelli. Rough night? Come by later, I can suggest the perfect lunch to help you recover… my best to Dr. Davies… and I just love the boxers, but you should try a smaller size, you're a bit over-exposed.

He laughed at his own embarrassment and Leylah's almost bitchy sarcasm that caught him off guard enough to notice the gaping hole between his crotch and the inside of his boxer. Embarrassed, he haphazardly pushed back on the railing causing man and chair to tumble backwards. She continued her morning jog with a trailing giggle, leaving him wordless and wobbly. He chose to make fun of his dopey reaction, content to chalk it up to Leylah's smooth delivery.

After breakfast and a quick shower, he went home and spent the rest of the afternoon planning his New York trip to coincide with the end of the semester. He wasn't hungry, but at around five he was on his way to Massimo's. He chanced an opportunity to be a victim once more of Leylah's sweet cynicism, hoping it would lead to some lively talk and a more routine friendship. He felt awkwardly penitent, as if he had cheated on her. Should he order some food, eat, and leave or offer an explanation. He would soon learn that decision wasn't his to make.

She sold him on the ravioli with a portion of cynicism as an appetizer. "I think you have Dr. Davies beat. I didn't think anyone could out-maneuver slick Catherine. I guess things do move at a much quicker pace in New York. I'm impressed. She would have worked you a little longer before you got to sit half naked on her patio. You must have pushed all the right buttons. Nice body for a man your age, by the way."

She accompanied her remarks with a wry smile knowing she had called him out. He had no choice but to reward her insistence.

"Okay, no sense trying to come up with a disturbing explanation, although the truth may be a bit much as well. It was an adult date if that's okay with you. We enjoyed each other's company as *adults* are allowed to do, all other interactions are personal... am I moving too quick for you? Now why is all this such an issue? Why the need to know? It's almost like you're some jilted ex-girlfriend."

"Ha! First, if I were your girlfriend, you would never allow me to become your ex, and second, your sex life is of no interest to me, couldn't you tell I was making fun? Now don't be offended, but any man who is weak enough to stumble into

Davies' house of mirrors, deserves never to find his way out."

"What is it about her? I mean, I get failing grades by association? What if I told you that it all went well? I had a pleasant stay with the lady, and I admit to being a bit weak in the company of an experienced socialite. I'm going to leave it at that. Besides, what about you and Paul Considine?"

"What about me and Paul? Where is this coming from?"

"I noticed how chummy you two were in the campus center."

Leylah felt instantly offended. Gianluca wished he could have taken back the remark.

"So, you enjoy spying on people... did you follow us? Were you lurking or are you some freak who enjoys stalking women?"

"I went to the campus center because I was curious about your relationship. If you must know, I was hoping it was more formal, I was hoping it was just about academics. I was wrong to follow you, to spy on you, and to make judgments. Can I have a check, please."

She looked at him puzzled, slowly pulled the check from her apron pocket, and left it on the table. He covered it with cash, looked up into her eyes and turned away. She followed him out the door lecturing to his back holding his doggy bag.

"So, you're talking about your feelings, and this is the way you let a woman know? If you're so convinced about the way you feel about me, what does it matter if I talk to Paul Considine? You're going to let your pride get in the way of your heart? Now that is nowhere near as romantic or courageous as your poets. If they had the same chance, they would have swept me off my feet. Instead, you whimper off leaving some half-baked clue that I'm supposed to figure out. Be a man and say what you really want to say! Wait, I'm sorry, it was rude of me to question your masculinity. It's what I would have said to a southern man. I should have said be scholarly and express yourself... is that better? I don't get it. Men like you want women to figure you out, dig deep into your soul to find me floating around in there. Then you expect to be rewarded when I fall instantly in love... how fucking convenient! Oh, my good Lord! just listen to my foul mouth. See what you've done? I haven't sworn since I was a teenager. Here, you forgot your bag!"

"I didn't ask for a doggy bag".

"Just take it!"

"Are you done? I'm sorry if I don't quite live up to your cowboy standards, your southern male prototype... the one with the muddy work boots, tight blue jeans with the big belt buckle, muscle shirt three sizes too small, and that ubiquitous beer bottle dangling from one of his fingers. The one who drives up in his pickup and takes you to the nearest bar to play pool. Yes, I am scholarly, and I am sensitized to the character of women. I admitted I made a mistake by observing. Why would I want to get between you and Paul if the relationship is amorous? Why would I act like I had a right to take a chance on you if you are involved? I would rather respect your choice than bust in and declare my affection."

He nervously paused, aware that his bravado had gotten the best of him. She had compelled him to admit to what he was arguing against. He had unwittingly declared his true feelings.

"See, now that wasn't hard. No need to hold back, second guess yourself, give too much attention to my reaction, and worry your silly heart should I pay you no mind. You people from New York are quick to condemn those who stereotype, and yet here you are pulling a Neil Young on southern men."

Gianluca knew what she meant when she referenced Neil Young's song *Southern Man*. The song is a harsh indictment of the southern male's poor record on human rights. Leylah wanted to make a point of the unfair nature of the song that lumps all men of the south into one stereotype. Gianluca had talked himself into an uncomfortable corner. He needed to escape.

"Sorry, I'd like to continue, but I have some work to finish. I need to get it done before leaving for New York at the end of the semester."

"Go! I'm not holding you back.

He gave up trying to kill the conversation, sat himself down on the bench facing the bay, and told his story.

"No, I'm going to be a father, and I want to be there when the baby is born."

She filled in the empty space next to him, too involved to go back to work.

"Well, that's just wonderful. Are you…? I mean, is she your… damn it, are you going back for good?"

"See, not so easy to get the words out when the topic is delicate. You sure you want a "sensitive guy" answer, or should I flip the top on another Budweiser, take a long chug, burp, and tell you it's none of your fucking business? I didn't mean to curse; I know you have a problem with that. Look, I should just leave… by the time this conversation ends you'll want me to stay in New York."

His tone betrayed a slight irritation.

"So, let me be the sensitive New York guy to ease your curiosity. It was a relationship. I didn't know she was pregnant until a few days ago. It was a bit underhanded on her part. She wanted a child and planned to become pregnant while we were together."

"Sounds like she was expecting more from you. I believe women settle for the baby when they can't get the man… common around here. For what it's worth, I admire your willingness to be a father. Are you going to New York to fix things?"

"Not exactly. We agreed it wouldn't be a family thing. She's involved with someone, but we felt the baby should know the real parents. Cassandra and I are very close. I didn't want to become the absentee father, substituted by a stepfather, only to resurface years later wanting to get back into my child's life. I will be her father, we know it's a girl, and I'll be there as much as I can. I'm ready to provide despite Cassandra not asking for my help. I still want to carry on with my own plans, and I'll try to be unselfish about it."

"Nothing wrong with that. Being in the child's life is the right decision, I believe. Cassandra... that's a beautiful name."

He had never dwelt on names, but now that she had made a point about Cassandra's, he felt compelled to ask about hers.

"Leylah, not a common name, do you know why your parents chose it?"

"Eric Clapton, one of my father's favorites. Dad's band played the song Layla to perfection. He sang it as good as Clapton. He was famous for his acoustic version in New Orleans. Dad did it way before Clapton, and he incorporated Creole and Jazz sounds. I would fall asleep as a little girl to his sweet version of that song. He loved it enough to make it my name, spelling it his way... *L, e, y, l, a, h.*

My father was all about the music. He grew up in Memphis, and he played several instruments with friends in so many of the clubs on Beale Street. We would go back every year before he got sick. I watched him play with his old buddies. It was such a thrill. He met my mom in one of the clubs, she was a singer in another band. They fell in love, they played the Memphis-New Orleans circuit, and made a modest, but happy living. I was born a few years later. When I was fifteen, dad started showing signs of the cancer that would eventually kill him, so we moved to Kingswick where my mom was born. We have family here and it was much easier taking care of him because we had some help. The treatments and his tenacity fought the disease for many years. I put my life on hold to take care of him at home while mom went out to work. I'm happy to get back to my life, but I miss him more than I can say."

She choked up; her pupils half submerged in tears accumulating on her bottom eyelids. "Well, I better get back... have work to do."

He had a tough time finding words. His feelings for her deepening as she spoke of her past. His heart filled with passion, and a love he had never known.

"I'm sorry for all you have gone through. I feel the cancer cut short a very happy family life. Your story has filled me with a deep sorrow." With difficulty he held back his own tears... the kind one sheds when feeling completely helpless.

She changed the topic. "I want to hear more about the comparison you made in class between our lives during the

Covid pandemic and the lives of Boccaccio and his friends during the Bubonic Plague. I mean, eight hundred years have passed, and I'm amazed at the similarities."

"Yes, I promise an interesting finale to the semester. I only wish we had more time." He touched her hand; she didn't pull back. He desperately wanted to taste her lips but felt that an attempt to kiss her was not the obvious next step.

It was a few weeks away from the end of the school year. He had his flight booked to land in New York two days before Cassandra was due to give birth. He would spend the last week of May in Manhattan, then depart for Italy; his parents were expecting him.

Spending a few weeks in Padova would give him some down time to sort things out. Florida was still a possibility, but the thought of a cold departure from Kingswick and Saint Simon gave him pause enough to think of Leylah. Learning about her past made an impression, and it was enough to push him beyond his earlier infatuations to deal with the phenomenon of deeply loving this woman. He was ready to set aside his delusions... he would fill his time with doses of her beauty, her voice, her haughty attitude, and her love of the life that surrounded her. Would she accept him? Could she find enough to love? He was ready to deal with the truth.

At nine o'clock on the morning of May 24, Gianluca became a father. The experience took him centuries away from his ideal existence. He then thought of how events had conspired in that long ago generation to alter the course of those lives, realizing that his grip on his own reality was fragile at best. Cassandra wasn't an institution like the Church or the aristocracy. Instead, in a very contemporary way, she was able to exert enough power to push him onto this unforeseen path. Now it was time for him to deal with it-fatherhood came calling like it or not.

Emilia weighed in at a very healthy seven pounds with a rose tint to her skin, and eyes wide open. Cassandra had chosen to honor the character of the same name in Boccaccio's Decameron. When he asked why Emilia, she spoke of her independent nature, her happier, less pessimistic views, and the joy she found in dancing and singing. Cassandra envisioned her daughter an *Emilia...* a happy child who would find joy in living each moment. Gianluca looked back to the lessons on the Decameron, and the how the temperament of the female storytellers stayed with one of his students. He agreed that the choice was a good one.

"I can tell by the look on your face you think she's beautiful. I was hoping you would be pleased about the baby and her name. I'm so happy you are here."

Gianluca sat on the bed next to Cassandra caressing her hand. "I can't get over how these hospitals have created the perfect room for a mother to welcome her baby into the world. Far cry from the days when women gave birth in a dark bedroom with a stern midwife running the show. You look exhausted... I can only imagine the work involved. The nurse told me your contractions started for real around three this morning and the baby was born six hours later. The pain must have been intense."

"Epidural, Gianluca, it's called an epidural... miracle drug for women with labor pains. Look at me, tell me we are good. I need to know you have no ill feelings about this. I can't handle causing you any stress. I mean it when I said I don't want Emilia to get in the way of your plans. We can all be happy. I know that whatever part you want to play in her life will be incredible. I don't need you here full time, I just need to know you will be there when we need you... when she needs you. Look, I want her to say I have a daddy, my daddy's name is Gianluca, he's a famous professor. She will always know the truth about who she is, that's why I want her last name to be Morelli."

He was overcome with humility as the nurse brought the baby into the room. Cassandra looked up at Gianluca and asked him to hold her. He cradled the tiny bundle in his arms, fixated on the smallness of her face. "*Emilia Morelli*, what a beautiful name. I'm surprised you want to give her my name."

"Why? She should have your name. It has nothing to do with us being married, husband and wife and all that nonsense. I'm not going crazy on you. I'll sign any papers you want saying you have no obligations to raise her or provide for her."

"That's silly, I would never deny my obligations. I welcome the name and all the responsibilities that come with it. This child will know she is loved."

Cassandra relaxed her nerves aware that she had gotten the reaction she had hoped for. "So, what are you plans? Are you staying for a while?"

"Yes, I'm staying three more days, then I'm leaving for Italy to visit my parents. I'll take some photos to introduce them to their granddaughter. I'm keeping my position at Georgia Maritime at least for another semester. There was something I meant to tell you when you first mentioned the pregnancy. There's this woman in my class. It's kind of weird since it reminds me of us. She's in her late thirties, came back to complete her degree after her father died. Her name is Leylah, she's…" Cassandra stopped him from saying another word. "You are fucking in love, or should I say you love someone." "You shouldn't curse like that around the baby."

"Never mind that, I'll stop cursing when she starts talking. You finally got your heart all fucked up, and I bet you have no clue what to do. My God, she must be some specimen to get you stumbling over your words and acting like one of your lovesick poets. Talk to me… what is it about her that turned you all mushy?"

"It's hard to say, there's more than one reason. It's a bit unusual with her being a student… I'm not even sure she thinks of me that way."

"It didn't bother you that I was a student. You wanted to hold back but then you settled in… do the same thing in the reverse. I came after your ass, now you need to go after hers. I'm certain she'll feel the same once she gets to know you better. Gianluca, there are so many wonderful things about you… let her discover them even if you need to make the first big move. Don't wimp out on me. If you fuck this up, you'll be

writing sonnets and poems to this chick the rest of your
pathetic life... I can picture you in your eighties with a twelve-
inch beard, one foot in the grave, smelling like shit, sitting at a
dingy old desk with papers strewn all over the place, adding
the finishing touches to a trilogy dedicated to Leylah who will
probably be long dead. What a fucked up ending to a precious
life. If you let that happen, I'll sneak up behind you and stab
you through the heart so you can finally rest in peace. You're
no spring rooster, and if I recall, I detected a few white hairs
on your balls, so your time is limited... fucking do something
with it. I curse like this only when you frustrate the crap out of
me. Love your poets, love their amazing masterpieces, but
leave it all in the past. Let those creations be a testimony to
those lives and their reality. You belong to the here and now...
as much as you would wish it, their reality is not yours. If this
Leylah takes you to the same place that Beatrice took Dante
and Simonetta took Botticelli, and Laura took Petrarch, then
you have the advantage of *having* her in *this* life... your odds
are so much better than those poor dopes, and do you think for
a moment they wouldn't want to be in your shoes... shit, we
even talked about it in your class-those guys would have
written those words even if they had married those women.
Ask yourself if you could love your Leylah with the same
intensity the rest of your life. If the answer is yes, then that love
would be the reason for your writings, not the fact that she was

never yours. Gianluca, you are so dense! Make her divine when she becomes a part of you, and not a part of heaven."

He laughed with pride at her words that always seemed to expose the idiot in him, and the lasting impact of his teachings. "Before I act on my emotions, I always think of you and your instructions. You know me so much more than I know myself. I'll give you an update when I get back to Georgia."

He walked down to the gift shop and returned with a bouquet of flowers and an envelope containing a check for a thousand dollars. Cassandra refused it until Gianluca made a good argument of it being the first contribution to the baby's college fund. He spent the next two days at Cassandra's side, sharing meals and taking pictures.

On May 27th he was on a nonstop flight to Italy, landing in Milan early morning on May 28, 2023. The train ride to Padova took little more than two hours. Gemma and Matteo were there to greet him. To his surprise, his parents had planned a getaway to their summer home in the alpine town of *Bassano del Grappa*. The one-hour drive gave him an opportunity to summarize the past year, and to share information and photos of Emilia. The snowcapped Dolomites hovered over the small chalet in the center of Bassano like an army of rugged, stone-faced guardians. The approach to the town sparked sweet memories of his childhood summers trekking into the mountains, shopping for chesses and wines at local farms, and hillside picnics alongside streams flowing with frigid mountain waters. Moving to New York changed all that. What would have been an easy, comfortable Italian middle class existence, became a demanding and tedious life in urban America.

Through his window in his dusty bedroom, he saw himself among the young people hanging around in the small piazza, reflecting on how little had changed except for the cell phones that kept them congregated but disengaged. He found some old notebooks from his middle school days. Gemma had moved much of his stuff from the house in Padova to the chalet. The poems and short stories he wrote during summer visits in his teens were waiting to be judged by an older Gianluca. The writings were juvenile and raw, as he recalled the youthful motivations that influenced his choice of words and topics. The name *Simona* came up as he read through the dedications, sending him off on a mellow journey to another time, awakening images of the girl from Venice who vacationed in Bassano. Her family spent two weeks each August at the Grand Hotel in the main piazza. It was a one-sided friendship in which he spent most of the time on her side of the piazza.

Gemma and Matteo were too busy editing their books, losing themselves in dozens of newspapers, or denouncing crooked politicians.

He and Simona wasted away the hours between dinner and her curfew sitting along the wall of the *Fontana Bonaguro* in *Piazza Garibaldi* dipping fingers in the water, chatting about the boredom of school, and making fun of their teachers. She wasn't allowed to venture beyond the piazza, so they promised to taste every one of the flavors at the local *gelateria*. The piazza hosted the summer concert series that failed each year to include music they liked. The international crowd speaking funny languages and carnival vendors kept them entertained just the same.

He had spent the summer of his fifteenth birthday without his dear friend, and before starting his boarding school years in London. The previous year was to be the last for Simona in Bassano. He asked about her at the hotel, but the clerk could only speculate that perhaps the family had decided to vacation elsewhere. He had no address or phone-no way of getting in touch. The commonality of the last name made it impossible to track her down. She faded with the years.

Her ghostly figure sitting on the fountain wall, skimming her finger through the water in figure eights and signing her name, spawned tender memories. He wondered if he had taken those years for granted, if he could have paid more attention to each moment, to each episode, committing more to memory by absorbing those seasons with the intuition of one who had understood they wouldn't last. He lamented the times Simona may have wanted to have her hand in his as they strolled the piazza, or that puppy love kiss that never happened. Had he done the same with other women, and missed all the signs? Had he once again ignored his heart's yearnings? As he drifted from one memory to the next, he no longer cared to deny himself whatever time he had left without Leylah.

His journey continued through those carefree days, flipping through the pages of his old schoolbooks when Gemma came to him wondering about his reactions to suddenly being back in Bassano. He spoke freely assuring her that it was all pleasant. She asked him into the salon where she and Matteo had laid out some documents and photos. They sat across from him with anxious energy.

"Gianluca, your father and I planned the trip here with a certain intention. We held back the truth for all these years. We are and will forever be deeply sorry for what we are about to tell you. You know we met while teaching at the University of Bologna. You have always been aware of the deep love we have for each other." She paused, glanced at Matteo who reassured her it was time.

"Just before we met, I had an affair with a man who also worked at the university. He was a cook at the restaurant on campus. I became pregnant with you. Two months after the affair, this man, his name was Massimo Brunetti, left Italy to work in America."

Gianluca hardly knew how to react. He slumped back into the sofa dumbstruck; his thoughts suddenly dropping him off at his favorite table sitting across from the same Massimo who knew Matteo, and who had lied about not knowing Gemma. He challenged Matteo to speak.

"Wait, did you know this at the time it happened?"

"Yes, your mother told me everything when we had moved into the same apartment. She wanted to keep the baby, and I wanted to keep her in my life. You were a blessing for us both. When we decided to keep the truth from you, it was convenient, but cowardly. I never regretted that decision until now. It was a mistake, we agree. We should have told you as soon as you were able to understand and deal with it. I have loved you as a father loves a son, but we had to make sure the secret didn't die with us. Neither of us would have wanted to tell you without the other, so here we are."

Gianluca stiffened up as he revealed his own disturbing truth.

"Well, your Massimo Brunetti lives on Saint Simon

Island, owns a restaurant in which I have been eating since I arrived in Georgia. Who, in conversations, has mentioned knowing Matteo, while denying any knowledge of Gemma Trevisan, and who is married to a local widow whose daughter I love!"

He paused, thought about what he wanted to say, adding a certain fury to his words. "So, what do you think of that? Some revelation! Now that we are on awkward topics, let me ask, are you two even married? Did you ever get married legally? Not some common law, hippie crap officiated by a Hindu swami, while all three of you stood naked in a stream somewhere in the Himalayas. I know you have been there, you always talked about that summer in Nepal. So, can I get some more truth out of you?"

They said nothing, looking at each other wondering who would answer. Finally, Matteo, who still spoke English with a melodious accent, calmly ignored his misgivings.

"Look, Massimo could never have imagined you would simply walk into his life unannounced. It wasn't so much a lie, as it was his inability to find the right response. You should approach him again now that you know.

We didn't have a Catholic wedding or a common law one; we didn't believe in an artificial ceremony invented by the government or the Church. You're right about our trip to Nepal. We did commit to each other in a Nepalese tradition called *Tika Tala*. We promised to each to be more than just titles, more than husband and wife. We settled on a mutual humanity, and the commitment to honor each other always as a man and a woman. I have never been less than a father to you. It was a choice I made with much love, first for your mother and then for you when you were born. Have you ever once felt we were not a family?"

Gianluca's confusion took him back to his boyhood days when he felt slighted and alone whenever he struggled with his parents' reasoning. Their 1960s non-conformist intellectualism was too heavy for him, too insistent on living marginalized by choice. For Gemma and Matteo no institution that imposed its will on people could be justified. It was the reason they hid away in colleges where there was the least amount of oversight... they could earn their salaries with little or no conformity.

There were times when he understood enough to let it go; then there were the times when nothing made sense... when their views were so eccentric, so far removed from the mainstream that he couldn't wait to be old enough to get as far away from them as possible. His teen years were strongly influenced by the Ronald Reagan presidency, a rebirth of American capitalism, the fall of the Berlin Wall, and the infallibility of American democracy. His parents were listening to Bob Dylan, wore Birkenstock sandals, Gemma could still fit into her bell bottoms, and they spent many weekends smoking pot on upscale hippie farms in the Catskills that had replaced the sixties communes now that most of their friends were rehabilitated revolutionaries who had inherited millions.

He soon abandoned the conversation retreating to his bedroom with a bottle of Prosecco. He tried to drink himself to sleep, convinced that finding a reason to be frustrated and betrayed would be a waste of time when he could instead prepare himself for his return to Saint Simon and the conversation he imagined he would have with his real father... and the comfort of kindling the relationship he hoped for with Leylah. There was one question he forgot to ask. He returned to the Salon.

"Does Massimo know? Does he know he is my father?"

"Yes, I spoke to him after he left for America. He knows of you, but nothing more. I told him that Matteo and I would raise you; that I preferred it that way. I asked him to keep to his plans and to forget the child. He wasn't happy with it, but he didn't object. I never contacted him again, never sent him information, no photos. He respected my choice. How did he end up on your Saint Simon Island, I thought he was going to New Jersey to work with his relatives?"

"It was by chance that he was offered a job in a new restaurant in Atlanta. He took it, worked there for many years. He would vacation on Saint Simon where he came across an opportunity to own an abandoned building which he turned into a restaurant large enough to cater even small weddings. The place is iconic to the area... *Massimo's Real Italian*. His food is as good as in New York. I can't believe I've sat across from a man I admire, had conversations in Italian, learned about his life, and I even live in an apartment in a building he owns not knowing I was looking into my father's eyes. This is nuts. How do I go back? What will I say? Maybe I should leave it alone. Shit, he knows you Matteo, and made believe he didn't know you, mother. That's why he was so uncomfortable the day we spoke of his work in Bologna. He's figured it out; he already knows who I am."

He gathered himself to deliver a more stable reaction to the two people who raised him. "Look, I'm good. I can handle the truth. I'm not yet sure how I can make it fit into who I am, and how to update my life. Matteo, you have been an ideal father. I never doubted who you were and are to me. I have lived a good life because of you two. I wish I had known sooner; I would have wanted to meet Massimo when I was younger. I am grateful for all you have done, but you have left me with so little time to appreciate other possible outcomes to my life."

Gemma wore a mother's face worn by regrets.

"I was selfish, I admit. I wasn't sure how you would react. I didn't think it would help you in any way, and that you would question everything at a very delicate time in your life. Besides, I knew nothing of Massimo. I had no idea of the kind of person he had become after leaving Bologna. There was a chance that he would have been a disappointment. Still, I can't justify my decisions if, in the end, they have caused you pain."

"Did you love him; did you have any feelings for him?"

"I was attracted to him. He was very likeable. I had just started teaching at the university, and it was difficult for women to fit in, to feel comfortable. I was lonely. I met Massimo and for awhile he was my only friend. He cooked food specially for me, and many times he joined me for lunch. Being with him was simple, kind, and without pretense. Most of the professors were snobbish intellectuals. The administrators were all males, distant, like feudal lords, mostly concerned with keeping their titles and high paying jobs... I had nothing in common with them. Massimo kept me there, kept me from running away, kept me alive. It was a convenient friendship; he was lonely too. He came from a small town in Calabria. The prejudices also weighed on him. We became lovers but we knew to avoid anything deeper. He was determined to leave for America; I was determined to make a name for myself. I wanted to teach and publish my books; he needed to escape his poverty. Our compatibility was limited to glasses of pinot and the bedroom."

Gianluca glanced over, expecting a reaction, or at least a few words from Matteo... nothing. Gemma's ghosts had troubled their younger years. With time, Matteo resisted the urge to become a victim, and it showed as he passively sat through her story.

With little else to discuss, they all felt it was finally enough truth for one day. Later they shared good stories and a meal in Gemma's favorite trattoria, chased a good bottle of pinot grigio with locally produced grappa. Later they strolled the piazza where Gianluca decided to break away to join the small crowd gathered around the fountain.

The evening was crisp and clear with a star speckled indigo sky. On the opposite side a woman, seated on the wall, carried on a lively conversation with a young girl. As the child scampered off to play with her friends, Gianluca watched as she skimmed the surface of the water with her index finger in figure eight motions. His reaction was instant: could it be Simona? It was one of the things he remembered most about her... the way she would fall into a trance as she orchestrated those ripples. He slowly approached and sat on the wall close enough to be heard.

"Chiedo scusa, ma lei si chiama Simona?" (*Excuse me, is your name Simona?*).

She gave him a puzzled look.

"Si, ma ci conosciamo?" (*Yes, do we know each other?*).

"Si, in un tempo molto lontano, sono io, Gianluca" (*Yes, in a time long ago, it's me, Gianluca*).

She took a closer look. With a heart full of jumbled emotions, she struggled with her words.

"Dio mio, ma sei proprio tu! Poco ci credo dopo tanti anni. Ma come abbiamo fatto a non vederci più? Ti credevo un fantasma, sparito, non so dove, forse in qualche posto remoto senza telefoni, senza posta, senza internet." (*My God, it really is you! I can hardly believe it after so many years. But how did we lose touch? I believed you had disappeared, not sure where… perhaps in a remote place with no phones, post office or internet*).

She took him into her arms with a heartfelt embrace, planting the customary kiss on each cheek.

"Mio caro Gianluca, mi viene da piangere." (*My dear Gianluca, I'm going to cry*).

"Simona, ricordo l'ultima estate insieme. Siete partiti con tre giorni di anticipo. Cercai qualche notizia di te, ma quelli dell'albergo non riuscivano a dirmi nulla. Poi siamo partiti per l'America, sono passati anni impossibili e ci troviamo qui per caso. Sono arrivato pochi giorni fa senza alcun itinerario, e tu?" (*I recall our last summer together. You left three days early. I asked for some news about you, by the people at the hotel knew nothing. We then departed for America, so many impossible years have passed, and here we are meeting by chance. I arrived a few days ago with no set plans, and you?*)

"Anche noi ci troviamo qui senza premeditazione. Quando arriva la primavera c'è sempre voglia di scappare in montagna. Abbiamo deciso proprio stamattina. Già, lasciami spiegare chi siamo in famiglia. Mio marito Alessandro arriva questa sera, sposati venticinque anni, mia figlia Lavinia e la mia nipotina piccola Simona. Abitiamo a Treviso vicino ai miei genitori. Non era più il caso di vivere a Venezia con tanti turisti e tanto casino. E tu... come hai passato questi anni?" (*We are also here with no plans. When spring arrives, we get the urge to drive up into the mountains. We decided this morning. So, let me explain who we are. My husband Alessandro who will arrive later tonight... married twenty-five years, my daughter Lavinia and my granddaughter baby Simona. We live in Treviso near my parents. It didn't make sense to stay in Venice with the tourists and all the confusion. And you, what have you been doing all these years?*)

"Vissuto a New York, mai sposato, professore alla New York University. Avevo smesso di insegnare con il pensiero di pensionarmi in Florida. Poi, a causa di un incidente sull'autostrada, fu necessario trascorrere una notte in una piccola città nello stato della Georgia dove incontrai il presidente dell'università locale e, senza tirarla a lungo, adesso insegno li. Fatto è che mi piace molto ed ho deciso di restarci. Non so, la vita non cammina una linea retta... ci sono tante deviazioni. C'è una donna lì che ammiro, a dire la verità, forse è più lei che mi attira a quel luogo... non so." (*Living in New York, never married, professor at New York University. I stopped teaching with the idea of retiring to Florida. Then, because of an accident on the highway, it was necessary to spend a night in a small town in the state of Georgia where I befriended the head of the local college, and without adding too much detail, I now teach there. Thing is I really like it and I have decided to stay. I don't know, life doesn't follow a straight line… there are many detours. There's a woman there I admire, and truthfully, she may be the reason I'm attracted to the area).*

"Certo, e il passare del tempo non aiuta. Invecchiamo senza aver contato gli anni. Poi, un giorno ti svegli e ti chiedi come mai sono arrivata a cinquant'anni." *(Yes, the passing of time hardly helps. We grow old not counting the years. Then, one day you wake up and you ask yourself when did I turn fifty?)*

"Dimmi, la vita per te, è riuscita come prevedevi? Sei contenta? Hai trovato l'amore? Se ricordi, ne parlavamo di queste cose da ragazzi. Ci chiedevamo spesso se si dovesse vivere come i nostri genitori, oppure se ci aspettasse una vita più a nostro parere." *(Tell me, did life turn out for you the way you predicted? Are you happy? Have you found love? If you recall, we spoke of these things as kids. We asked ourselves often if we were to live our parents' lives, or would life work out as we would choose).*

"Gianluca, la vita prosegue a parte dei sogni. Secondo me, sono strade parallele, e per molti non intrecciano mai. Si, avevo delle idee fantastiche, e tanta voglia di creare una grande opera con chissà quali risultati. Purtroppo, ho imparato che non esiste un assoluto. Cioè, la nostra vita appartiene più agli altri che a noi, e quindi miei genitori mi introdussero a quest'uomo che volevano loro e anche se non fu un grande amore, man mano è cresciuto il rispetto, e abbiamo creato nostra famiglia. Non per colpa sua che mio marito non sapeva amare, fui la sua prima. Mi tratta con dignità, provvede per tutto e chiede poco di me. Senti, mi sto quasi confessando... perdonami." *(Gianluca, life takes its course despite our dreams. In my opinion they run parallel to each other, but for many they never intersect. Yes, I had these fantastic ideas to create something great even with uncertain results. Unfortunately, I've learned that there are no absolutes. I mean, our lives belong more to others than to ourselves. So, my parents introduced me to this man they wished for me, and even if it wasn't love at first, slowly we learned to respect each other and we created our family. No fault of his that my husband didn't know how to love, I was his first. He treats me with dignity, he is a good provider and demands little of me. Listen to me, sounds like a confession... forgive me).*

"Figurati. Dopo tanti anni, è naturale che ci fosse qualcosa da svelare con un passato che continua a improvvisare. Per me c'è poco da festeggiare." *(Please, after all these years it's only natural that there would be things we want to talk about, with a past that insists on improvising. For me there's little to celebrate).*

"Che c'è? Anche per te qualche delusione?" *(What is it?*

You too have some disappointments?).

"Ho saputo proprio oggi che Matteo non è mio padre. Infatti, mio padre è un uomo che ho conosciuto per caso in America di nome Massimo Brunetti. Lavorava come cuoco all'Università di Bologna quando ci insegnavano mia madre e Matteo. Brunetti e mamma divennero amanti per chissà quanto tempo. Lei restò incinta con me, e lui partì per l'America." (*I learned just today that Matteo is not my real father. In fact, my father is a man I met by chance in America named Massimo Brunetti. He worked as a cook at the University of Bologna when my mother and Matteo taught there. Brunetti and mom became lovers for who knows how long. She ended up pregnant with me, and he left for America).*

"Ma questo Massimo lo sa che sei il figlio?" (*But this Massimo person, does he know you are his son?).*

"Credevo ne avesse qualche idea quando in un discorso ammise di conoscere Matteo, ma poi forse mia madre non ha il coraggio di dirmi tutto. Io parto dopo domani e certamente ho molto da chiedergli." (*I believe he has an inkling when, in one of our conversations, he admitted knowing Matteo, but then again, my mother perhaps doesn't have the courage to tell me everything. I leave after tomorrow with much to ask him).*

"Caro Gianluca, mi dispiace se la verità ti ha portato del dolore, ma ormai ti resta solo di confrontare tutto di modo che si normalizzi tua vita." (*My dear Gianluca, I'm so sorry if the truth brings you some pain, you have no choice but to confront it all so that you find some normalcy in your life).*

"Vedremo. Che piacere trovarti qui. Spero di ritornare per Natale, forse ci vedremo più spesso." *(We'll see. I'm so happy I found you here. I hope to return for Christmas, perhaps we will see more of each other).*

"Si, lo spero. Però quest'ultima cosa lo devi sapere che in quel tempo della nostra gioventù, sei stato il mio primo amore. Non vedevo l'ora di starti vicina, di trascorrere tempi spensierati, aspettando e sperando che tu mi baciassi. Quel bacio e quel sogno purtroppo non si sono intrecciati." *(Yes, I look forward to it. However, you must know this one last thing. In our youth, you had been my first love. I couldn't wait to be close to you, to spend silly time together, waiting and hoping that you would kiss me. That kiss and that dream however, never did intersect).*

Her nostalgia drenched narrative left him hollow… with an emptiness he knew he couldn't rehabilitate. He may have been negligent in fostering dreams of his own, but he chided himself for not connecting with hers. He looked back on how he had done the same with Cassandra; how he had missed the signs so selfishly. When she decided on the pregnancy, she did so catering to her dream alone, having no choice but to factor him out except for the sperm. It was too late for any word or action that could make up for all the blind spots in his head. Feeling unsettled and pathetic, he walked her back to the hotel, bidding her a sweet farewell, as her lips welcomed his tender, apologetic kiss from another time.

The long flight back to Georgia offered time to convene the ghosts of things that would have been. He could tell that Simona had earlier grown into a beautiful, modest woman, and now an elegant, yet unassuming young grandmother. There was much to like in her, and he wondered if destiny had conspired to keep them apart. It was clear she had settled for a good man and, like many Italian women from that generation, she learned to trade in her dreams for a stable home. It seemed that choices for women hadn't changed much over the centuries. He imagined even Dante's Beatrice having been forced into the same decision in her time. Love was at best a fleeting fantasy often accompanying the hopeless romantics to their graves. Gemma was a rare exception, and finding Matteo made it possible for her to follow her passions, have her affair, be in love, choose an out of wedlock pregnancy, and build a family that straddled the norm... suffering no stigma.

Gianluca's fifty years had traveled a route that ignored the intersections and the shadowy truths that never found him. Now those ghosts were in his face dumping on him an uncomfortable past. Gemma had coldly introduced him to his real father. Matteo had played his-make believe-fatherhood so well while quietly enduring the truth that the woman he loves gave birth to another man's child, and Simona's stable, but loveless marriage had forced her to be in denial for twenty-five years. He would soon ask Massimo to unshackle his ghosts.

The hours spent appreciating the vastness of the atmosphere outside his window seat, offered the chance to consider how secrets had become a part of the way people lived. Gemma, Matteo, Simona, Massimo, and even Leylah made efforts to hide away fragments of life. He thought of the power in keeping secrets. One would have the option of discharging those mysteries with unpredictable effects on others or choose to bury them in a common grave.

All was falling into place: his age, the idyllic Saint Simon, genuine friendships, and Leylah. It was time to set aside the agonizing quest to live love's greatest torment: to be denied the woman that inspires every atom in his being. He was finally capitulating… no longer willing to censure his feelings and manipulate his emotions. He now yearned to live his remaining years in the company of the woman he would have otherwise miserably eulogized.

Life had become suddenly brief, and within that timed domain, the purest consummation of love was being performed by souls meant to intersect. Leylah had come into his world either by divine design or haphazard chance. It no longer mattered... she had seeped into his veins, exposed, and admonished his ghost, and freed his heart to act. Unlike the women of his poets, there was nothing impeding his courtship. Still, he cautioned himself that he needed to learn more about the woman with the power to redefine him.

CHAPTER 10- *BEATRICE TRANSFORMED*

Clarence Hightower would use any excuse to travel to Atlanta to meet up with his sons. In the texts he exchanged with Morelli, he learned he was due back in a few days. He booked a hotel room, spent the day catching up with his boys, and the following afternoon he was at the airport to pick up his colleague. It was mid-June, and Clarence was eager to know if Gianluca would stay another semester. He pulled up to the terminal where his friend greeted him with a fatigued smile that couldn't hide some irritation.

"Bad flight?"

"Have no clue, I slept most of the way. It doesn't take much... my usual strong Bloody Mary and next thing I know we are pulling up to the gate."

"How did your reunion with your parents go?"

"That's another story. Clarence, this remains between us for the time being. It will eventually become known... it's just that I need a little time to sort out some stuff.

Our dear Massimo started his cooking career in Bologna. My mother started there as an adjunct professor in the mid-seventies. She met a man who worked as a cook in the university restaurant."

"So, she knows Massimo... world keeps getting smaller."

"Yes, but it's not that simple. They became close... they shared some common ground: he arrived a poor young man from the south; she was a woman breaking into a profession dominated by stuck up males. They helped each other get through, deal with the prejudices. He would cook her foods she liked, and often he would join her for lunch. The friendship led to an affair. Mom got pregnant; Massimo left for New Jersey."

"My goodness, Massimo is your father?"

"Yes, by my mother's own admission, Massimo Brunetti is indeed my father."

"What are the chances? My God, Gianluca... it's not like you came to Saint Simon purposely because you knew your father was here. I'm floored! I hope this kind of thing doesn't surprise you or cause you to become unbalanced in any way. I've learned to be prepared for the shocks and to control our reactions. My first bout was when I learned Amelia was dying. I had to set aside the trauma if I was going to be any good for her in her final days. I had to accept and carry on. There would be plenty of time afterwards to pity myself. For what it's worth, I suggest you try the same. What good will it do to confront Massimo as if he did something wrong. He is a victim of rough circumstances, and of a consecrated destiny. Massimo was meant to be here... your mother was meant to follow her instinct; Massimo was a short but welcomed detour for her. Look, it worked at the time for both. They gave each other the strength to stick to their plans. The affair was part of that. Put yourself in that world, at that time. The companionship, the discussions, the intimate moments, and yes, the sex... all contributed to their perseverance. They provided what the other needed, and while some might say it was opportunistic and selfish, I say it was all grand, beautiful, and very, very human.

You mentioned going to New York to meet your child, to bond with the woman who delivered you a daughter. You had already decided to be known to her, to be a father involved in her life. Modern sensitivities have made it possible for you and Cassandra to openly profess how you will live your lives and the attitudes that will guide you. There's no shame in choosing an unconventional relationship. Your mother's actions were guided by the norms of her time. Massimo was leaving an Italy that couldn't provide for him. Think of the fear, the uncertainties, the road each had to travel to catch up to the stars and live out their fates. Wait, but how does Matteo fit in?"

"He and mom fell deeply in love. Matteo accepted the pregnancy and raised me as his son. I never doubted their affections. I can't remember a time when things turned bad. They never argued. They were dedicated, but they still allowed for personal growth. They never married institutionally. There was a ceremony of sorts somewhere in Nepal in the foothills of the Himalayas. Something about the cosmic union of souls. I didn't ask for an explanation. That doesn't concern me... it was fifty years ago, and they are still together. I can admire that. Matteo sat silently when my mother told me about my past. She spoke of her days with him freely while he seemed to passively endorse her monologue. I wondered if he was ever bothered by the fact that she slept with another man and bore his child." Clarence dished out a little more wisdom.

"Look, it's like I said earlier, we learn to manage the situations, especially the ones that cause us the greatest heartaches. You can let countless episodes in life erode you, strip you of your dignity, make you fearful of taking the next step. Your natural reaction is to fight it, to confront it when instead you learn to live with it, and you may squeeze a few more drops of happiness out of life. So, you learn to coexist with the things you find awkward. Isn't all of America built that way? Not all is to our liking, but we make room for differences and often we learn to accept and even appreciate them. We would otherwise be a nation in constant chaos. Matteo has done just that. He has contributed to a stable relationship with you and your mother, and in return his world works, he avoids the chaos. His decision to remain in love with Gemma, and to be a caring father to you was never a decision to accept and live miserably. He denied his ego and chose his heart. I see the nobility in that, and for me that beats wanting to castigate him for keeping secrets.

I'm sure you have a few secrets of your own. Are your going to lock them up and throw away the key? Thing is you're so bad at keeping them… everyone knows your shit around here. What about Leylah? She still one of your big secrets? Look, you don't get many chances with a woman like her. She moves at the speed of light… she has plans, and one of those is to settle down. If you keep falling behind, you'll see nothing but taillights. Listen, she is much more complicated that she appears…that veneer is on thick. You must know that winning over such a woman is a hell of a challenge. With Leylah, I caution not to be guided by your ideals, your fantasies. You've also got some competition, so be productive with your time."

"After being slapped around with the truth about my past, I sobered up about Leylah. Clarence, that woman has reshaped everything. I had a sense at first that I didn't belong, and that thinking of her as anything more than a friend was plain foolish. A few months go by and this place, you, Massimo, even Catherine Davies have stripped the pen from my hand and written the next chapter in my life. I had nothing to do with it, and yet I'm completely altered. I was such a buffoon to think that I could remain in total control of what happens to me and never consider that other forces could intervene, get in the way, send me off on a different path. You have all wickedly conspired to keep me here, and I am playing the willing victim.

My friend, I have this need to stay, wondering if this is where the rest of my life belongs. It's the only place where I can unburden myself. I want what you had with Amelia. I never thought I could dedicate myself unconditionally to one person, so I gave up long ago... never gave it a real chance. It didn't help that I believed people felt the same way. Then I fall out of the sky and land on Saint Simon and here you are proof that two human beings can free their souls to become one... to create the greatest of intimacies that survive even beyond death. You've made me understand that death doesn't stand in the way of your love for Amelia, and that she still fills your life with joy. I was wrong to think that the greatest expression of love was to give it painfully to the one person you love even if she is not yours. Until now I have refused to commit to what was too easy, too obvious. Leylah has thankfully thrown me off course. She is the roadblock I can't get around. Look, I'll risk sounding desperate, but how will I know if she will feel the same, if she can love me? And why shouldn't I be guided by my ideals?

"With Leylah you won't know, but you can't leave it at that. I will tell you that there is a mysterious side to her, a side she shelters jealously, and a side that won't dovetail with your ideals. You're afraid there is no one beyond her, and that learning she has no feelings for you will numb your heart and doom you to writing sonnets about the woman lost to fate. My dear man, you need to approach this with a certain spunk, a dose of determination, and above all with your truth. Create time together, get her to feel comfortable in your company... find some common ground. She needs to come around on her own. Gianluca, she will never want to fit your image. If you are ready to love her, she will demand that you love the person she has defined for herself. I have watched her grow into the woman she has become. Any attempt to reimagine her will turn her off, and she will give you reason to forget her. You don't have to fall in love with her to feel her disdain... ask any of the professors who have had her in class. I've sat through a few of her grievance hearings-baffled at the transformation. She was all business, leaving her more likeable character on the other side of the door. You take a risk with her, but if the stars align, you may be on the receiving end of her good graces. You mentioned she had strong reactions to the literature in your class. Find a way to keep those discussions fresh and interesting. Being around her isn't difficult; you're in Massimo's quite often. Ask her to meet for a drink at the Inn... she loves it there.

For now, you need to come to terms with your real father. My advice is to ease into it. I'm sure he knows who you are, and he may have already decided to bring it up. You have my support and my blessings."

After unpacking and a quick shower, Gianluca decided it was time to approach Massimo. It was a quiet Monday afternoon at the restaurant. Only Leylah was there to greet him. Massimo and Emma had taken the day off to visit friends in Savannah.

"Professor Morelli, welcome home. How did things go in New York?" He was cordial in his response and made no secret he was overjoyed to see her.

"I would love to hear only my name from your lips."

"Fine. So, Gianluca, how did it go in New York?"

"My daughter, Emilia, is healthy and quite beautiful. Her mother is doing well. Fatherhood is a sweet revelation."

"Well, congratulations and I applaud your decision to be a father. She will never have to go through life wondering who you are."

"Yes, I can't say the same for me. Are you aware that Massimo is my father?"

Gianluca got right to the point, but Leylah wasn't surprised.

"Yes, I am. He brought it up after you left. I'm not sure what to say, but I can imagine your discomfort. Here I am praising you for taking the responsibility of fatherhood seriously, yet you were denied the privilege of knowing your *real* father, and I'm truly sorry for that. You may know that Massimo figured it out when you first mentioned the names of your parents. He became paralyzed… had no idea how to handle it, so he left it alone."

She showed genuine sympathy as he struggled for a direction.

"I left New York after the birth to spend time with my parents… little did I know. My mother… she told me everything during my stay."

"I know, she called and spoke to Massimo. That's when he gave me the whole story. It was weird thinking of you as someone who just happened to find himself in the same place as his natural father purely by chance… maybe it was all meant to be. I believe in fate bringing people together."

"She called?"

"Yes, you obviously told her about Massimo, and it was easy to find him. She spoke with him this morning. It was a long conversation with many apologies and recommendations on how to handle the situation. He had planned to talk to you tomorrow evening. He shed a bucket of tears. They'll be back from Savannah late. How did you leave off in Italy?"

"Strangely, I remained calm after finding out. They expressed remorse, but it didn't matter to me. I dealt with it and kept the relationship normal. Too many years have gone by to feel anger. I chose not to dwell on what would have been and to accept what is. I'm fine with it all, I just need to hear Massimo's version and to avoid the awkwardness, if possible. I don't want to have to go through a clumsy transition from friend to son."

"Are you okay? Can I get you something?"

"No, thank you, but I could use your help and advice with this. Massimo may be my father, but you know him a lot better than I do. Do you have time to meet for a drink at the Inn later?"

"Yes, I can be there around eight."

"I'm not imposing, I hope."

"No, not at all."

She walked him outside just past the benches.

"I'm looking forward to our drink, I want to get your opinion on graduate school."

Several cars were just pulling into the parking lot.

"Sure. It's getting busy, I'll let you get back to work, and thank you."

As he walked away with a tickle in his heart, he turned back to notice she was avoiding Paul Considine as he got out of his car. He was saying something when she turned with her hands raised, yelling at him. He got up close, grabbing her by the arm. She pulled away forcefully. He followed her into the restaurant. Gianluca's curiosity would have led him back to Massimo's but decided against it.

That evening he arrived at the Inn early to spend some

time with Ernie. He enjoyed the conversations, and the bartender wisdom. Gianluca knew he had crossed the line from admiration to infatuation, to finally admitting his love for Leylah. His poets had taught him that to love a woman, one needed to restrain the heart's drive with a duty to reason… that one must follow his passion guided by logic. What value was there in allowing the heart to roam freely, unencumbered by sound judgment?

Ernie poured him his usual glass of Chianti, detecting a bit of anxiety.

"Doctor Morelli, you normally come in here happier than a clam at high tide, but this evening you look like a banjo everyone's been pickin' on. What can I say to switch it up?"

"Sorry, I have some things on my mind… just got back today from my trip. Ernie, when I met Leylah for the first time, you made it sound like anyone who has ever been attracted to her would regret the waste of time. What is it about her that makes it end that way?"

"Well now, you've caught the bug, and it seems like you're running a high fever. Look, you ain't the first, told you that way back. With any luck, you may be the last. I usually take care not to mention things I learn about others… you know, sort of a client privilege to keep my mouth shut… worked well for me all these years. I'm sure you know that Leylah comes here late on Fridays to unwind after a full house at Massimo's. While you were away, she mentioned you during one of our conversations. I was kind of surprised since she hardly talks about men. Most of the time I just listen offering only a few comments, but when she started asking about you, I had to add my two cents."

Gianluca became eager.

"Can you tell me more?"

"She was just plain curious, like how sincere a person you might be. She let it slip that you were going to New York because you were about to become a father. I have no problem bringing it up, chances are most of the town knows by now. She admired you for the way you dealt with it, and that there may be some hope for men after all. I said that I wouldn't have expected less from the likes of you. I've become an expert of sorts over the years figuring people out after listening to their stories, and I could tell early on that you were an upstanding man... one with a conscience. I said that I didn't think you had a nasty bone in your body."

He paused, preparing to get something off his chest. "Look professor, guys like you make me laugh. You spend years studying, writing books, getting who knows how many degrees and titles; you teach others, and you hand out diplomas. Yet with all that, you still don't have the smarts to figure out women. Leylah isn't a simple recipe... flour, eggs, and water. She's been adding all the extras over the years turning her into a souffle, if you know what I mean. Things can only stay complicated with a woman like her, but there is still much to like. Don't add to the complication. The more she senses your strong feelings for her, the more she will turn away... everyone knows that about her. Not for nothing that Jane Austen is her hero. Any man will struggle to make her commit to a relationship. She can't be tied down... you can't take her home like some masterpiece to hang over a fireplace."

"So, it's not even worth trying? That I should abandon all hope like Dante did at the entrance to hell?"

"Okay professor... you're talking like I've been sitting in everyone of your classes... the only Dante I know is Dante Pearson who owns a small farm just outside of town. Good, hard-working man with a wife, three kids, and a weekend drinking problem. Don't think he's the one you're talking about."

"Forgive me, I'm making unfair assumptions. My Dante is a poet who wrote the Divine Comedy. One of the books is the Inferno. He writes of himself, still living, who gets the opportunity to travel through hell, purgatory, and heaven. At the entrance to hell, he reads a sign with the words- *abandon all hope ye who enters*. So, I'm just saying that with Leylah, I too should abandon all hope."

"Now it ain't all that serious. If anything, Leylah will show you the way to heaven if she falls in love. You know, I've had enough conversations with her, and I have a strong feelin' she's ready to settle down. She volunteers at the church, and they have a program that shelters women who have been victims of domestic violence. Leylah works with those women, and I'm sure those stories have had an impact on the way she sees men. She's smart enough to know that not all men are like that, but it may be the reason why even the good ones have gotten nowhere with her. Still, I see her happily married with a kid or two."

"I'm meeting her here in about twenty minutes. Ernie, I've come to believe that the accident, getting off in Kingswick was all meant to be."

"My advice? Don't fall in love too fast, take it slow, she won't like being smothered with all the soft stuff. More than anything, she would want a man in her life who can be her best friend. She got a late start after taking care of her father, so she has a lot of catching up to do. She's an independent soul with a ton of energy, and if you can be the reason she smiles, well then, you're moving in the right direction."

"What can you tell me about her and Paul Considine? I saw them arguing in Massimo's parking lot today."

"That's already an old story. Look, Leylah's problem is being a thirty-seven-year-old student. Professors look at her in their classrooms and they see a woman, an amazingly appealing woman. Makes it hard to concentrate on anything else."

"I know, I've been there."

"He needed to replace Catherine after the divorce. Paul's a good-looking guy, still in his forties, and despite there being other single women in town closer to him in age, he concentrated his efforts on Leylah. He knew she comes here on Fridays to have her usual and unwind. Well, for awhile Paul kept coming by making like he was doing the same. Leylah has a good heart with just a small portion of it on the naïve side. I could tell Paul had it planned, but to her he was just one of the college professors. Having a drink with him seemed innocent enough. Problem began when he was doing it often enough that it started looking like the two were dating. I even confronted her with it, and she brushed it off saying that he needed to talk to someone after his divorce, and that she was good at listening. She felt that all the talking was just helping him out and the fact that she had taken several of his classes made him a good friend. It wasn't my place to keep my opinion alive, so I let it go. This went on most Fridays all last year. They would meet here often and then leave together."

"Did you ever notice them argue?"

"Can't say it was a full-blown argument, but the Friday before Christmas they met to have the usual drinks and to exchange gifts. I recall she got him a Georgia Tech hoodie…

his alma mater. When she opened her gift, she didn't break out in a smile. She put the little box down on the table and just walked out. It was the kind of box you put a ring in. My guess he either got her a very expensive one or it was an engagement ring. In either case I could have predicted her reaction. He worked her for a whole year, came across as the cool professor with a soul, rebounding from a relationship gone bad, and in need of someone to soothe his sick heart. Leylah fell for it until the ring; that snapped her out of it. Paul's just another man who would do whatever to steal her away from herself. She might have even liked him enough to give him a chance, but his ego kept getting in the way."

"That ended last year, but then why all the animosity? I mean, he was livid in the parking lot… you would think he'd gotten over it by now."

"Well, that anger may have nothing to do with being rejected. It gets a bit more complicated. You see, Paul never really got over Catherine. I don't think the man is capable of real love. He's more interested in the appearance, you know, the whole perfect couple thing. He dresses well, has the fancy car, the upscale house, the full head of hair… lost mine years ago. He needs a woman to compliment all that. Catherine was perfect-she shared the same addictions. She came to her senses eventually and outgrew him. She toned it down as she got older, and I have to say, she is a much more pleasant woman now. Lately he's had a rough time with Catherine because they run in to each other at the college. Then the rumors started getting to him."

"Rumors?"

"Yep, college kids started talking about an affair Catherine had with Leylah."

Gianluca was stunned. As liberal as New York had conditioned him, the lesbian affair was something he wasn't ready to process. Perhaps he didn't want to think of Leylah that way, or he understood where it would leave him if it were true, but all he could do was to sit wordless as he waited for a follow-up he hoped would completely dispel the rumor. Ernie had nothing more to say on the topic. When the rollercoaster in his head finally came to a stop, Gianluca needed to know more.

"Ernie, tell me it's just a stupid rumor some disgruntled student started on a Facebook page to get back at Catherine or Leylah. If it's not a rumor, is it still happening? I mean, are they still…"

"Professor, my take on it from what I've heard is there was something going on after Leylah rejected the ring, but that it didn't last long. More importantly, Paul got totally screwed in the head dealing with Catherine divorcing him, Leylah rejecting him, and then learning that the ladies had gotten involved. I don't want to pity the guy, but he's batting zero when the two women in your life dump your ass and practically celebrate it with a lesbian affair. That's gotta hurt... I wouldn't commit suicide over it, but I would hate to be that subject on the lips of people, and I'm sure Paul now blames her for killing any hope of getting back with Catherine."

"Shit, I don't know where to go with this. I'm meeting her in a few minutes, hoping to start something... and now all I will be thinking about is that I know so very little about this woman. It makes sense in a way why she doesn't seem to trust men. I feel so stupid right now thinking it was simply a guy liking a girl thing. No wonder she feels that being in love with a man would make her less free and keep her from being herself. I can't say I blame her... women have been abused by men for centuries. There's no way I can compete with that kind of thinking, especially if she sees me as just another of those men. Now I have no clue how to act around her... I'm a such a mess." Ernie kept him balanced.

"You need to know the truth, and the only one who can give it to you is Leylah. So, with nothing left to lose, go ahead, and ask the questions... worst that can happen is she tells you it's none of your business. Ask a few more questions, and if you get the same answer, then you'll know it's time to turn the page, pack your bags and get out of Dodge."

"You're right. I want to know as much as she is willing to tell me."

"Well, you won't have long to wait, here she comes."

Gianluca was eager to talk, but he didn't want to give her a reason to retreat… to blow him off. He kept in mind Ernie's advice.

"Hi, thanks for coming."

Words he had carefully chosen to use before the meeting turned into a box of scattered Scrabble letters. Her face, the curly locks that settled softly on her exposed shoulders, the perfume and the loose summer dress got to him. He nervously complimented her appearance, as she ordered a glass of Pinot Grigio. With her back to the bar, Ernie sneakily gave Gianluca the "she looks so hot" look, poking the air with his index finger then pulling it back shaking it like it was on fire. Layla took a sip of wine, depositing a cloudy scarlet lipstick print on the glass.

"So, are you staying for the fall semester?"

"Yes, I decided to stick around at least for one more. Clarence has become a close friend, and I enjoy teaching here."

"Did we perform as well as your NYU students?"

"There were many similarities. I enjoyed the questioning, the differing opinions, and the fact that here, in the south, the topic of romance is taken more seriously. In New York there seemed to be a cautious disconnect, almost a fear of becoming romantically involved. The reasons are not lost on one if you live there long enough. I think New Yorkers prefer short lived friendships with the occasional sex. The culture forces people to spend most of their time trying to make it beyond just surviving, and that fosters much independence which is jealously protected. That's a very personal, mostly lonely task. Then the competition is fierce, so losing or failing can be devastating. I don't see that here."

"Don't be fooled, it exists here, but it's not as obvious. The custom is to keep your shit... sorry, the word pops out every so often, in house. The main difference is that people in these parts rather spend most of their time living, and not scrambling around for fame or fortune."

"I've come to understand that, and I find it addictive. It's one of the reasons I've stayed. The thought of joining a bunch of retirees in Florida became suddenly unappealing after a few months on Saint Simon. Are you happy here, I mean, do you have any intentions of leaving?"

"Only to finish my degrees elsewhere. I can take some graduate courses at Maritime. They don't offer enough, but it's a start. Otherwise, I plan on staying. I love my life. I love the people. Massimo is like a father to me. The restaurant is more a therapy than a job."

"I know, I've watched you work the floor. You are so good with people, and I'm sure you're one of the reasons the place is so popular." He hesitated, but then found the courage to ask. "I noticed you in the parking lot earlier today. I'm sorry to pry, but it seemed you and Paul were arguing about something. Are you two..." She cut him off.

"Paul and I are trying to be friends. I have taken all his classes, and I enjoy his company. After his divorce he started acting differently. He wanted more... more than friendship. I refused to be dragged into that. Catherine is all too conspicuous, and he hasn't completely gotten over her. I felt bad for him. I lent him an ear and offered to help with diversions. He took the breakup badly, and I know he's still hurting. I told him I would never be more to him, and that if he insisted, he would lose me as a friend."

"How far did his insistence go?"

"In this very room he pulled out a ring and proposed. I told him he was nuts, and I walked out. He refuses to give up. The argument in the parking lot happened because he's been asking me to a weekend away in the Bahamas. I explained that it would only make things worse, and that he needed to stop. He didn't like what I had to say, so he went off."

"You were never involved amorously?"

"He thought it was heading in that direction, but with the situation at Maritime with Catherine, and me being his student... it just didn't feel right. So, no, it never got to that point, and I'm glad now it didn't."

"Did it impact your relationship with Davies?"

"In a way it did. I took one of her courses. I thought I

did some good work in that class, and she gave me a crappy grade. I grieved it. Paul was the adjudicator and he ruled in my favor. Catherine never got over it. I'm sure she thought he changed my grade because there was something going on, and things with her never got fixed. She avoids me on campus, and she's spread rumors about me and Paul. Look, I never gave him a reason to think there was more to us, that we would ever become lovers."

"It seems you've had your share of suitors."

"You could say so, male and female, but I never led anyone on. People seem so desperate for something, for someone. I can't satisfy those needs."

"It's easy to like you. It may even be easy to fall in love with you."

"Is that what's happened to you? Have you fallen in love, professor?"

"Not sure what to call it. Maybe I'm fearful of the term, it involves so many unchecked emotions."

"Come clean, say what's on your mind, speak the words floating around in your heart. Now's not the time to shy away and end up composing volumes of what could have been with the woman you didn't have the guts to conquer."

"You make it all sound like everything will happen as one wishes."

She softened up still more, touching his hand across the

small table.

"So, you're afraid of rejection? You can't handle being told that you're not someone's type? You worried that I may brush you off like some everyday encounter? Well, that's not me. What if I told you I won't reject you? Does that make it easier?"

"I knew I couldn't trust myself from turning this into a head game. Look, there's something, something hard to define, even understand, but when I'm around you I turn into that awkward high school boy at the freshman dance alone, leaning up against the cinderblock wall of the gym wishing I had the guts to ask that one standout girl to dance… the one that sits in the front desk across from me in all my classes. You know, the one whose name you write all over the inside cover of your notebook. The girl whose every mannerism turns you on. The one you never had the courage to sit next to during lunch, and the one who ends up being some other guy's girlfriend. I know it sounds ridiculous, but I don't know how to describe the adult version of that pathetic fifteen-year-old."

She absorbed his dilemma. "We should walk back to the harbor, it's so beautiful around this time." During the stroll, she brought up the Massimo situation.

"You also wanted to talk about how to approach Massimo when they return. He is the sweetest of men. Kind, gentle and aware of whenever someone is troubled. Sometimes

I think he is too good. At least on Saint Simon everything he does is appreciated… people love him. I think you should give him a chance to explain how you came to be his son. He was probably as lonely as your mother, and often people just need someone to get them through. Massimo is not the kind of man that would have had a one-night stand with your mom. Even if it wasn't love, there had to be some affection and respect. I've watched him closely and learned from him."

"I'm already over it. Now that I know the truth, I only need to normalize my relationship with him. It will be hard to replace Matteo, my mom's husband. He is as good a man as Massimo."

As they approached the harbor benches across from Massimo's, they ran into Paul and Catherine leaving the restaurant. Gianluca tried not to act surprised.

"Paul, Catherine… hi."

Paul spoke as Catherine stood stoic choosing to turn her gaze to the harbor waters.

"Welcome back Gianluca, you have been missed."

"Thank you, it's good to be back."

"Leylah, you look great."

"Thank you. Catherine, love your shoes."

Catherine said nothing and walked away.

"She drank a little too much wine. Well, you two have a nice evening. Gianluca, will you be on campus at all this summer?"

"Yes, I'm going in tomorrow to work on a new syllabus, and to continue editing my book. Will you be in?"

"Yes, I'll stop by to catch up."

Leylah led Gianluca to one of the benches.

"Are they back together?"

"No, they come to the restaurant and dine together every so often. I try not to serve their table… it's kind of weird. They are colleagues, I guess, and I've never witnessed any hostility between them. It's not uncommon to see them together, even having coffee in the campus center. Enough talk about them."

She pulled a chocolate mint patty from her purse. Broke it in half, teasing Giancarlo to open his mouth. His instinct was to pull back, but when her expression turned deliberately erotic with her sticky glossed lips slowly parting, creating a slight slit exposing the tip of her tongue, he gave in. She smiled and asked if he was Catholic. He nodded.

"Well then, make like you're receiving the host at communion. No hands, open your mouth and show me your tongue. He obeyed. She gently placed the piece on his tongue then pulled it back leaving him with a hint of mint that left a slight sensation. He parked his tongue back into his mouth when she urged him again to expose it. He nervously obeyed one more time. This time she let him keep it half melted as she slowly licked her two fingers clean. The remainder of the patty ended up between her teeth entreating him to bite off the half he could see. Their lips touched; she bit down releasing the protruding part into his mouth. Gianluca struggled for a moment with her intentions but decided to remain suctioned. The playful struggle matured into a tingle inducing kiss, the kind that ancient high school freshman must have imagined each time he sat behind the girl that made him sweat.

She eased up to let him catch his breath only to come right back, hooking her teeth into his bottom lip with tender pee wee bites anesthetizing the membrane. The thorny pain became surprisingly enjoyable. He opened his eyes shocked to behold hers studying him. He felt as if the seduction gave her the time to analyze the effect it was having... was she spying him the entire time? Gianluca craved the moment for what it was, but there was a stitch of weirdness. This woman was now contradicting much of what he thought he knew about her.

She backed off, her eyes stalking his thoughts. She came back at him running her tongue in slow motion from left to right along the crevice of his lips. She brushed away the strands of hair from her face, then came back across from right to left, leaving his lips wet and throbbing.

"We can't keep doing this on this bench. I know the apartment you rent from Massimo, but I've never seen the inside."

The out-maneuvered New Yorker dug deep for his usual reasons to resist, but this was Leylah. The fantasy that had settled into his detoured bones when he first came upon her in the salty harbor town had become a puzzling reality. The woman biting down on his lip was quickly shedding her outer skin. Her mannerisms, the humble way she interacted with people, and her wholesomeness spoke of a woman incapable of even a little radical behavior. Yet, as she played on his weakness, he found his easiest and sweetest surrender. He was ready to give up on caution and take chances. In his mind there could be no better reason than Leylah.

There was no hesitation once inside Gianluca's apartment. She slowly let her dress slip down from her shoulders, exposing her nakedness as it fell to the floor, completing the intended tease. He held on nervously to a glass of wine. She wore no bra or panties... not even a thong, he thought. She owned his gaze; unable to turn away, or blink. His body rejecting his mind's intrusion in an erotic freefall. She owned the moment; she was too good, and he knew he was a long shot competitor at best.

Leylah had trashed his expectations, presenting him with a version of herself that had his nature battling his intuition. The tattoo just below her belly button didn't help.

She sensed his interest, so she moved in for a closer look.

"Pleitho, the Greek goddess of seduction. I was expecting the Virgin Mary."

"Funny, is that how you thought of me?"

"Not to that extreme, but pretty close."

"Well, I guess you had me all wrong. Tonight, you'll find out why. I'm going to take a quick shower. I see there's room for two in there."

Shades of Cassandra, he thought. What was it about women and showers? Water and hands caressing a body must have much to do with it. They must enjoy being delicately stroked with soapy hands. It also crossed his mind that he never took the lead with women.

The shower was almost too much to handle. He expected being roughed up by this updated version, instead she surprised him once again by taking her sweet time.

"Show me your hands."

She poured bodywash into his cupped palms.

"Wash me."

He played along spilling the liquid onto her breasts, her stiff, sprouting nipples responding to his schooled finger pirouettes. In short time, his conspicuous arousal invited her sarcasm.

"My goodness, professor, you hid this well in class despite those tight jeans... talk about making an impression, my goodness! Now that is worthy of so much more attention."

With those words his body became her playground, and each time he attempted to reciprocate, she boldly pushed away his hands with an expression that had him feeling unnaturally vulnerable. Her sweet caresses probing below his waist with both hands, succeeding in changing his mood and any hesitations he may have had involving her intentions. If Gianluca had been better trained in the art of deciphering the duality of character, he would have detected the camouflaged Leylah sooner.

"Talk dirty, talk dirty to me" She pulled closer, pushing her ear to his lips.

Gianluca had no clue. No such request had ever been part of his past entanglements. He didn't have the vocabulary nor was he equipped to match the eroticism, so Leylah took the lead she wouldn't relinquish.

"Professor, tell me if you like this."

She slowly tightened her grip on his penis while she sucked and then bit hard on his nipple. He pulled back to his side of the shower in pain. Distracted, he was losing the buzz. She took notice, flipped it a few times with her finger, succeeding in reviving his erection. She turned and pushed up against him. He hesitated.

"Gianluca, shall I show you the way, do you need a GPS? Are you going to fuck me or not? I can't believe I used that word... damn it, Gianluca... you're messing me up!

He panicked again. Should he forget himself, get raunchy, take her expectation for granted, fuck her like he had done to no woman in the hope that it would transition to love? Was love her motivator? Would he soon learn that it would be just a fuck, and nothing more? How could he deal with the disappointment? She sounded so weird saying *fuck*. There was no escaping the moment, he was in it, and he knew he could play no part in the outcome... it was her show, her impulse, her game, her manipulation. He blamed himself for never being the initiator, for allowing the female to always take the lead. He thought he might be able to figure it out once she was done.

He gave her his version of a slower, more romantic intercourse thinking it would give her the orgasm she desired. She rejected his methodical approach slamming her butt against his crotch with a rhythm and force that had his backbones punishing the shower wall. He concentrated, but his erection failed him again.

"Gianluca! I don't understand!"

She turned, grabbed his penis, and with power thrusts she tried masturbating it back into the mass she demanded. With his eyes shut tight, concentrating on getting hard again was of no help. She finally let go as it came to rest exhausted and bruised on his swollen testicles.

"I can't believe you! What kind of man gives up that easily? I spent an entire semester waiting for you to get the courage to finally make your move, to make me want you, to know that sooner or later we would be doing this in every corner of your apartment. I would have made all the moves had I known I would have to wait all this time for this. You northern men think too much, and you don't act enough. You need to let your dingaling do the thinking for you. I've been horny on you for so long. I bet you thought all this was the prelude to us falling in love. You have these illusions that you can have a woman like me that will blow your brains out in bed, and then use love as a pretext to own me. Have you ever been with a woman that can give you the best sex and love you at the same time?"

"Yes, I have."

Leylah lost some control.

"Bulldung! You keep thinking that... nothing but a lie. That woman exists only in your delusional head. I can be that woman, but I choose not to. I don't want you drooling over me with your trivial poetry and your bloated romanticism. No woman can deal with that much cotton candy affection... not for a short while, and definitely not for a lifetime. Think for yourself, Gianluca... don't worry about my feelings... I don't need that from a man. I asked you to bed, and that's what I wanted, a good man in bed. That's all I asked you to do. I won't ask if you love me, I won't ask if you still feel the same a day later, and I won't ask you for a long-term relationship… I'm asking you to *fuck me*! That's all… what don't you get?"

The man who thought he was prepping for the rest of his life, wrapped himself in a towel and sat dejected on the edge of his bed. He couldn't set aside the thought that her cursing, the word *fuck* didn't carry the nastiness it was supposed to. Her pronunciation was that of a person who hardly used the word. It seemed an act, an audition. He tried to downplay the new Leylah, but it was too unexpected, and he hadn't been around her enough to completely reject it.

"You must know. I was, rather I thought I was, in love with you. It was almost at first sight. It may have been unfair, but it was your beauty, the kind I had never seen, and I gave no consideration to character, to the person you may truly be… I didn't want that to matter. I buried all other considerations; your beauty was enough. Then, the more I learned about you from others and from watching you go about your life, the more I wanted to love you. In class I stole glances each time you looked down into your notebook. In the restaurant I was amazed at your interactions with people… I thought of how much affection you received from just about everyone, from all walks of life. I mean, old folks, the sanitation guys, truckers, parents with children, the college baseball coach… they all lit up like the Fourth of July around you. Whenever I mentioned you, I got volumes on your goodness. I was in awe that you didn't let any of the praise fatten up your head. So, forgive me for planning the rest of my life around you, it's a perfectly normal human endeavor. You can call me an idiot for thinking that I could meet a poetic ideal in a woman, but it was never meant to be an impossible standard. I placed you there, in the literature, and I admit to comparing you to those women, to make the past contemporary and real. What a head game. I'm stupefied that I am even telling you this… I have been a pathetic fool… I was making it all up in my mind. I must apologize for creating a Leylah that isn't real. You even warned me in your reactions to the course material. You said that women were forced to fit the images men had of them, and that those women may not have been the perfect creatures we think them to be in those writings. Well, you have given power to that theory."

He couldn't help the paradox. "I'm baffled, is the Leylah that prances around in public as the angelic spirit that makes everyone and everything take notice and smile, real or manufactured? Who is the Leylah I just showered with and who asked me so unconditionally to fuck her? Which is the real one? You owe me that much."

"Talk about head games… Gianluca, you will be playing them forever. For women like me there is no time to love, be loved, or fall in love. I'm too selfish for that. I don't want to be some man's woman, or wife or lover or concubine. I want to be me first; go after the things and the people I want with no infatuations, no commitments, no need to set up house, no need to ever use the word *love*. It ruins everything. This night would have worked out if you had given up on all your bogus obsessions about love and women.

I choose the time and the place; I choose who I want to bed... man or woman. I can make those choices because of who I am, because of the way I look. I know I'm irresistible, and that's what gets people like you to bite. I want you to bite, I want you to taste me and be tasted. You get the opportunity you want, and I get to own you only for a short time; I don't want any of it to last too long.

I let people think of me as they want. They need someone like me to balance out all the shit in their lives. People have to deal with the ugly in their lives almost every day... I give them that little bit of the beautiful. You see, I'm their invention. I'm their light at the end of a dark tunnel; their Mona Lisa surrounded by graffiti; I'm their prayer when there's little hope left, and their dream when there have been only nightmares. Old men look at me and wish they could still run their hands over my body; old women look at me and think of the first time their offered their young bodies to their lovers. Townspeople gaze at me and think all is good and pure.

I give them what they want, and they can have it.

When it comes to me, I want to be the woman that drains partners of all their energies; that destroys their self-control; that turns them wild with some primitive fever. I want them weakened to the point where I'm in complete control. You see, I need that power over men... and powerful women. It's my way of washing them out of my system. The best part is that they always want more... more sex or they want me. The worst is when they expect me to fall in love or they think they're in love. That's when it gets messy because I need to find a way to get rid of them without the drama."

Gianluca had only one reaction.

"So, I'm just another jackass who fits all those descriptions. Sounds like you really hate men and are jealous of women with authority. Why do you have a need to use me? You could have just ignored my interest, brushed me off, and I would have given up. You could have let me walk away without all this."

"There's no fun in that. You don't get off that easily. You got involved, you think I didn't pick up on your heartsick shit? You think I didn't notice the times you were eyeing me? I wasn't taking notes in class... *he's looking at me again; he thinks I'm taking notes; he thinks he's falling in love; I'll pull my skirt up a little, let's see how he reacts. Funny, he can't handle it, he's stumbling over his words. At the end of class, I'll tell him how much I enjoyed his lecture.* My notebook is full of these silent thoughts. I wanted to give you the few seconds you needed to keep looking, to keep spying what you so desperately wanted. I can recall each glance. I allowed you the tease to keep you coming for more. How often did you stay up thinking of me? How often did you come to the restaurant just to be around me? How often did you think of making love to me? When did you start thinking that we would be together forever?

So, now you know. The real Leylah was in that shower ripe and wet... yours to have, yours to explore and inhale. You did nothing, lost in your own miserable confusion. There was nothing to figure out, you filled that small space thick with hesitation and frustration... not even the warm water could cleanse you. Why would I want to live like that? Your nature is to be that kind of person, you can't help yourself." She paused waiting for a reaction. Nothing.

"My dear professor, you ask too much of a woman. You seek to mold her to your image, make her perfect for your needs. See, you're no different than your poets. Things for women like me don't change unless we force it. I want to prove how pompous intellectuals like you, Davies, and Considine can't see or understand life outside of yourselves. People on Saint Simon have me figured out the way they want, the way that makes them feel good about teaching their morality to the next generation, so I let them have what they want.

When it comes to the classroom, to your lectures, snug in your interpretations of everything from a piece of literature to the thoughts of poets long dead to justifying the habit of past societies, it turns my stomach that you use your pulpit to shut us down. That's why I don't want to be your ideal. You want this one-sided relationship, your invention of perfection to give you an object you can praise… to provide the motivation to elevate your experience. Admit it, Gianluca… my perfection serves to complete your perfection. You can be the best of poets, the best of husbands, the best of lovers only if you possess in life or death the best of women. Would Dante have written a word about an ugly Beatrice? She had to be perfection for his motivation. Now why would I want to give you that same pleasure? Why would I want to serve the same end that generations of women have done before? Why would I want to sacrifice who I am to give you that opportunity?

Gianluca, look at me… I am a human being first, free to define myself as I see fit. You want to keep me a woman first, so you get the power to define me. I know you didn't expect all this. You could hardly fathom that I would turn into this monster, this beast in your eyes."

She stood her ground in front of her dejected target still wrapped in a towel, slouched on a mattress that struggled to stay firm. Without warning she pulled his face towards her breasts and nestled it neatly in her cleavage. She ran them slowly and delicately across his cheeks several times pausing only to give him a fleeting taste of her nipples. In his trance, she pushed him back onto the bed, digging her long, sharp nails into each side of his naked chest... her momentum scraping the tips of his nipples, causing the kind of pain that sends shivers through your teeth.

He pushed back, but she wouldn't budge. She ran her lips over his still wet crotch persuading him to abandon the fight. His hands could only busy themselves tugging on the bedspread as she worked him into a frenzy and bursts of heavy breathing. As his body was lulled into a debilitating daze, she abruptly plucked, then sunk her teeth into the skin of his penis. He tried to absorb the pain, but the poor man's only option was to yank her away by the hair as he tried frantically to rub away the burn.

She remained seated on the floor. He looked down at her, taming the throbbing in his groin. Her expression turned erotic again as she spread her legs compelling him to pay attention.

"I can't do this. I can't look at you teasing my pain. Do you understand I'm in pain? What pleasure do you get out that? What is this? It's not love making, it's not sex, it's not what people do to each other. Is this your definition of who you are? If it is, then you may like it, but I don't. What value is there in being this kind of... of... I want to say woman, but it just doesn't fit. You need to leave, please."

She walked to the other side of the bed. Slipping under the covers, she invited him to do the same. He hesitated, but eventually gave in... a man too forgiving to stand his ground, seeking the elusive love in all that was happening. With the tips of her fingers hovering over his skin, she gently guided them with soft landings to all parts of his body, then mounting him she finished him off with a two-handed massage of his temples. The climax stimulating gel she pulled from her purse helped him get over the injuries, and the slow, perfectly spaced suction kisses coated in her warm breath, awakened his disobedient erection, as she felt it drumming her lower back. She responded, sliding down backwards smothering it, disappearing inside her. Leylah had worked herself into a foreplay hysteria... with measured trampoline trusts and clitoral strokes increasing in tempo and assertiveness, crushing what little control Gianluca had left to guide his penis through the turbulence.

Her orgasm was an explosion of gyrations, spasms, and curling fits that ran the length of her body, dispatching her arms upwards, erect, and stiff... her separated, scarlet tipped fingers like thermometers measuring her fever.

He cushioned her movements, mitigating as best he

could his tenderized phallus. The seismic tremors kept him numb and erect but with little incentive to reach his own orgasm... he was too focused on her expressions, of the selfish nature with which she claimed her pleasures. Depleted, she collapsed onto the empty side of the bed.

"See, I make no secret of the fact that the weaker you are, the more I can control you, the greater my climax. Tell me, are you still in love?"

Gianluca had reached the outer limits of his confusion and exhaustion. Her performance seemed so poorly rehearsed... what was she trying to prove, why the theatrics? He struggled to speak... his weighty words hardly making it past his lips.

"I'm not sure. Probably not. I thought I was, but I had no clue this is who you really are. Look at me-you carved your nails into my chest, and you left your mark on my penis. Your orgasm was powerful, but it was all about you, and it didn't turn me on. Was I that ridiculously idiotic to believe that we could work out? You admitted that this is who you truly are, and I would have welcomed it even as I foolishly recreated you in the image that made me want to love you... because I so *desperately* wanted to love you."

She spoke on edge. Her frustration adding volume to her words.

"See, you seem to be learning important lessons about

women. I don't want to be that image in your head. I don't want to be loved the way you want, because that is even more selfish than my orgasm... and at least my orgasm is honest. Your love is deceitful; it could never be honest. You think that making up your mind to love me, to make me your woman, your bride would satisfy my goal in life. I'm so sadly disappointed in you. You teach about love, about romancing a woman, but you never allowed yourself to look beyond the words, to consider that all those women memorialized by your snobbish poets didn't want to be treated as objects of their passions, that it wasn't important to them. You came to those conclusions through the eyes and the writings of your boys, but did you think of looking deeper into the lives of the women, and the attempts by some of them to break out, to become independent thinkers, and to aspire to be the women they imagined themselves to be? I bet Beatrice had no intentions of taking Dante as a lover! I did the research-there is no information, no proof that she ever exchanged any messages, any letters. I could find no evidence that she ever expresses any love for him.

Still, you find no peace in your relationships. You so hysterically want to keep that woman alive in your head that you have become so good at convincing yourself you can create her out of nothing. Shit, Gianluca! Fuck, I said *shit* again. God, you are so aggravating! You have me cursing like a cowboy at a rodeo. Tonight, I will wash my mouth out with soap... I'm so angry at me!" She paused to recall where she left off.

"Right, if that's who you want, you need to pursue Catherine Davies. There's a woman yearning for a specimen like you. She would capitulate after a few more dates and long weekends. She would allow you to mold her, give her a purpose, make her obedient. Paul was too much a fool. You have everything she wants, but she'll want you to work damn hard before she gives in... and she *will* give in.

I went after her to prove how easily she would drop all the fake liberated, feminist shit. She's no feminist, never been liberated and will always be a slave to dicks of all kinds and sizes. If she's not married to a man, she needs one around all the time. Oh my God, nasty words again... my filthy mouth...I can't keep talking like this... I won't be able to sleep. Where was I?

You think that just because you're ready to love me, to settle down, to Pottery Barn an apartment together, to start the perfect wine collection, and play house, I should praise the Lord, get down on my knees and thank him for my good fortune? To me that's the most pathetic way to live. Instead, I get into your head and under your clothes, feed my desires, choose to love you, or dump you, accept the results or the fallout, and move on. If I choose to love someone I can't have, then I will, just like you, get others to show me some compassion." She took a deep, heavy breath, flapping her lips as she released it.

"I'm paying tribute to the generations of women that were abused in real life, and then used by egotistic romantics like you and eulogized to get your readers to pity you, to admire your sacrifice, and the steadfast bull poop love you took to the grave. That's cataclysmic, and men are so good at inventing their own immortality. It's never about the woman, it's always about you. You're a student of history; how many women have had the opportunity at immortality? The sick thing is that those women-Beatrice, Laura, Fiammetta made those men famous. The women remain immortal only as objects in literature, and since they never became involved with the poets, they had no clue their names would live eternal. That's my point, they had no say in how they became famous. That blows my mind! It really does!"

In the time it took Gianluca to consider abandoning the conversation, he came up with an argument he felt would straighten her curls.

"So, you're stroking your theory by being the woman who destroyed the men who had the courage to love you? You reject the notion that I can love you, possible or impossible? If you choose to love a man who loves you unconditionally, is that a sign of female weakness? Is it weakness if I did something to make you love me? Is it weakness if you choose to live out your life in the company of a lover, a man, a husband? Will you grow old alone? Will you give up on the chance of creating something greater than yourself or waste away your years selfishly, unable to dedicate any part of you to another human? Do you also reject that we come to know the best of ourselves in the eyes, the arms, the heart of another? You're right about the lost opportunities for women throughout the centuries, but I would never belittle any attempt made by a man to demonstrate his love for that one amazing creature that captured not only his heart, but his entire existence.

It's only by good fortune that one encounters such a person, and those lucky few who do, do not piss away the feeling or the fortitude to confront and own their destinies. To me there is nothing that can rival love's seizure... the greatest mental and emotional convulsion is when two give themselves so willingly. In a spiritual way everything falls into place. There's an undeniable completeness. Few ever cross that threshold.

It pains me to say it was what I have felt for you since we first met. The Leylah you presented so openly in public and to my senses, took me captive. All my beliefs, all the truths about love found their aspirations in you. You were suddenly there, in my life, in my world. I loved you instantly-your eyes, your expression, your hair, your walk, your voice, your nature, your body, your scent... I tried to find something about you that would have me question your perfections. I was hoping for some flaws, for something that would bring me down to earth with a lesson on male infatuation and stupidity. Nothing, there was nothing about you that would keep me from loving you… until now.”

He paused, probing for a sign of remorse to keep him from saying more. She refused. He had to finish.

“I'm thankful for your sad lesson. It may be your lone truth, but it is a truth I want to desperately avoid. As much as you refuse to be loved by a man for his own selfish reasons, I know I can't love this real you. Talk about misery… what are you afraid of? What are you hiding? When did you lose your trust in men? Without a good enough reason, none of what you are doing makes any sense.” She hid none of her outrage in her response.

“You parked your sorry butt in my space thinking you were being delivered by some mystical power into the arms of the woman you deserved because only you had what it took to love me. Life was supposed to come to a standstill on Saint Simon while you indulged your fantasies and performed your courtship. In your constipated thinking we were all supposed to watch in awe as you swept me off my feet, and to the delight of these people, we would have put ourselves on display. '*My goodness*', the women would say, '*aren't they so perfect for each other. She was smart going for the older, educated man. He'll always appreciate her youth, her beauty. He will love her till his dying day, never unfaithful'. 'Never want for anything more than Leylah'*, men would say.

You got what most men in this town wish for. You think I don't know how many of them and some women wonder what it would be like to have me naked in their beds?"

She got up, continued talking, walked into the bathroom to pee leaving the door open.

"Why would you want love, commitments, marriage, children, a silly mortgage to interfere with a happy, satisfying life? Then again, at your age it would make sense. Amazing, that's probably what you thought you would get with me... Jesus, Gianluca... how did you convince yourself? How did you come up with that neat, opportunistic mid-life conclusion?"

She flushed, went to her playlist on her phone, and slipped into the shower.

"Com'on, your life is getting shorter, come shower one more time with me, show me you can get it up twice in one day... you may not get another chance."

Humiliated and deflated, he said nothing, quietly dressed and walked left the apartment and made his way to his office. They had passed the night without sleep... the sex and the head games had conspired to keep them awake.

As he swiveled his office chair toward the large windows looking out on the Saint Simon coastline, Gianluca felt at ease and secure, away from the ominous Leylah. He was too exhausted to give the events organization or to find sense in her behavior. He shut his eyes still wondering if her performance was real. As he invited his mind to take a short vacation, a knock on his opened door forced him to abandon the attempt.

"Gianluca, is this a bad time?"

"Paul... no, please come in."

"Are you okay? You look like a bad hangover."

"Perhaps, but not because of alcohol."

"Leylah?"

Gianluca lacked the alertness in that moment to dodge Paul's intuitiveness, so he came clean.

"Yes, Leylah. I spent the night with her, or should I say with her evil twin." He paused. "If you know her well enough, help me understand. Drop me a clue... who, what is she? How could I have misjudged her so badly or is she that good at disguising her true nature? How does an angel fall from grace so unannounced? I mean, she did everything in her power to make it easy for me to walk away, and yet she haunts me in such a way that I still obsess about her. How does one so taken by such a woman begin to let her go, to give her up? This is so far from normal, or maybe I have no clue what normal is anymore."

Paul smiled, took a quick sip from the bottle of water he carried.

"You spoke the magic words. What is normal? You and I, Catherine as well, have been presented with a new normal, a new reality that has us trapped, desperately seeking a way to fit in. You will come away hollowed out... no heart, no soul, cold blooded, and hesitant to go back for more, yet incapable of walking away completely."

"I'm aware that you have had a relationship with her, but how is Catherine involved?"

"My dear man, she seduced Catherine as well."

"So, the rumors were never rumors."

"Correct. They were conveniently allowed to become rumors because in a town like this no one wanted to believe it, except perhaps Ernie. *'Oh, that's just a silly rumor'*, they would say. *'Women always hold hands and have sleep overs and go to the bathroom together'*. The narrative contradicted the rumor, and it stayed that way. Truth is, she went after Catherine when we divorced. Catherine never hid her tendency to like women, but she never acted on it... as far as I know. When Leylah signed up for her class, she covered many feminist topics, and one of them was the different manifestations of lesbianism. Her lectures telegraphed her passion for the topic, and someone like Leylah picked up on it. She fabricated an objection of the final grade Catherine gave her. The disagreement landed in my lap as the adjudicator. The grade was clearly honest and fair, yet Catherine begged me to change it. By that time, she had become infatuated with her student. She played it up, you know, the angry professor pissed off about my decision with references to fake nasty exchanges between her and Leylah in order to deflect attention. Meanwhile, the affair was powerful and had a secret life of its own. They did an excellent job of covering up, and the most that came of any talk were instantly dismissed as rumors."

"So, what happened, did it end?"

"It did, on many a sour note, but Catherine kept placating her by staying attached, knowing that sooner or later Leylah would lose interest and abandon the relationship. It was Catherine's way of wiggling out with no damage. Leylah did it to prove she could seduce even someone as in control of herself as Catherine, and when it finally satisfied her sick curiosity, she did indeed move on. When Catherine told me, I looked at her in total disbelief. I was shocked that the woman I knew, and my ex-wife could stumble so easily."

"Did you know this before you got involved with her?"

"No way… had I known, I never would have given her a chance. Catherine didn't reveal her situation until after Leylah was done with me-she had to keep it from getting out. She's a few years away from retiring with a cushy pension, and a solid reputation… no way she would risk that."

"What do you mean-*done with you*?"

"Does any of this sound familiar… she loves to take showers with you; she will sit, stand, lay naked in your face to get a reaction. She lectures you on how you're lucky enough to bed her, and she will work you until you're so sore, there's no firmness left for an orgasm. She will continue to tease you until it turns nasty and almost evil. She will call you names, tell you how disappointing you are, make a point that you're old, and how fruitless your effort would be to love her.

I even got to the point of a proposal, afraid of not acting quickly enough before someone else could put a ring on her finger. Looking back, I still can't come to terms with how pathetically disjointed I had become… to think that I would find happiness with her. She strung me along to prove some sick theory. When my emotions got the better of me, and I refused to step away, she asked Clarence to intervene. In probing, the poor man had to insinuate that I was being generous with my grades because of my admiration for her, and not because she earned them. She took two of my classes, I gave her an *A* in both courses; one she deserved, the other was a bit of a gift. Point was that she had those grades to back up her claim, and I had nothing but a stupid look on my face. I tried approaching her, but she kept brushing me off. Clarence then asked me to walk away from it, fearful it could have gotten worse. I'll talk about it, but deep down I'm devastated by the humiliation."

Gianluca sat stunned. "Why didn't you confront her, tell her you were no longer interested? What about Catherine, did she have any problems?

"That would have meant exposing too much. Around here no one does any exposing. Everyone has secrets. See, if you don't expose, you don't get exposed... pretty simple. Catherine understood that her only choice was to stand down, to neutralize Leylah. I was too juiced up to do the same. I confronted her, and I ended up having to explain myself to Clarence."

As Paul finished his words, Catherine walked in. "Sorry, I'll come back later."

"No, please, come in. Do you mind if Paul stays?"

"I'm so used to seeing him around he becomes a blur. He's like that souvenir refrigerator magnet you bought in Florida... unless I stare at it, I totally forget it's there."

She turned to Paul. "Stay, fido... no, just joking. So, you two seem involved in some heavy head banging... what is it, a new essay on Dante? Is he now Jewish, gay or transgender? What's the new theory?"

Gianluca smiled. "Not even Dante is immune to rumors. I... rather we, have been discussing our relationships with Leylah, and you came up."

She pounced on Paul. "What did you talk about? I can't believe you would discuss my personal life with anyone. This is one of the reasons why we didn't work out. You have no clue, no limits. I confided in you, and you alone! Paul!... fuck!"

Gianluca intervened. " Catherine, please. Paul meant no harm, it's just that we compared notes, and it seems, in a mind-numbing way, that Leylah has some deep-rooted issues. Look, I fell for her too. She had me the moment I met her. I too am ashamed of admitting to a weakness. I'm coming clean... I need to know more. I just got done spending the night with her in a bizarre affair. She defied every expectation... this morning I had no clue who she was."

His words calmed her down. "Fine, it was a matter of getting over her, and over the whole ordeal. I'll admit to my little lesbian fantasy, so Leylah did to me what she did to you two fools. Early on she was everything I ever imagined about making love to a woman... then she sprinkled salt on my slice of sweet watermelon. She did it to own me, and I sold myself cheap. I considered she was a student, but I also considered she was a thirty-seven-year-old woman... how many excuses is she allowed; how often can she ignore her age and claim to be a victim? How is it that we can talk about this openly, and at the same time be consumed with the guilt of not having employed the greater morality? Do we truly have an obligation to justify our orgasms with a mature woman? So, I engaged. I thoroughly enjoyed her body, her nature, every one of her sighs, her squeaks; exhaling… slithering on my bed, imploring my lips, my hands, my skin. If you didn't feel the same, I'm sharing all this with two liars."

Gianluca's bewilderment spoke for him. "Are there others? Has she been involved with other men, other women?"

"I would have to say no. It would have come out, and we would have known. She focused on us. After Paul and I divorced, she knew we would both be rebounding, not for another serious relationship, but for some easy, no strings attached flings… nothing stupid with commitments, talk of love, marriage, long term shit. She picked her time and made her move.

We think it had much to do with her feelings about men and conformist women with power. It's hard not to believe she hates us, or she just can't come to terms with what we represent… like some psychotic anger that builds up inside, and then she puts in motion a series of actions that changes your mind about her. That pure, healthy female image dissipates, and you're left with a good dream that ends badly.

I'm not out to completely condemn her as some freak. I still believe that she is a fragile creature looking for happiness, maybe even love. In her confusion, and her fears of investing her feelings, she finds it difficult to trust her emotions with any one person. I also believe the lesbian thing was spontaneous. I don't believe, given her performance, that she has any real intentions with a woman. Under her clothes she was equipped with the most seductive outfit which on that body became totally obscene… in a good way. Who could resist? Her attempts at pleasing me were amateurish at best. I let it go, there was still so much of her to enjoy. Paul came away feeling the same way."

As he listened, Gianluca made comparisons to his own experience. "She did the same with me. I sensed it was all very much a show. I can't say she came across as a woman who had done this sort of thing often enough to be at ease with it."

Gianluca turned to Catherine. So, how did all this end up? "Nothing really. She said something to Clarence. He called us in. We sat there stunned, wordless, and I never embarrass around Clarence, but that day I couldn't make eye contact. Our only hope was that he would be the only other person to know. He didn't overreact and didn't ask us to resign.

About a week later Leylah called Paul and asked to meet. They met at the Inn." She turned to Paul.

"Tell him what the meeting was about."

Paul took an agitated breath. "We had a few drinks, and for the first hour she said nothing about us. She talked about the class material and her choices for graduate school. She said she didn't want to continue working at the restaurant,

and that she was sick of being around Massimo. Then she
apologized for getting involved and that she had no intentions
of us being a serious thing. I sat there totally confused,
wondering if there was more. She gave me that penetrating
gaze, said nothing for a minute or so, then got up walked to my
side of the table, kissed me gently on my lips, and walked out.

Gianluca once again looked at Catherine.

"Yes, my dear she did the same with me. It was all
bittersweet. I sat there knowing it was over, but I didn't want
to let go of her." Gianluca couldn't dodge the confusion.

"This is sadly bizarre... why would she force herself on
the two of you when she could have anyone?"

"She doesn't want just anyone. We figured it out. She
chooses those of us with resources, a comfortable venue,
unmarried, and no kids... no family to get in the way. Look at
us, doesn't it make sense?

Suddenly the story was no longer just about Paul and
Catherine. As much as he wanted to brush it off as something
he could walk away from, Gianluca needed get into Leylah's
head. Back in his apartment, her scent lingered. The towel
hanging on the bathroom door was damp with hints of her
perfume. The bed, however, was a complete mess with pillows,
sheets, books, and the pages to his new syllabus thrown about
as if to make a statement. He sat on the edge of his naked

mattress replaying the events of the previous night and thinking that perhaps he had misjudged her intentions, and unfairly dismissed her anxieties about love. But why unleash a storm in his bedroom? He either had to let the relationship die a quick death or search for something worth salvaging. He walked out unwilling to search for answers.

On his way to the restaurant, he slowed his pace to think of how he would approach her. His fear was taking it too far; to the point where she would be so turned off, there would be little to fix. As he entered, he was immediately greeted by Massimo who had returned from his trip to Savannah. He had become accustomed to calling him by the Italian *professore.* This time he greeted him as *Gianluca.*

"Ciao, Massimo. Welcome back. Is Leylah here?"

"Gianluca, please, come to my office. Please, I want to talk with you."

Not seeing her around, he decided to give Massimo the time he begged for. The topic would be no surprise, and it was a chapter of his life that needed a final paragraph.

"Of course, we do need to talk."

In his office Massimo was equipped with the best of his collection of sprits. He poured two glasses of his favorite grappa.

"Gianluca, by now you must know who I am to you.

Your mother called to tell me about your visit, and about the years we spent in Bologna. Me and Gemma... we became good friends, and then we became more than friends. She did not tell you the whole truth, so she asked me to talk to you. When Gemma was pregnant with you, I asked her to marry me. I was supposed to come to America, but I said I would stay with her and the baby. I didn't make much money at the university, but I knew we could be happy, and I wanted to be a *papà*. I said to her I would find more work in a restaurant on the weekend so we would have enough. She was a *profesoressa*, and me... I was only a cook, but I promised her I would be the best husband and father. Then she look at me very sad, and she said *'Massimo, you are a good man, but I do not love you. I'm happy for our time together, but I do not want to be married, I do not want to be a wife. You may not understand, but this is the way I want to live my life. I will love and cherish this baby, but you need to go to America.'* Your mother did not want you to know this. She did not want me as a husband, so I could not be your father. I understood I would only be in the way of her dreams. So, I decided to leave. When I arrived in America, I called her. She told me she meet someone and that it was serious. I gave her my number and my address, and she promised to send me photos and write letters about my son. I never hear from her again. I felt very bad, but what could I do? I had not so much money, and I worked seven days a week in my uncle's pizzeria.

The years go by, and I found my new life in Saint Simon. I forgot about Italy… I never went back.

I expect no forgiveness from you. I have no excuse, only what I told you. Maybe I could have done more to be a real *papà*. I lost that chance. I don't know if we can be a normal father and son, but I would like to try."

Gianluca sat pensive, believing his story about Gemma. He remembered the words Clarence spoke about not placing blame. He had no stomach for the circumstances of their past lives; that time belonged to them, and if he was the result of their actions, he would need to leave it at that.

"I have no other choice it seems. How can I make any sense of all this? The past is so behind us… can't bring it back, can't be undone or reworked… it was never mine to own and to mold. I can accept the heritage, but it will take some work before I can become your son. I have no idea how to start this, or what direction to take. Massimo, right now I'm completely lost. We can take this up gradually. I want to talk to my mother again. Forgive me for abandoning this conversation, but I need to talk with Leylah, is she back?"

Massimo peaked outside his door. "Yes, she is sitting at the bar."

His intention was to approach her with a clean slate and to find a calm path to the heart of her actions.

"We need to talk." He whispered in a voice on the edge of an irrational delirium. Leylah, still seated, pulled back calmly.

"You need to sit your ass down and change your tone if you want to talk. Now, explain the attitude in your voice... you are making me very uncomfortable."

"You left a sick mess in my bedroom... you tossed all my shit around, even my class papers, and they were in my bag. You went through my bag! Does that give you a strong hint why I have an attitude?"

"After showering, I went back to bed thinking you were coming back with some coffee and breakfast. I fell asleep only to awaken to the sight of me alone in bed. I freaked, I hate being in bed with a man all night and waking up alone... I went nuts. I jumped up on the bed and started with the pillows, then I pulled the covers off your bed and when I saw your bag, I opened it and emptied it. I took another shower, got dressed and left. I guess you didn't see the stab marks in the mattress."

Adding some angry volume to his strained whisper, Gianluca couldn't believe her words.

"No, what stab marks? You stabbed my mattress? Why? What did you stab it with?" She answered as if he was overreacting.

"So let me guess, you thought I had some psycho episode and decided to destroy your bedroom... because I'm out of my mind... I'm crazy, right? I used the kitchen knife on the counter... it's really thin and sharp. Let me guess, professor Gianluca, so in control of himself, so well put together now has the right to pass judgement on some jilted woman who took out her rage on his mattress of all things. If I were that demented, don't you think the police would have found your body this morning with a dozen stab wounds? I must have a had a good reason to cut up your stupid mattress instead of you. You just can't accept the life and people around you as we are. You need to analyze every action, every thought, every expression to satisfy your expectations. Do you understand why it would be a complete torture to be married to someone like you… to live any length of time in the same place with you? Now that's what you call crazy." She was on a roll. "You had your chance, you got me to respond, to be interested, and now I'm satisfied it wasn't worth it. You stood gazing at an oasis, and you chose to die of thirst. You're dead, Gianluca! You have no life left in you. You're a corpse filled with literary clichés. Go back to your office, back to your classes filled with feeble hearts, and bloated brains."

She paused as more people approached the bar. "We can finish this in my father's office." He followed her. Massimo looked up from his desk, and saying nothing, walked out. Gianluca still had his words stuck in his throat.

"That's what it's all about? You needed to prove how self-absorbed I am, how pompously I present myself in class, and how blinded I am to what I teach? So, after convincing

275

yourself of the things you hate in me, you choose to use your greatest assets-an inquisitive mind, precious beauty, and an alluring femininity to seduce and then punish me? ... amazing! What's the point? Where's the majesty in that? What theory have you proven to the world? Do you believe for a moment that your actions will ease your anxieties about who I am? For every one of you there are ten who are inspired by my teachings."

As those words spilled from his mouth, he could only think of Cassandra. "I'm very much alive, Leylah. I chose to nurture the love I had for you. I acted on those feelings unaware of how fake you were. So, who's the hypocrite here? Who's the one who is dead to herself? You killed off the real Leylah to create this sick, pathetic version to escape your own truth. I never intended to mold you into my image of the perfect woman... I had accepted you as you were, in awe of your own creation, and not what I expected you to be. Why does it bother you so much that my feelings would turn to love? I didn't go back to my apartment each day reimagining you, tweaking you to be more of what I wanted. You went about your business, acting, reacting, interacting with people, sitting gracefully in my class... all I did was to absorb all of you, and it was magical. I had no reason to question the person I was learning to love... can you blame me? Yes, I naturally had, and still have, an image of a woman who could make me eternally happy... but I never intended it to be a one-sided, selfish arrangement. I stood ready to make myself worthy of such a person. Condemn me if you must, but I did think of us as natural lovers... content and fulfilled in who we are with no expectations beyond that. How can you be angry with my conditioning, my bouts with the past, with heartbroken poets, and deprived romances? How could I dare take you for granted? How could I have wanted to change you when you already spark the sentiments bouncing around inside me? I was ready Leylah, I was damn ready to give, to dedicate, to commit, to break myself down into humble pieces and to rebuild what was left of my life in praise of your unblemished simplicity. You could have thought me foolish and way overconfident, but I was even ready to deal with a rejection and move on... a better man for the feelings you inspired. There was no need for the alter-ego, for the unpredictable and strange Leylah. In the end, you may have wanted to destroy things you find unappetizing about me, about Paul and Catherine, but I can tell you that you have only made me more aware of where *not* to look for happiness."

His changing mood tried to lasso the whirlwind of emotions swirling in his head.

"I have no fear of the truth. In fact, I would consider it testimony of a life best avoided, and a sad reminder of how you destroyed the best of who you were... at least in my eyes. I don't pity you, but I do pity the Leylah you will not allow to love or be loved."

His monologue buried her in an avalanche of truth. Her only response was to land a powerful slap across his face, the sound bouncing off the walls of the large office. She attempted a replay, but he caught her arm in motion, stopping it before it could reach its target.

"Do you really want to slap me again? Do you? Fine, go ahead." With that, he let go of her arm. She got up close, in his face, angry enough to press her forehead to his. He looked up at her determined expression, challenging him to react, to show some anger.

Gianluca was never one to completely lose his composure. He got up and walked away saying nothing. She followed him outside unwilling to let him shut her down.

"Go ahead, walk away… I figured you would choose to give up, to act like you're so above even an argument. Are you still in love with me? Do you still want to marry me? Am I still the woman you expected me to be? Com'on Gianluca, turn around and rise above all this petty poop. Show me how much you can take. You claim that your love of the perfect woman has no bounds, that it lives forever. Are you still convinced I'm perfect? You still convinced that the women loved by your poets were all so perfect when you know so little of them? Any romantic dickhead can create a false perfection in a woman if it makes him feel good. You did that with me. You made me perfect in your tiny, bulldung world, and now you know the truth... this is who I am, this is the real me... can you handle it? Can you fucking handle it? God can't take much more of this foul mouth!" The dining room fell silent as the patrons looked on stunned with a growing curiosity.

Gianluca kept walking towards the exit; Leylah kept pace, raising her voice.

"I didn't think so. Perfect doesn't exist, Gianluca! It doesn't fucking exist!... get over it. Let it go so that you can come to terms with who you really are, because right now you are living in denial, and you will take it to the grave. I understood you after our first class, so I played into your ideals... you were so involved, so weakened by your vision. It opened the door to manipulate your head and your heart. It was so easy... I let you brew like a good bourbon."

Depleted, she stopped. He turned to face her. As much as he wanted to disappear into his apartment, Gianluca gave her the audience she demanded, and she added another dose of her madness.

"Hope I've given you enough material to write about me. Some poems, sonnets, maybe your own Divine fucking Comedy. I hate cursing! I hate it, but with you it just feels right. Make me immortal, I beg you. You have what Paul, and Catherine don't have. You have what it takes to make others want to read about women like me. How amazing would it be if I can carry the torch for all those faceless females who got into the heads of your writers and picked apart their hearts. I bet most of those women had no idea their names would be on the lips of people far into the future without a voice of their own, or a chance to make a name for themselves. I'll never give up that power! If Dante had some balls and made his move, even if it meant giving up his life, it would have been real, not in his delusional fantasies… doing that would have given us the real Beatrice, not some spirit he meets in Heaven. Jesus, Gianluca! We can all make an argument that anyone we choose to place inside the gates of God's kingdom is a damn special person. So what if Dante makes a big deal about her being in Heaven, we still have no clue who she really is. That's what I reject; I reject anything intruding on *me,* on putting up roadblocks that want to keep me from a destiny I can control."

She took a deep, exasperated breath, exhaling furiously before pounding him some more.

"See, it won't matter whether future generations know the real me, they will only know the me that you write about. I'm so *fudgeing* angry at all that I've learned in college and readings of how women were forced to live constantly in fear all these centuries! I'm really pissed, Gianluca… really pissed, and you had a lot to do with that! Women were beaten by their husbands, raped by soldiers, beheaded by kings, and demonized by the church… and worst of all we still allowed you to fall in love with us… and we loved you back. You ignored the degradation, and you continued to stroke your egos telling the world you had chosen one of us to love… what a fucking blessing! What woman would deny herself *that* pleasure? My God, Gianluca Morelli, you have me cursing more in one day than I have my entire life!"

Exhausted, she paused, turned away from him, to face the bay, contemplating how unappealing the whole business of love had become. He couldn't dismiss her, nor could he walk away from a good thesis. She then followed him into the apartment.

"You know, I did stab your crappy mattress to death because I hated you for taking me for granted, for thinking that I was supposed to live up to some dusty standard in your head, and when I failed you, you got turned off, and you fell out of love instantly… that's why you got up and left. I wasn't worthy of your company, of sharing a breakfast, of spending a day together. You couldn't accept the true me, my sexuality, being your equal to perform as I wanted, and not as you expected! So, was I too much, a huge mistake? In your dead-end thinking, my independence disgusted you, something to walk away from, something a man like you shouldn't have to deal with."

In her frustration she started biting her nails. "You're such a disappointment, Gianluca... a real, depressing disappointment... the kind that can't be fixed. I almost had you different; a man who doesn't pigeonhole his women... no such luck. This is a total *shitzu*! I can't keep making excuses for men." She walked towards the door.

"Wait, don't walk away, please." Gianluca called out as he got close enough to touch her.

"Oh my, I feel another curse coming on. Fuck you. Move on with your life. Go ahead, keep feeling sorry for yourself. You act like you're such a martyr to love... like you're owed something because you've suffered, looking for than elusive person. Well, guess what... we all want the same. We all want to love and be loved... but I want to be loved for the person I truly am. I didn't ask you to perform; I was willing to accept your uptight, Yankee ass as you were. Why is that too much for people? Why do I have to become a beauty pageant contestant that performs for the judges? I don't want that kind of scrutiny; I just need your brain to convince your heart to love the real me. You know, I never knew that cursing this much could feel so good."

She turned her back to him as she strengthened the levees in her eyes to keep the tears from escaping... fighting back the temptation to fall apart. Gianluca's Renaissance mind conspired to touch her, to caress her shoulders, to tighten his arms around all of her. As his mood continued to thaw, Leylah would have none of it. She turned and repeated a much harsher version of the earlier slap. He stood mummified.

"You just can't help yourself! I'm another weak, helpless woman that deserves your sympathies, your forgiveness, your pity... however temporary it may be. Well then, one more *fuck you*! You can't love me because you'll never know how to. Use all you have learned, all your power lectures about the ultimate experience in love, and you still won't get an ounce out of me. Look at you... you couldn't be more pathetic."

She left, slamming the door with enough rage to send shivers through the vase sitting on the kitchen table. Gianluca followed her retreat through the living room window when he received a text message alert on his cell. He opened it to a half dozen photos of his three-month-old daughter. The last one had her laying asleep in her mother's arms. The image owned his eyes and his attention for several minutes. Tiny Emilia restored some balance and offered an emotional escape from the lashing he had taken from Leylah.

He tumbled exhausted onto the sofa reflecting on his experiences. Wasn't it a given that in true love a person should be eager to mold to a loved one's expectation because there was happiness and satisfaction in doing so? He thought. It took him back to the notion of submission; that one submits to the burden, the contortions, and the work involved in love... that love is not static, but constantly evolving into the other person; not passive, but actively connecting… and he had always been good with that.

Gianluca had spent a lifetime sculpting himself to the demands of parents, friends, priests, and his profession. He felt there was greater devotion in relationships motivated by love, and that they contributed to social stability. There was a certain neatness to it that appealed to him. When he measured it up against Leylah, he asked himself if there was anything in her worth loving. Disillusioned, he faced the stark reality that he had been so wrong about matching his ideals to her. Could she be right about his women in literature? Could Beatrice have been a spoiled bitch? Had Dante embellished the image based on her beauty and what little he gleaned from occasional encounters? Considering the era, the class difference, and that she was a married woman, how well did he really know her? Gianluca had to admit that in his readings, Dante had met her only a handful of times, and none of those encounters were intimate. Was Lelylah right then? Did Dante need his version of Beatrice to fit his famous narrative?

Gianluca judged himself harshly for missing out on those considerations. But then, he thought, the realities would have stood in the path of the poet's fantasy… there would have been no great works of literature, just a collection of lies. Was Leylah also right about the selfishness of making a woman the object of a writer's infatuation? If Beatrice didn't have a voice of her own in the thirteenth century, was it wrong of Dante to give her a voice? Gianluca couldn't dismiss that there would have been enough encounters, and interactions even if the great poet had just been listening in on her conversations or picking up some gossip to provide enough material to give us a truthful image of his Beatrice. The embellishments would have been products of his admiration… and why not? Couldn't a man love a woman not his, as he sees her, as he is stirred by her presence? Is it necessary to know her fully?

As he sat annoyed at the unexpected confusion creeping into all his teachings, he planned to meet with Leylah to clear the air. He decided to avoid the restaurant and the bar at the Inn, opting to invite her back to his apartment.

His phone signaled another message from Cassandra with more pictures of Emilia. He decided to call.

"Hi, got all the photos… love them. She is so beautiful, so much like her father."

"Funny, you never did have a sense of humor, and you still don't. Tell me, how are things going at the college… are you still staying?"

"Well, I did make a commitment to stay the fall semester. I'm going to keep to that promise, but I'm not sure about the spring. I mean, I truly like it here. It fits my mood, my older person mood. I sound like a retired fart right now, but I feel younger here. I'm surrounded by this magnificent nature, and not by steel and concrete. I do miss the energy in New York. I feel good about myself. I found my real father here."

"I think the slower pace and the strong sun is screwing up your brain. Whattaya mean you met you real father? Isn't Matteo your real father?"

"It turns out he's not. My mother became pregnant while teaching in Bologna. She became involved with one of the university cooks. One thing led to another, they became intimate, and then the pregnancy. I was born out of wedlock. with a stand in father. Matteo and Mom fell in love, and he gallantly chose to be a father to me. My real father, named Massimo Brunetti is the owner of the restaurant I go to often down here. I had no clue; he had no clue until my parents told me everything on that trip to Italy after Emilia was born. When they mentioned Massimo, you can imagine my sick reaction. What were the odds? How the hell did I end up in a small town in Georgia purely by crazy chance to meet my real father?"

"No fucking way! What did you do?"

"What could I do. I'm fifty years old, they're in their seventies, and I'm supposed to freak out? I kept my cool and accepted things as they turned out. I'm good. I can't change any of it, they gave me a great life, and Massimo is a gem of a man. They were victims of their time and place, and they did the best they could. It could have all turned out much worse, so I'm grateful for my good fortune."

"What about Massimo, how are things with you two?"

"Good, I would say. We had a nice talk, and we will work at it. Not easy to go from a casual friend to being his son. I suppose we want to try it out and see how things go."

"Wow! You have been through a lot of shit. You know, I forgot how much I enjoy listening to your Brit English… then you throw in that little Italian thing, and I still get that strong tingle."

"Too funny, my sweet Cassandra… you always find a way to lesson all the drama."

"So, what about your squeeze, your flame, your lady? You still trying to get her to notice your sad ass?

"Well, I need your help on this one." Gianluca gave her a complete summary, the full Leylah story.

"Gianluca, if it were anyone but you, I would have thought you made this up. Okay, turn everything off, don't answer the door, go to your computer, and get me on video chat." He followed her instructions.

"Hey, looking a little shabby, you've aged." Gianluca didn't take too kindly to the comments. "Just joking, you're a beautiful man, just a little more vintage.

Listen, your lady is acting up. The performance is the

only way she can prepare herself for someone like you. She needs to test you out. You have everything she wants, but she's not convinced you're real. She's too afraid of investing all that good stuff she shelters so well. The nasty stuff you spoke about, the cursing, that's all a show... you even noticed she wasn't good at it. I curse the right way, she's an amateur from what you tell me.

She doesn't want to be a statistic... you know, divorced in less than five years. She doesn't want a brainless macho dumbass with a giant prick who comes in five seconds then false asleep. She wants a man who can be a friend, a lover and still handle fatherhood. Don't let her fool you, she wants a family... she's pushing forty.

She wants to love you-you can take that to the bank. She doesn't know you all that well, but from what she's seen, and listened to in your classes; the classy way you speak and present yourself, and the fucking topics of love in your curriculum that you spin like a magic potion, is a drug to a woman who is a deep romantic but has learned to hide it because basically, men suck. You need to come to grips with the fact that women get exposed to a semester of lovesickness in your class that is more powerful than any soap opera or Hallmark movie because it's organic... in your poets there is true suffering by real people in real situations with powerful complications. No woman with a tender heart can resist it.

She's coming out of hibernation; this is an awakening of all the deep sentiments a woman keeps to herself until the right man shows up. All the talk she gave you about women having a voice is a feminist escape-a way of mitigating the possibility that you feel nothing for her. She used those arguments when she didn't know you well enough. Then she softened up before acting out in bed like she was some super liberated new age slut. I can't imagine she fooled you one bit. The lesbian thing was another attempt at self-discovery. Many women go through that stage. I did too. When we conclude that men can no longer offer a woman a gentle and sentimental relationship and have no clue how to unravel the secrets of the clitoris, we can be tempted with a woman. With the right lesbian experience, you will never miss the penis. I can tell you, however, she's no lesbian.

She's probably had a shitload of dickheads make a move on her, and not one was in her league. I know I'm right when I think of southern women as being more needy when it comes to men. She's in her late thirties, she doesn't trust men enough to settle down, but it's probably what she wants most. Then you come along, and you *monkey wrench* her world. You offer something stable: a man with a soul, with a heart, and one who has a deep understanding of how to keep a woman coming back for more.

Gianluca, bottom line is you're too fucking normal.

Then you have that way of genuinely listening to a woman's head as well as her heart. I'm not talking about just yessing her to death... I know you really listen because then you talk about it, and women need that. For you it's hardly ever about the sex... never once did you initiate like the usual Neanderthal in heat... I had to practically violate you. This is not stupid female shit, it's what makes a relationship work.

So, you need to take the *bitch* out of her since it wasn't meant to be there to begin with. That means you have to find a way to let her know you're in it for good. She can love you, Gianluca, but if this is it for her, then she can't handle it not working out. You have what she wants-this isn't some insignificant infatuation... women act out this way only when they know it's right. If you love her, and you know you can for the rest of your life, then confront her and let her know it. Don't back down. Let her react, even get pissed. Let her know you're not buying her schtick... it's what she needs. It's the only way she will completely trust you. The acting out will stop, and she will return to her nature... the one that owns your heart.

You can't deny you've always wanted to be in love, but your mistake has been to think it needed to be elusive. Well, this one is real, so drop the fantasy and don't lose out on this chance to live for the love of a woman who doesn't believe in the impossible. I've told you so many times to not fuck it up...

this is the last time I'll use those words. She's your girl, Gianluca… and if she is, then you live forever in each other… see, you can have your *tiramisù* and eat it too. You get her and the immortality of a love experienced, not fantasized. So, this is it, you're on your own, and you don't have enough time to find another Leylah."

A very contrite Gianluca reacted to Cassandra's feminine wisdom.

"I get it. How uncomfortable it must be for her to deviate so haphazardly from her true character. So, she never intended to act out. It seems she has no choice but to take that approach. She has so much to offer, and with the wrong man, she would have risked everything to a miserable existence. "

To him this was no textbook love story for the sake of a love story. It was an overdue mingling of two souls finding a purpose. Cassandra's reality check served to remind him of how he had mistreated the future. He had foolishly held to his warped ideal that *mortality* was nothing but a buried corpse if one didn't see it as a chance at *immortality*. Then Leylah appears, and mortality becomes a point in time defined by love of life, love of another human being, and not a prelude to an afterlife roll of the dice. With her, immortality beyond life loses its appeal, and death becomes immortal. It was the lesson Clarence had laid out so convincingly when he spoke of his

Amelia. In death, Amelia lives forever in him alone because of the lives the two dedicated so completely to each other. There's no finality in death, the two live on immortal as one. He returned his attention to Cassandra.

"I have all these flashes and mini explosions going off in my head. I missed all the signs... Leylah was right all along when she urged me to look beyond the images, to see the real her. When I stubbornly held to my beliefs, she proved she could get me to react to a version of her I was uncomfortable with. She shattered her own image to make the point. It worked, and I didn't see it.

I have no words that can describe your friendship. You have every right to treat me indifferently, even hate me for the way I took you for granted. I'm so sorry for my behavior."

"My dear, dear Gianluca. I can't imagine anyone capable of hating you, no less wanting to avoid your company. You are an oddity, but a very cute one."

"Are you good? Can you forgive me?"

"I'm the best I've ever been. Emilia is my total joy. My mom has been amazing, and her granddaughter has injected new life in her. After my dad left, she spent most of her time wondering what went wrong. Now she measures only the good. My teaching career is amazing. I love it, and it gets me back to Emilia early enough to be a good mother. I talk about you all the time and I make sure she knows her daddy.

I didn't tell you... I'm keeping the boat. With summers off, I get to book fishing trips and charters that bring in some good money. Besides, I love being out in the Sound, and I want Emilia to get used to it. It's something I think she will love."

An inquisitive Gianluca had to ask.

"You haven't mentioned Ritchie."

"Well, his ex-came back into the picture, and reading the writing on the wall, I backed out immediately. I don't want any part of that scene. Our relationship was more about creating one family than it was about love, so getting out of it came easy. I'm good with the way my life is. It was never about needing a man. I would have invited a meaningful relationship, but unless you've been around the person long enough to get a true sense of who he is, I refuse to take that chance anymore. I mean, I do miss the sex, the love making, the playful stuff, but again, not enough to take chances. Maybe I'll try the lesbian thing again."

"Again? So, you really did try it."

"It lasted a couple of months. It was with one of the chicks in our class... not telling you who. It was good... she was good. I was the amateur and I let her take the lead. Some of the best sex I ever had. Then you took over. You were the best of both worlds, a fucking woman in a man's body. You may not have been aware, but except for the blabbering about your poets, you did everything else right... but don't let it go to head, you still have ghosts under your bed.

So, I have most of what I want out of life; I doubt many people get everything they want. I'm batting eight hundred, top of my game, and I'm perfectly happy. Now you need to get there too.

Gianluca, you have a daughter that will always know who you are, and with whom you can create your perfect relationship. I will never get in the way of that. If this thing works out with Leylah, I will welcome you both. Fuck, this is like an episode of *Modern Family*. That's fine, it doesn't need to be conventional if the feelings are conventional. Anyway, hugs and kisses you adorable man. Let me know how it goes."

CHAPTER 11- *"Open your eyes and see me as I am. The things that you have witnessed have given you the strength to bear my smile." Paradiso-Beatrice to Dante Canto XXIII.*

There was little left of the past he held so dear that could be applied to the present. It was no longer about visions pushing a dying fantasy. He couldn't ignore the wasteful way he had handled the last twenty years of his life. Whether he could have built a solid relationship, a family, a long-term plan into old age, was nothing more than conjecture. He had denied his flesh to appease his spirit, but he had little to show for his dedication... not even his daughter. Emilia was the result of Cassandra's intrigue... there was no planning on his part.

Sadness overcame him thinking he had no right to sign his name to his greatest creation. He thought about giving up, turned off by all the work that would be needed to fix things with Leylah. But what if Cassandra was right? What if Leylah was acting out, convinced that even the right man was too much of a risk. Could he counter her hesitations, and would she be responsive enough to give him the chance he was willing to take? He decided to give her some time.

He spent most of July exploring the areas to the north and south of Saint Simon. He ventured to Savannah and stayed for several days, then turned south to the beaches of Saint Augustine. He took a room initially for a week, then extending it to two at the *Saint Augustine Beach Bed and Breakfast*. The property was beachfront, good for lengthy strolls on sands that ran north-south for miles. On his stretch there were no other hotels, only private homes which made for very thin crowds and a raw, genuine connection with nature. He spent hours under his umbrella reading, tweaking his syllabus, and adding pages to his book. In his most peaceful moments, he would set aside his work, move his chair at high tide inviting the ocean breeze and the foamy water to caress his body while he affectionately recalled his early affections for Leylah.

He wondered if in the new semester they would cross paths. She was enrolled in two graduate courses offering a chance he would run into her at a hallway intersection long enough to make eye contact or drop a quick salutation in the hope it would be received with a smile. He asked himself if his perceptions were indeed self-serving, and if he had wrongly discounted the messages lurking in her unorthodox actions.

"Could it be I'm still missing the signs? I'm guilty of having done so with Simona years ago, with Cassandra and those in between. Shit, maybe I don't know how to make her feel secure. I never considered myself the man that could eliminate the risk to women serious about a relationship, until now. I can see the apprehensions that would turn her hard, and indifferent. She toughens up even more when the expectations contrive to either get her into a bed or own her. That's when the other Leylah appears; when she senses no return, no covenant for the feelings invested. The acting out is just a cover up, a way of saying 'fine, I knew it wouldn't work out… there was no love', and she gets to start over, managing the pain.

Shit, have men become so oblivious? Am I one of them? I've spent the past twenty years teaching about a woman's quest for unconditional male love, and yet here I am blindly making it elusive. It's what women like Leylah are conditioned to accept-the fact that few men can have her feel secure about being in love.

So, Dante rewards Beatrice with a place in Heaven because only there can he unmask his feelings, and where she is free to acknowledge the lover he might have been. Isn't that what Leylah was talking about? That if we lean on our perceptions, we force only the other to be worthy, when the quest should be for us to be worthy of each other, to make us lovers in this life. That's the guarantee she was begging for.

She tested Paul, but he had no clue. She knew that the proposal was a desperate move to own her… unwilling to give her up to another man. Paul's love was sterile, one dimensional. Beyond what worked for him, he had nothing intimate to offer.

I was the one she believed in. She gave me a chance. I didn't respond as she would have wanted. I offered no guarantees."

He drove into Saint Simon early evening the first Monday in August. It had been more than two weeks since he last spoke to Leylah. The absence of calls, texts or emails only added to the uncertainty of where they stood. He wondered if she busied herself working at the restaurant, catching up on her readings, or worse, if she desperately gave in to Paul's marriage proposal. He dismissed his anxieties, deciding to dine at Massimo's.

His father greeted him bearhug style like a son returning from a tour of duty. The old man was all smiles, and visibly emotional. He walked him to his favorite table and sat with him. He called over the waitress. Gianluca noticed she was a new face, which led him to quickly survey the rest of the restaurant searching for Leylah.

Massimo kept him busy with small talk, and pushing plates of appetizers around the table, urging him to eat. Ignoring the small feast and his hunger, he finally asked about her, learning she was out running some errands. There was a sense of relief since the sight of the new waitress had him thinking Leylah had decided to leave Saint Simon.

"Massimo, you have a new waitress." "Yes, her name is

Serena, very nice girl and very good with the customers. Me and Emma, we meet her in the restaurant in Savannah during our trip. We started talking, and she says she wants to move down to Kingswick to be close to her boyfriend. I say to her come see me and maybe you can work for me. Emma keep saying we need more help. I was surprised when Serena show up last week. I said, let's try- you come to work and we decide if you like the job. After one day we said she is perfect, and she give us a big smile and that's it... now she live with her boyfriend and she work for Massimo's. What about you? You will stay in Saint Simon, no?"

"Well, yes, at least for now. I like the college, and I sense that Clarence would want me to stay. There are so many good things about living here-the people, the weather, the beach, and the ocean, and of course Massimo's."

"Gianluca, please stay. You are my son-I'm not afraid to say it. Yes, you are my son even if you no feel the same. You are my only family. Mamma and my Papà died, and I have no brother, no sister."

Gianluca made room for Massimo's need.

"The time I will spend here will give me a chance to build the relationship you desire. I have a more difficult task. Matteo has been everything a father should be, and I'm certain you would have been every bit the same. You are a good man, Massimo, and I sense I have much of who you are in my blood.

We will find the father and son in us."

"Bravo! Your words make me happy." He swung his arms around him one more time and planted a *papà* kiss on his forehead. His son had mixed feelings to the tender expression. Matteo was a good man, but incapable of such intimacy. Massimo had now granted him the fatherly affection natural for one who has never known his son. There was much to love and admire in Gianluca, and Massimo didn't shy away from showing his pleasure, while holding back on expressing his pride since in his mind, he had yet to earn it. He couldn't make up for a lifetime, but destiny had at least granted him a rebirth, and it was only a matter of whether Gianluca could evolve with him.

Massimo's affections, Leylah's spirit, and the warmth of the family feel of the restaurant were reasons convincing his unsettled heart to stay. He now came to terms with the odd possibility of seeing himself happily married, living comfortably in a house close to the beach, and even having more children. He sarcastically laughed at the thought, as he nibbled on the antipasto, turning his head towards the entrance each time someone entered-expecting Leylah to come prancing through those doors.

When two hours passed with no sign of her, he decided to go home to unpack. As we walked over to the bar to leave a message for Leylah, Emma noticed him from the kitchen.

"Gianluca, welcome home. Can we talk, do you have a

minute?" "Yes, of course."

She led him into Massimo's office where she handed him a letter she pulled from her apron with a footnote. "This is from my daughter. It's what she left for you before leaving for Memphis. Massimo didn't have the courage to tell you she was gone." "Memphis? Why Memphis?" asked Gianluca in complete suspense of the information that turned him gloomy.

"She spoke to me about the two of you, and how she was falling in love. I learned of how shameful she felt about her actions, about the way she came across. You know, that's not my daughter, that's not how she is or has ever been. I'm not sure why she acted that way, but I must make sure that it will never taint your opinion of her or of us."

Gianluca countered with a tender response. "Emma, I had already reached that conclusion. All she said and did were the actions of a woman fearful of being disappointed. I was initially too oblivious to see it. You must know, I began loving Leylah almost from the moment we met. You may dismiss it as some unfiltered infatuation, but my experiences told me it was very real. I was the one who messed it up, unable to read her, keep her from thinking this was just another waste of time.

I now understand she was willing to invest all of herself, and that she viewed me as the man who could make that commitment and start a productive life together. I couldn't be more convinced of that now. The two weeks I spent alone on the beach in Saint Augustine, shutting down my phone, blocking out the world; gave me time to reset, to think of how worthless life truly is if lived alone." He paused, turning to Emma for advice.

"What should I do? Do I go to Memphis?"

"I think you should read her letter first, then decide. There are several pages, she poured her heart out. I've never seen her so involved with her feelings... she must have felt something for you-it's not like her to give a man that much attention."

He decided to read the letter in his office. He did most of his reading there, and facing the beaches always added clarity to words.

"Dearest Gianluca. So sorry for leaving while you were away. I didn't hear from you. I wondered what happened. All I knew is that you had taken some vacation time. It would have been decent of you to let us know where you had scampered off to, and how to reach you. I called and left many messages. You ignored the calls, or you lost your phone... not sure- I hope you did lose it. I can't imagine not wanting to take my calls not matter how we left off.

I know you were sincere when you said you loved me from the first time we met. All your silly, boyish actions told me much about the way you felt around me. I confess, I felt the same whenever we were within feet of each other. I was stupidly bitchy in class only because I knew about Catherine and your affair. I figured I had no chance with a woman like her… she has so much to offer a man like you. Not that I want to make an issue of your age, but she is closer in years, and my thought was that you two would be compatible and happy… maybe I was wrong.

While you were gone, Cassandra had been trying to reach you for several weeks. When you didn't respond, she knew about Massimo's so she contacted the restaurant. I was there to answer, and when she said who she was, I knew we could talk. She knew about me. She told me all you said about us. I learned about your feelings better from her mouth than from yours.

What I have to say now needs to sink into your numb brain. The more I listened, the more my heart broke for this woman. Not only does she know so much about your life, but she also has your soul completely deciphered. I tried, without success, to get her to say something negative about you. The only remark was about how you have fanatically tried to pattern your life with your stupid poets… something I already knew, and still she thought it was cute. I called it pathetic; she insisted it was cute… that's love.

Look, let me be the one to tell you how dark your life will be if you don't get your ass back to New York, and back into the arms and the beauty of this woman, the mother of your daughter. How can you be so fucking unaware and careless with her? I'm fucking cursing again, and I will keep cursing you out until you lose the shit in your head and reward yourself with this woman's love. What have you done to your heart? It's like you performed several bypasses when it came to Cassandra.

She spilled all her memories of the time you spent together with no doubt they were the best days ever for her... in love with you, and as she put it... 'the only time she wanted to love a man so completely'. It was clear she was telling me all this to make sure I would feel the same for you. She did all the talking. Her voice lit up like a firefly each time she mentioned some moment you shared. She was selling you, marketing you to me with all her truth. There was no remorse, and if there was, she didn't even give a hint of it... again, that's love.

You asked her advice on how to handle me. She made me cry when she urged you to come after me, to not give up, and that I was your girl. She was convinced that the love was real, and that you needed to make the next move. Well, how dense can you be? Didn't it dawn on you she was trying to nail the coffin shut with those words? That she was finally about to bury you for good so she could move on? She chose to be courageous and considerate while all along it was breaking her heart. She was holding out, Gianluca, she held on to a slither of hope you would come to see the brilliance of loving such a woman. How can you fuck that up so badly? Fuck, fuck, fuck... there, happy? All you make me want to do is curse! I had to calm down before finishing this letter!

So, I will already be in Memphis by the time you read this. I decided to get out of Saint Simon, and to follow in my parents' footsteps. I can sing, so mom set me up with some old band members to audition. My singing will keep me from the silly business of men and love, and I can connect with my daddy's ghost. He will help me know him better through the music and just being in the same clubs he played.

Gianluca, please know that I am not running away. This was a decision that came to me one Sunday as I sang in church. It was one of my best performances. It was a packed house, and the standing ovation had me in tears. I totally broke down. The pastor and other choir members had to hold me up... I wanted to fall to my knees and praise God's glory. I never gave myself a real chance at this. I brushed off the fact that I was born of two very musical persons, both with wonderful voices. I will find a calling and I know it will bring me satisfaction and happiness.

I am so deeply sorry for the way I treated you. I acted out in the shadows of my fears. I was so tired of the same sick attention I have received from men my entire life. It made me cautious, and cold. I hope you can find the real me again as you shuffle through our time together. I so want to remain the best of friends and a part of your life. For what it's worth, I strongly agree with Cassandra that you are the best of men, and that you are so easy to love. I did fall in love until I understood my love was nowhere as intense and meaningful as Cassandra's. You worked hard at getting my attention; you did nothing to have Cassandra love you... she didn't even have to tell me; I knew it just from listening to her... her voice filled with the same passions that owned her entire body whenever you two were together.

I know about your weekends away in Newport, and how she didn't want them to end. Gianluca, can you open your mind to this? Can you accept that she is your fucking Beatrice in the flesh? We may have shared some feelings of love, but they were hardly skin deep, so undeveloped. It would have taken much more work for us to bring it to the Cassandra level, and I'm not so sure it would have gotten there. Not sure how my sex ranks with you. I know I enjoyed every minute, but it wasn't love.

Don't have Webster's Dictionary define the word fool with a reference to you and use your life as an example of one who lived foolishly. Go ahead, I challenge you to try to live out your life without her, without the pleasure of watching your daughter grow into a woman. You can't do that part time; you can't show up on holidays and then tell yourself you were a good father… that's bull dung and you know it.

Your ass will sag soon, and wrinkles will show up unannounced. This is where you decide on how much more you're willing to sacrifice to your fantasies. You even lectured about how improbable it is for two souls to find each other; to beat the odds, to experience the intensity of love that can't be defined. Now that's fucking incredible, and it's what you have with Cassandra. Open your heart, Gianluca… time is your enemy.

I did my research, and I'll be taking graduate courses at Rhodes College. I need a backup in case the singing thing fails me. I will send you information about me once I settle in. I'd like to see you when I start performing… wish me luck. Call me after you read this… I want to ball you out some more.

You will always have my bittersweet love to keep your spirit cozy, and your heart focused on what will bring you happiness.
Eternally, Leylah.

With his indifference unmasked, Gianluca was forced to confront it. Not only had Leylah made powerful arguments against the one-sided romancing of women by men bent on making a name for themselves, but she had also debunked his conviction that love was embodied in an image rather the person.

He had disaffected the lone individual who had chosen to love him without imposing an ideal. Cassandra's affections were born entirely from observation and interactions. They came to life in the classroom, migrating to the Poet's Cafe, and left smoldering in the Inns of New England.

She kept her feelings under control with difficulty, avoiding too much talk of love, commitment, long term plans or family. Beyond adding those topics to their casual discussions, she wouldn't allow them to be seriously considered, in her determination to keep him in her life. Unable to deny her feelings, she tolerated his detachment from the present and from her. The pregnancy was a planned alternative to losing him entirely.

When Leylah was introduced, there was no bitterness. She dealt with her heavy heart by granting Gianluca the support he sought, despite carelessly leaning on her as a good friend. Comfortable in the thought that Cassandra had found her destiny with Ritchie, he had snugly left her behind in New York. He now thought of the hurtful insensitivity of that assumption.

There was little left to decipher. He needed to fix himself and fix things in New York.

CHAPTER 12- *"Now turn around and listen well, not in my eyes alone is Paradise." Beatrice to Dante Canto XVIII.*

He imagined himself back with Cassandra in New York either pathetically attempting to convey the hard lesson learned from Leylah, or as a newer man genuinely coming to terms with his sad inadequacies. He stared down at the letter, the words pricking at his conscience.

Cassandra had presented him with every reason to love, if not her, then to simply love. He could no longer avoid the sincere and powerful truth that she loved him. He flipped to the image of Emilia in her mother's arms. He finally broke down, emotionally depleted... suddenly repulsed with his miserable manhood, and the arrogance with which he repelled the love and the life this woman was willing to share. Emilia was not the product of a selfish act. Cassandra made certain the child was born of her own love, but also of the love she imagined Gianluca would have as a father. She never factored him out, keeping him involved even when he saw himself more as a benefactor than a parent. He thought back on how many references she made to Emilia *knowing her father,* and the promise that she would never hinder that process. He couldn't help but think that Cassandra would have considered any other man a total *dick,* in her words, for the way he handled the arrival of Emilia. Instead, she set aside his clinical approach, and endowed him with all the glory of becoming a father, embellishing him beyond what was deserved.

Before packing his bags, he met with Clarence. He asked him to read Leylah's letter. He handed it back to Gianluca wearing a proud smile.

"I would have bet the entire homestead that she would bring you to your knees with her truth. You see, with Leylah, things and people need to look for and find a prophetic fit. She understood there was something grand about you, but she didn't feel that fit. She wrote the letter because she understood Cassandra better than you ever did. She only needed to open your eyes to it. I know of no one better equipped to follow through successfully on that task.

My good man, this is your *Amelia* chance in life. You're lucky to get one opportunity at this… and Leylah is asking that you do not squander it. You once said to me that you wished for yourself what I had with my wife. Well, you should thank that wonderful girl if she has indeed enlightened your heart to that precious reality.

I'm assuming you are now heading to your apartment to pack your bags. Coming back to us is nowhere as important as fulfilling the destiny that awaits you in New York. You have my and Amelia's blessings… If she were with us, she would have set you on fire with all her good reasons, and her wisdom would have accompanied you north. Now go, feel the love, and give it in abundance… God is watching!

The following day Gianluca took the late morning flight from Atlanta into LaGuardia. He *Ubered* to her mother's house in the Bronx, arriving midafternoon. She came to the door holding Emilia with her right arm, the little girl harnessed to her hip.

"Oh my God, you're Gianluca. I recognize you from the pictures Cassandra took when the baby was born. This is a surprise... don't know what to say, please come in."

"So sorry for showing up unannounced. I wanted to come up to see the baby before I started a new semester. I'm sorry, but I don't even know your name. May I?" "Regina, but everyone calls me Gina."

She passed Emilia into his arms. His daughter was only three months old, but she could sense his was an unfamiliar face. He was amazed at how this newly arrived tiny human could summon unfamiliar feelings. He was overcome with a sudden urge to be a father, to start the process of raising Emilia. In a daze he imagined himself growing older paging through her life from adolescence, into her crazy teen years, and finally into womanhood. The thought of not being a part of that turned him gloomy and scared. Suddenly, he was doing the math in his head: when she's ten, I'll be sixty; when she's twenty, I'll be seventy... what a sick reality, he thought.

"Is Cassandra here?"

"No, sorry. She's out on the boat in City Island. She had a group of three guys out on a fishing charter this morning. She should be pulling into her boat slip in about an hour. I expect her home around five. She tells me you're teaching in Georgia... how do you like it?

"I miss New York, but there's something very appealing about a small coastal town, long summers, tame winters, and that homey feel to everyday life. The people are very kind, they could be a bit nosey, but that comes with the turf. I like this part of the Bronx; I've never been here. It's almost like a separate town that belongs in Westchester."

"Everyone says that. Pelham Bay has always been like this because it borders on the Long Island Sound, and the thruway on the other side makes it feel separate from the rest of the Bronx. I've lived here my whole life... this was my parents' house."

"This must have been awkward for you... Cassandra and I not being married, with her having the baby without me around. I hope this hasn't dampened your feelings about me."

"Cassandra explained what she did. I lay no blame on either of you. She says only wonderful things about you. Getting pregnant is not what I would have expected, but after explaining it the way she did, I began to understand. When Emilia was born, all that stuff went away; it no longer mattered. This beautiful girl was meant to be here." She turned serious and somber. "Gianluca, the three of us are very happy... please help us keep it that way."

Gianluca sensed the anxiety of a loving grandmother. She thought perhaps he had come to impose some sort of joint agreement on raising Emilia.

"Please understand that Cassandra and I have spoken about our relationship and how we feel about Emilia living with her mother. She has released me from many obligations, but we both insisted I remain as active as possible in our daughter's life."

"I know. She said she wanted to make sure Emilia knew her daddy. I know you agreed to all those things... I wasn't sure if you were here now looking to change all that."

"Not at all. I want things to stay as we agreed, with only more participation on my part. I want to be available whenever I'm needed... in any capacity."

"You know, I can't remember Cassandra ever falling in love. When she was a teen, she dated a couple of guys, but it didn't last. Throughout her college years and into her thirties, she never brought a man home for me to meet, and she hardly dated at all. She worked, came home, ran her boating business, read a ton of books, and worked on her degree... that was it until she met you. I saw the change. It was so obvious. She couldn't stop talking about you, your classes, the way you taught. When you started dating, she started dreaming. She would say *'Ma, I really like this guy... you know, I think I love him. I don't want to make a big deal about it, and I don't want to get my hopes too high, but I can picture us together... you know, as if it was meant to be'.* I shouldn't be telling you this; she would kill me if she knew. I tried to change her mind since you were her professor. I just didn't think it was right. But then I said to myself, she's in her thirties so she should know who she wants. All I know is since the baby, she hasn't even mentioned wanting somebody or marriage, and I think that's good for her. Emilia has given her all the happiness she's been after these past years. You must know about her dad… she has been bitter about him after he left. Listen to me, exposing all our dirty laundry… I'm so sorry."

Gianluca could have smacked himself in the head for being so detached, so unaware of the depth of Cassandra's feelings. He felt sick thinking that she kept her disappointment so well hidden, ignoring the pain, putting her heart out there like a target. He thought about how many shots it had taken, and that his may have been the one to cause the greatest injury.

Leylah had no such intentions. She sheltered her heart by stifling her feelings in anticipation of things not working out. Cassandra instead took chances, took the hit but cured herself with the greatest antidote… a daughter.

"Gina, can you tell me where she docks her boat?"

"At Rudy's Boatyard. After crossing the bridge make a sharp left. It's right there."

He drove off with an edgy impatience. He wanted things to move quickly; maybe to make up for lost time. He knew what he wanted to say, but he had yet to come up with the words. His mind wandered as he turned into a bundle if nerves. This was unusual; he had never felt uneasy with her. The episodes from the past played out like a scrapbook. His eyes were on the road, but his mind had wandered off framing only images of Cassandra.

This time he grew sad, to the point of shedding uncommon tears. He turned overemotional, laboring at containing the anger he turned on himself for his nauseating disregard for the woman who had exhausted every hope settling on being his greatest cheerleader. His alter ego took over, forcing him back into his head.

"You have loved this woman all along. You were just so fucking full of yourself, so convinced of some higher order perched on your literary throne extoling the bullshit virtues of female divinity. Get it into your thick skull: divinity is beyond your reach, it's not real. Cassandra is real. She is of this world, of which you are still a part of. I can't believe she ever gave you that much attention. Do you realize that for her to keep offering her friendship, to want to have a child by you, and to keep from giving you the bloody nose you deserved, that this woman's love for you has survived every attempt by you to extinguish it? The revelations should make you sick to your stomach… you should be throwing up your guts! Here you are exposing all the dumb shit you've done to yourself. You've hit a new low. This is pure misery… I can't stand to look at you!"

Approaching the City Island bridge, he snapped out the mental daze. He found Rudy's Boatyard, parking his car where he could see the boats pull in. He didn't have to wait long. Cassandra was steering the thirty-five-footer as expertly as any merchant marine into the tight slip.

He delayed. His hands stiffened around the steering wheel while his nerves compelled his stomach muscles to spasm. She appeared as he had never seen her in her fisherman's overalls, bucket hat pulled down to just above her eyes, and white deck boots splattered with the blood of fish she had filleted for her clients. She busied herself securing the boat, unloading equipment, and sprinkling ice over the catch of the day in zipped plastic bags. The men helped with some of the chores after which they disembarked to load up their pickup.

Gianluca could wait no longer. Risking a performance in front of an unsuspecting audience, he emerged from the car, walked on to the marina platform to get her attention as she hosed down the deck.

"Hi."

With her back to him and an ear bud drowning him out, she appeared to ignore him. He added some volume and a little attitude to his voice.

"Hi, hello… Cassandra!"

Perched on the highest part of the deck, she turned, baffled at the sight of him standing there. She was startled but there was no excitement in her reaction.

"Gianluca? How… I mean, what are you doing here? This is weird. I never expected to see you anywhere in New York, least of all here. Why? Why are you here?"

He pulled his sunglasses from his face nervously folding and unfolding them.

"I came here to tell you that I love you. I mean, I'm in love with you... that I have always loved you... I just didn't know it. Wait, that didn't sound right... I meant to say that I always knew, but I wasn't aware... wait, that doesn't make sense. Cassandra, I don't know which words to use." He took a deep breath, annoyed at his loss for words and the hesitations.

"I know what I feel, and you know me well enough to figure me out... so please, put me back together, because right now I'm just falling apart."

Poor Cassandra felt herself splitting in two. She understood his frailty, and the clumsy attempt to package his feelings. She was also furious at the sucker-punch and the fact that he wasn't even aware he had delivered one. She let him have it right back.

"Are you out of your fucking mind? You show up out of nowhere acting like some bullshit Romeo who has finally come to his senses about who he wants to love in this life, and I'm supposed be so grateful that this is finally happening? Holy shit, how can you be so fucking oblivious... how, tell me how it is that you get to live inside your cloistered mind, detached from the rest of us, selfishly preparing to proclaim your love only because now you're ready to do so. Alleluia! Gianluca is finally ready. Let's get down on our knees to thank God for this amazing man. This one-of-a-kind creation."

The frustration made it impossible to hold back the tears. She spoke as she cried, snot dripping from her nose, wiping her face with her fish blood hands.

Gianluca giggled at the sight. She blasted him again.

"I can't believe you find this funny... you are fucking laughing at me. How can I take you seriously?"

"It's just that you spread lines of blood and guts across your cheeks and now you look like one of those Amazon warriors ready to slice me in two. It's kinda scary."

"You're such an asshole, you know that... a total asshole." She gathered herself to deliver a knockout. "

"I sent you away! I pushed you away! Fuck, I gave you up! When you told me about Leylah, I closed the book on you... I set you aside, and I knew it was forever. You made me get over you, but you never understood that I never did. I didn't bother you with it... I didn't want you to change your life because of me. I let you go with all my blessings, Gianluca... with all my blessings while I stumbled into limbo... and you continued blissfully looking for your Beatrice.

I can only imagine what happened. Leylah didn't want to take that chance with you. She wasn't willing to invest, to find out if the woman you wanted was a ghost or was real. She's real, Gianluca, and in her mind you were still chasing ghosts. I was willing to challenge the ghosts... that's what you weren't aware of, not the fact that you didn't know you loved me... you had no clue that I was as real as your ghosts, and that all you had to do was see me, and not see through me."

She paused again to wipe her face. She looked, but couldn't find a towel, so she used her slimed hands adding another layer of guts and blood. She sensed the freakish transformation on her face. There was no containing her anger. She pulled a filleted porgy from the bucket at her feet and flung it with the fury and determination of a Dodgeball player. The very non-athletic Gianluca didn't possess the aptitude to duck. Within seconds he stood hunched over facing the boat spitting fish juice into the water. He yelped like a wounded soldier asking for his mother. Cassandra picked another projectile from the bucket. This one had the bulk of its entrails still attached. She held it flat in the palm of her hand, walked to the boat's railing putting her within a few feet of her target. The more massive porgy hit his face vertically with the entrails wrapping around his neck. The fish tumbled to the platform, but the insides slid slowly down his neck, slithering in between his chest and his button down. He squirmed and danced, unbuttoning his pants, pulling out his shirt attempting to discharge the blob that had reached his belly button.

Detecting his disgust, she turned the hose on him.

"How does that feel? Does it feel scummy? Does it? Now you know how I feel with you coming here to shit all over me. To make me feel like it was nothing but a delusion to love you... that wanting a life together was the misplaced desire of a confused woman. Well, I'm not confused... I know exactly what I want. Was I confused when I wanted Emilia? No, Gianluca, no... I knew I wanted her, and I knew I wanted you in my life.

So now you're no longer confused, you had your epiphany, whoop-de-do! That's a fucking accomplishment. I wish I could stop crying... I hate crying when I'm with you. I get weak, and all I want to do right now is kick you ass. I wish I could hate you; I wish I could get you out of my system. I was good, now you show up, bust in on me to tell me you love me. What am I supposed to do? Huh? Tell me Gianluca, what am I supposed to do with you? All I wanted was a man I could teach to do things, teach you to swim, to drive a boat, to fillet a fish, to have you know all of me, unveiled and naked with nothing to hide, and no other agenda than to love you the rest of my life... the rest of your life. You never understood that... how is it that you understand it now?"

"So much has happened to pry open my eyes and my heart. All I can ask of you is to consider my love, give it a chance. You must know that I feel so inadequate. Look, I know I don't deserve you. I can only hope it's not too late."

Her courage in breaking him down added a sense of righteous justice to her tears turning her crying into gasps for air. The sight of her struggling humbled him further, looking for the opening that would allow him to climb the boat.

She rolled her eyes at the pathetically inept academic.

"Don't move, just stand there for a second. I can't believe I'm about to do this. Get on your knees."

"Why?"

"You have no right to question anything I ask you to do, so get on your fucking knees."

Gianluca obeyed, as was his way with women.

"Okay, now propose. Ask me to marry you."

This time he refused to be guided by his stale convictions. He took his knees to the craggy and stony concrete pavement, thinking the last time he did so was in church as an altar boy. He tried to fix his drenched hair, parting it in the middle with his nails. He tucked his waterlogged shirt back into his pants, the slime dripping onto his boxers.

"My dearest Cassandra, will you fix this man and this heart, make me worthy of your love…"

She flung her arms at him in frustration cutting him off. "Jesus, Gianluca! Can you please stop with all the shit poetry, and just ask the damn question!"

He anxiously composed himself, inching his knees in any direction that would blunt the pain.

"Cassandra, marry me. Be my wife. There, I did it"

She smiled, thinking there was finally no hesitation in his performance.

"Yes, yes, against my better judgment, yes… I will spend the rest of your old fart life making you miserable."

Gianluca had come full circle, newly captivated by the complete beauty of the woman he loved, the wife to be and the mother of their child.

She looked down at the silly man, slipped the suspenders off her shoulders… the rubber overalls bunching up at her feet. She hosed herself down standing in her wet t-shirt and thong. Dripping and shivering, she suggestively glanced his way as she invited him to follow her below deck.

LEYLAH

John Dolgetta

Can be reached at **johndolgetta@yahoo.com**

914-330-1727

Other Publications:

BRONX RIVER NORTH 2016

MERECA' (AMERICANO) 2020

LEYLAH 2022

LEYLAH

LEYLAH

LEYLAH

Made in the USA
Middletown, DE
25 June 2023